By Henry Daniel Archunde Jr

Six Minutes Late

It Doesn't Rain Forever

Six Minutes Late
By
Henry Daniel Archunde Jr.

True North Writings
★ ✪ ★
Arizona

All rights reserved. No part of this book may be reproduced, distributed, or transmitted in any form or by any means, including photocopying, recording, or other electronic or mechanical methods, without the prior written permission of the publisher, except in the case of brief quotations used in reviews, articles, or scholarly works.

This is a work of fiction. Names, characters, places, and incidents are products of the author's imagination or are used fictitiously. Any resemblance to actual events, locales, or persons, living or dead, is purely coincidental.

Published by True North Writings
Edited By: *Ana Archunde*
ISBN: **979-8-9934077-6-0**

Book Design By Mr. & Mrs. Archunde

© 2025 True North Writings LLC.

For those who arrived six minutes late and still showed up anyway. For the ones who forgive themselves slowly. For every heart that learned showing up can still be enough.

And for my mother, who encouraged me to begin writing when it was still only a quiet idea finding its way to the page.

Table of Contents

Six Minutes Late
Foundations
The Patient
The Sessions
Chance, or Something Like It
The Line Breaks
The Night We Couldn't Leave
Fractures
The Collapse
Relocation
A Shadow in the Walls
Whispers in the Walls
A Labyrinth of Shadows
The Chessboard
The Trap
Six Minutes Revisited
The Last Move
Epilogue

Six Minutes Late

Six Minutes Late

4:06 P.M.
Thursday.

Six minutes late.

The clock on the wall pronounced it like a sentence. Precise, unbending, impossible to appeal. Each tick sounded like judgment rendered. The room had already memorized her absence by the time she entered; it took a moment to unlearn it.

Up close, I could see the rain had left a constellation of dark specks on her coat. Small, star shaped stains that would dry hours later, long after she'd left this room and pretended to forget it.

A single strand of hair had curled into a question mark against her cheek, trembling with every breath she didn't mean to take. The leather of my chair exhaled when I shifted. The lamp's pull chain tapped softly against its stem, a sound too gentle to matter, and yet, it did. Every noise in that office had the same peculiar weight.

Domesticated, harmless, suddenly significant, like witnesses that might one day be asked what they'd heard. Claire's eyes wandered before her words did. They latched onto small, solid things. The brass clip on my clipboard, the faint crack running down a picture frame, the square of weak light that escaped through the blinds and fell across the rug like a door to nowhere. It helps them not to fall.

"Would you like some water?" I asked.
She shook her head, then, after a moment, nodded.

The choreography of ambivalence. I poured the glass and set it before her. The water stilled. She didn't touch it. Watching it remain perfectly still felt more honest than anything either of us could say.

"First sessions can feel like a test," I offered. "They do," she said. "And I never studied for this one." A gust of wind pressed against the window, making the pane hum. Rain trailed down the glass like a thousand stories surrendering at once. The faint scent of her coat made of wool, wet pavement, faint perfume with the ghost of something floral and human filled the space between us.

"Tell me what brought you," I said. My voice carried the practiced calm of a man who had built a profession out of steadiness, a learned cadence that kept the storms of others from breaching my skin. She tightened her grip on the strap of her bag. "I keep thinking I can't be this tired without dying," she said. "And then I keep not dying." The sentence landed like a confession disguised as science.

Something in me went still. "I'm not going to hurt myself," she added quickly, a reflex reserved for rooms like this. "I'm too… careful." She almost smiled. It failed halfway. "I'm just… late. For everything that might have saved me." Her gaze found the license on the wall, that framed piece of paper with my name embossed in authority.

Once it felt like ballast; now it looked like a relic. "You ever feel like peace is a door everyone else has a key for?" She asked. "And yours is… jammed. Or fake." "I know what it's like to stand outside a door a long time," I said.

She studied me for a moment, not the way patients do, but the way survivors do when they sense another of their kind. Silence followed. Not empty. Not safe. The kind that breathes. The radiator clicked through its slow argument with the pipes.

Down the hall, someone's drawer opened, closed. The clock ticked, the one constant sound that refused shame. "Try this," I said softly. "We won't start with everything. Pick one moment from your week, something small, something invisible to everyone else. Place it here, between us, and we'll look at it together."

Her shoulders dropped slightly. Relief. "Tuesday," she said. "The elevator stopped between floors. Only a second, I think. But the light… it flickered. And I thought if it went out, I wouldn't know where I ended. That I might dissolve." She looked down, almost embarrassed. "People laughed when it started again. I laughed too. But later, I couldn't remember how to breathe."

"Where did you go when it flickered?" I asked. She turned toward the window, toward the city that never let itself go completely dark. "Nowhere," she said. "That's the problem." I wrote two words I didn't show her: edge work. Her throat moved and then came the apology, always the apology.

"I'm sorry I was late," she said again, as though time itself were something she had failed to keep alive. "I don't want to be the kind of person who keeps people waiting." "You're here," I said. "That matters more."

For a fleeting heartbeat, she believed me. The truth softened her face; then, as quickly as it came, fear reclaimed it. "Can you… not make this into something I have to pass?" She asked. "If I fail here, I don't have another here." "I don't grade," I said. "We build a map. You tell me what hurts when you can, and I'll listen when you can't."

Her eyes glimmered, not with tears, not yet, but with something awakening from distance. I should have glanced at the clock. I didn't.

Instead, I watched the pulse in her throat, the small muscle at the hinge of her jaw that betrayed effort, the way her fingers toyed with the skin at the base of her thumb, a small, private pain to distract from the greater one. "Tell me one thing you want," I said. "Not a plan. Not a fix. Just something that fits in your mouth without choking you."

She thought carefully, as though the wrong answer might collapse the room. "To sleep without bargaining," she whispered. "To sleep without convincing my body it's safe to leave me for a while." "Okay," I said. "Then we'll aim there." "And if I don't make it?" She said quietly. "Then we aim again," I added reassuringly.

The words came out plain, unadorned. Truth doesn't need decoration. Something loosened in her shoulders, not much, but enough. Behind my composure, the old machinery of my mind turned and sparked. I thought of my father's silence, my mother's trembling hands, of the vow I'd made to never let quiet become cruelty again.

I thought of Eva's photograph from last week with paper stars strung on yarn, Saturn ringed in glitter and taped crooked above her bed. A galaxy held by thread, still called a system. "Homework?" Claire asked, half dread, half hope. "Not yet," I said. "Today you leave with nothing to do but be. You came. That's the work."

Her breath hitched, almost like a sob learning how to disguise itself as gratitude. When I ended the session at five, it wasn't because we were finished. It was because time said so. Ending felt like tearing a page that hadn't been written yet.

At the door, she paused, framed in amber light from the hallway, her shadow cut into bars across the floor. "Thank you," she said carefully, like the words were fragile and could break in the wrong hands.

She didn't say see you next week. The future was too large to fit in her mouth. After she left, the room changed shape. It didn't empty; it remembered. Her silence remained like a temperature. My phone chimed. *6:30. Ballet.* I gathered myself back into usefulness.

★ ✪ ★

At home, the night smelled of Lo Mein and shampoo. Eva's feet left small rosin prints on the hardwood. Her paper stars drooped above the window, dust softening their edges. She told me about pliés and penguin-sliding girls in socks and physics that tasted like joy. When she saw my smile falter, she fished a perfect dumpling from her carton and dropped it onto my plate. "You like them crispy, Daddy." Love, in its truest form, is always unguarded. "What did you do today?" She asked, serious as a journalist. "I met someone brave," I said before I could stop myself. "Were you brave?" She asked. "I tried," I replied with a small smile playing on my lips.

She nodded, satisfied, then yawned with small, perfect, unburdened. Later, I tucked her in. "Story?" She murmured, already half asleep. "About what?" I asked. She considered. "About a moon that was late but still caught up." I smiled. "I can do that."
   So I told her about a moon that missed its orbit by six minutes and thought the sky wouldn't take it back, and how the ocean forgave it, and how light returned anyway. She fell asleep before the ending. I whispered it anyway, for both of us. Love expands the room; fear shrinks it.

That night, both were present. When the apartment went still, I washed the bowls, wiped the ring my mug had left, and tried to make order from a day that had undone me.

My phone buzzed once, no caller ID. A single vibration. Like a pebble tapping at the glass of my life from the dark. I didn't answer. I didn't need to. Some messages speak even when they're never read. I sat at my desk. The license on the wall caught the lamplight, the gold seal glinting like an accusation.

I opened my notebook and wrote: *4:06 p.m. Six minutes late*. Then stopped. The ink pooled like blood where the sentence waited. Outside, sirens wept through the city. Inside, the air held her voice, the trace of her perfume, the ghost of rain on her coat.

I told myself I minded. I told myself she was a patient, a story, a mirror. But the truth, the quiet, dangerous truth, was simpler. I was already a threshold.

And she was already crossing.

Foundations

Michael Harris was born into silence. Not the kind that soothes, that gathers like a quilt around a sleeping child, but the kind that presses. That seeps through walls and into the marrow. The kind that teaches a boy to hold his breath without knowing he's doing it.
His parents, Gerald, and Ruth Harris were schoolteachers in a small, unremarkable New Jersey town, a place where the streets emptied by eight, where the seasons arrived on schedule, and where every family seemed to know which window not to look into. Theirs was a house of tidy appearances and invisible fractures.

The lawn trimmed to exactness, the curtains drawn at dusk, the kind of order that came not from pride but from fear of what disorder might reveal. Dinner was at six sharp. Always. His father at the head of the table, his mother opposite, the space between them filled with unspoken things that had long outgrown their words.
Gerald Harris was a man carved out of discipline and disappointment. He graded papers the way other men prayed: methodically, ritualistically, with the belief that precision could keep the chaos of life at bay. The red pen never left his hand, even at the dinner table.

Each mark across a student's essay was a small act of control in a world that had denied him larger ones. A glass of Jack Daniel's kept him company, sweating into the coaster, leaving faint rings on the oak like the ghost of something spilled and never cleaned.
He always drank it with a side of Coke.

A small ritual of control in a house that had none. His eyes were tired, not from work, but from the burden of unmet expectations. His own and everyone else's. Ruth Harris was the opposite and the same.

Where Gerald wielded silence like a blade, Ruth carried it like a burden. She knit constantly, scarves, mittens, anything that required repetition. Each stitch was perfect, symmetrical, and tight, as if she were trying to repair something that had never been broken properly.

The rhythm of her needles filled the air where laughter should have lived. Click, pull, breathe. Click, pull, breathe. They loved each other once, perhaps. You could sense it in the way they avoided meeting each other's eyes, as though the memory of love was a mirror they couldn't bear to look into anymore.

Their affection had calcified into ritual, birthday cards signed in the same handwriting, hugs replaced by polite nods, apologies lost in the static hum of the refrigerator. The clock on the wall did most of the talking. Its tick was omnipresent, patient, impartial. It marked time like a judge, counting the seconds between words not spoken.

When conversation came, it arrived in fragments: *"Pass the salt." "Lights out by nine." "Don't forget your homework." "Your teacher called." "Your father's tired."*

Love was never mentioned. Not once. In that house, love was implied in small, brittle gestures. An extra pork chop left on his plate, a blanket tucked under his chin, the faint smell of starch on his father's shirts ironed without complaint.

But implication fades. And for a child, silence can sound like indifference. Michael learned early that quiet could both protect and suffocate.

He learned that not all pain leaves bruises, and not all absence means neglect. Sometimes, it means the people who should teach you how to speak have long forgotten how. So, he made his own noise.

At first, it was drawing faces that could smile back, mouths that could say what his parents never did. He'd sit for hours at the kitchen table, sketching eyes that looked alive, that seemed capable of forgiveness. The graphite smudged across his fingers felt more honest than words ever had.

By then, he'd filled a box with sketches of people he imagined could listen. People who might stay. But drawing was only a temporary language. The silence always returned. At night, he would lie awake and listen to it stretch through the house. The faint clink of glass from the living room, the steady tap of knitting needles down the hall, the sound of two people managing not to speak until sleep took mercy on them.

In school, Michael learned to observe rather than participate. He memorized faces, tones, hesitations; the microscopic shifts that gave away what people meant but didn't say. He became fluent in the subtext of sighs, the weight of pauses, the small betrayals in body language.

By fifteen, he could tell when someone was lying before they spoke. By twenty, he had decided to make a profession of it. He told his parents he wanted to study psychology. Gerald barely looked up from his papers. Ruth's needles stopped mid-stitch, then resumed without comment.

"That makes sense," his father said finally. "You've always been good at listening." It wasn't praise. It was a statement of resignation. When he left for college, no one cried. His mother packed sandwiches and slipped a folded note into his suitcase that read, *Remember to eat.*

His father handed him an envelope with a check inside and said, "Don't come back until you know what you're doing." He didn't. He spent years trying to fill that silence through education, through empathy, through the illusion that helping others could make up for everything he never received.

He built a life out of listening, a career out of healing strangers, a reputation for being calm when others weren't. But silence doesn't disappear. It waits. It changes shape. It hides behind professionalism and polite restraint.

And sometimes, like the night Claire Alden walked into his office six minutes late, it resurfaces. Not as emptiness. But as recognition. Because when she spoke, when her voice trembled under the weight of its own confession, it sounded like home. The same quiet desperation he was born into, dressed in different words.

And for the first time in his life, the silence inside him answered back. Michael grew up teaching himself what love should sound like, what it should feel like. He pieced it together from fragments: a teacher's soft encouragement, a neighbor's wave through a rain-speckled window, the way sunlight lingered on faces that smiled without reason.

He became the boy who stayed behind after class to help stack chairs for tired janitors, the one who carried groceries for widowed neighbors without being asked. He never did it for praise; he did it to fill the echo of absence with something gentler.

By high school, he was the quiet constant in other people's storms; tutoring kids who struggled, not for money or recognition, but because he couldn't stand watching someone drown in the same silence, he had grown up in. He'd wait beside them until the numbers or words finally made sense, smiling softly when they did, like it was their victory alone.

People gravitated toward him, not because he was loud or charismatic, but because he listened. He had that rare kind of patience that made others slow down, open up, breathe. That instinct carried him into adulthood.

He worked for everything he owned. Scholarships earned through the bruised hours of study, degrees built on caffeine and exhaustion, his name eventually engraved on a therapist's license that wasn't granted by chance but by relentless determination.

He had a gift: he made anyone sitting across from him feel seen, as though their pain wasn't a burden but a story worth unfolding. Where his parents had been withholding, Michael vowed to give. Family became his compass, something sacred, something he would not repeat his parents' mistakes with. Love, for him, wasn't grand or performative.

It was steady. It was showing up. It was remembering intricate details and meaning them. Still, sometimes, when the house went quiet and the hum of the refrigerator was the only sound, a familiar ache would settle in.

The kind that reminded him how hard it is to unlearn the silence that raised you. With Eva, he was endlessly present, the kind of father who showed up even when the world gave him a thousand reasons not to.

He'd braid her hair before school, clumsy fingers fumbling with strands that slipped through like silk, until she giggled and told him she liked it anyway. He'd tuck folded notes into her lunchbox and scribbled hearts, little reminders that she was loved beyond reason.

Every recital, every school play, every small performance in a cafeteria that smelled of floor wax and crayons, he was there. Always there.

Even when exhaustion clung to him like a second skin, he would sit in the dim light of the auditorium and smile as though nothing in the world could matter more.

With Evelyn, before the seams began to fray, he tried to build the home he never had, a softer kind of place. Sunday breakfasts with too many pancakes, laughter echoing through the kitchen; late-night talks that lasted past the comfort of coffee; the quiet brush of hands in passing that said I'm here.

He wanted love to be something you practiced, not just promised. Michael was not perfect. But he was good, good in the way that counts. The kind of man who tried to do the right thing even when it cost him sleep, pride, or the uncomplicated way out.

The kind who carried guilt like a pocket watch. Something heavy, old, and always ticking, reminding him of the moments he wished he could rewind. He was good in quiet ways. He was the man who stayed late to help a patient no one else wanted to see.

The man who returned a call at midnight because someone said they were "fine" in a voice that clearly wasn't. The man who remembered the birthdays of his colleagues' children, who never left the coffee pot empty, who paid attention to the smallest cracks in people and treated them like things worth mending. He believed integrity wasn't a virtue, it was oxygen.

Without it, everything else suffocated. Every inch of where he stood in life had been earned; carved out of silence with patience, empathy, and a stubborn refusal to let the world make him cruel. He had seen what cruelty could do. He had grown up in its shadow, watching his father drown behind the armor of responsibility, his mother smile through her own quiet erasures.

He had promised himself he would never be like them, never let disappointment turn to bitterness, never let kindness rot into duty. And for years, he kept that promise.

His apartment was modest but clean, the walls lined with books that bore underlines in the margins and folded corners like conversations paused mid-thought. He read philosophy beside his daughter's bedtime stories, poured whiskey beside warm milk, balanced the ache of adulthood against the light of a child who still believed he could fix anything.

He wasn't a saint, not by any measure. He lost his temper sometimes, in small, human bursts. He forgot to eat. He let emails pile up. He cursed at the news. He stared at his reflection some mornings and thought: You're still not enough.

But goodness, to him, was never about perfection. It was about persistence, showing up, even when it hurt. Listening, even when he was too tired to care. Loving, even when the world made love feel like a liability.

And yet sometimes, when the house went still and even the ticking clock seemed to hesitate, a question stirred quietly beneath the surface of that goodness. A question he never spoke aloud that lead to more questions.

What happens when doing the right thing isn't enough? When honesty costs you what you love most? When compassion crosses the line between healing and harm? When a kind hand lingers one moment too long, and the world, or worse, your own heart, refuses to forgive it?

Michael had built his life around boundaries, around principles that were meant to keep him safe from chaos.
But boundaries blur when loneliness moves in.

Principles bend when a voice trembles across from you and you see not a patient, but a person. Sometimes, he thought goodness was less a virtue and more a burden. A soft armor that the world kept testing for cracks.
And lately, he could feel it splintering. The pressure of choice. The weight of empathy. The unbearable truth that sometimes, the right thing doesn't save anyone.

It simply breaks you slower. Michael grew up learning that feelings were things you folded neatly and put away. He learned that a calm face could be armor, that silence could pass for strength.
His parents didn't teach this lesson aloud. It was written in gestures, in pauses, in the way his father's jaw would tighten instead of speaking disappointment, in the tremor of his mother's hands when she tried not to cry.

Michael watched, memorized, translated. He became fluent in silence, fluent in everything unspoken. By sixteen, the quiet no longer fit. It burned. There was a restlessness in him, a thrum of anger he couldn't name. It wasn't directed at anyone in particular, just the weight of holding too much inside for too long.
Rage became a hum beneath his skin, coiled and waiting, like static looking for a wire. Basketball gave him an outlet for a while. The rhythm of the ball against the pavement was something like a heartbeat he could control. The squeak of sneakers on polished wood, the slap of hands, the sweet, momentary flight when he rose toward the rim. It was all noise, motion, freedom.

For a few hours each day, he could outrun the silence that raised him.
Then came the *pop*, a torn ligament, sudden and merciless.

The doctors said it would heal, but something else broke that never quite did. The gym lights faded, the team moved on, and Michael found himself in the stillness of recovery.

Alone, aching, and forced once again to sit with everything he couldn't say. The silence this time was different. It wasn't external, it was inside him, pressing against his ribs, daring him to find a way out.

He turned, almost out of desperation, to books. At first, anything would do. Tattered paperbacks from yard sales, mystery novels with cracked spines, stories that let him disappear for a while.

Then, by chance, he stumbled onto the psychology shelf in the school library. The titles were dry, academic, even strange but there was something electric in them. Words like projection, repression, transference felt like keys he'd been waiting for.

For the first time, the silence of his life began to take shape, to make sense. It was there, under the dim hum of fluorescent lights, that Michael Harris began to understand that people weren't born broken, they were simply unheard.

And he decided, quietly, that he would spend his life listening.

The books came first. Thick texts with cracked spines and underlined passages where other hands had lingered before him.

Margins crowded with questions, arrows, and half-legible notes that made him feel less alone, as if someone, somewhere, had once been asking the same impossible things.

He read greedily, as though the pages could teach him what life had refused to explain. He carried the books home in a worn backpack that always seemed heavier than it should have been, sneaking chapters between classes, between dinner and homework, between the long breaths of an empty night.

Why did people break? Why did they hurt the ones they swore they loved? Why did his parents, who said they cared for him, feel so impossibly far away even when they sat across the same table?

He would watch his father sip Jack Daniel's with a side of Coke; always the same, measured ritual, eyes fixed on a stack of ungraded papers, the smell of whiskey, cola, and ink mingling in the air. His mother would knit beside him, her needles clinking softly like a metronome for their silence.

Each stitch seemed a plea for peace, a quiet bargain with the universe that if she just kept weaving, maybe the family would hold. Michael began to wonder if families could shatter without anyone ever raising their voice.

If heartbreak could happen in whispers. Those questions didn't fade, they sank into him like seeds buried in damp soil. He filled entire composition notebooks with restless thoughts, margins lined with borrowed wisdom.

Freud, Jung, Maslow, they became his secret companions. His handwriting pressed too hard into the paper, smudging ink along the edges where his palm dragged across the page.

The words weren't elegant, but they were honest, small attempts to make sense of a world that never made room for softness. Teachers began to notice.

They saw the boy who stayed late after class, asking questions that had no easy answers.

A guidance counselor once told him he was "too serious for his age," though her tone carried a hint of admiration, as if she sensed that his seriousness was less a burden than a kind of calling.

For Michael, it wasn't seriousness. It was survival. It was a hunger to understand why people unraveled and whether anyone could ever truly be put back together again. College became his escape.

Columbia University.

A scholarship was his golden ticket out of the suffocating quiet. When he stepped off the train in Manhattan, the city swallowed him whole. The thunder of traffic, the pulse of subway brakes, the chorus of a thousand strangers moving with purpose. For the first time, silence wasn't a cage; it was a choice. The city vibrated with everything he'd been missing.

Steam rose from the subway grates like ghosts of forgotten energy, twisting in the winter air before dissolving into the skyline. Streetlights buzzed in intervals, halos of amber bleeding into the mist. Taxi horns bickered with sirens, each claiming its own desperate urgency, while the rhythm of hurried footsteps filled the gaps between.

New York did not sleep, it pulsed. And in its pulse, Michael Harris found something that almost wanted to belong. He walked the streets with his collar turned up against the wind, his breath coming out in clouds that disappeared too fast. There was a comfort in the anonymity of it all.

Thousands of lives brushing past him, each carrying its own noise, its own burden, its own secret ache. Here, he didn't have to explain himself. Here, no one cared who his parents had been or what he'd left behind in that small New Jersey town full of whispered disappointments.

For the first time, silence was not a punishment. It was freedom. He rented a small room above a laundromat on Amsterdam Avenue, barely more than a bed, a desk, and a window that looked out over a fire escape tangled in ivy.

At night, he could hear the city breathe a distant laughter, the whoosh of buses, the faint clatter of bottles somewhere below. He loved it all. The imperfection of it. The life in it. The noise.

Columbia's library became his sanctuary.

The scent of aging paper and ink-stained ambition clung to its air, the quiet hum of fluorescent bulbs merging with the slow, steady rustle of turning pages. There, beneath the towering shelves of psychology and philosophy, he discovered the sound of his own thoughts.

He read until his eyes blurred; Jung, Kierkegaard, Maslow, devouring theories about meaning, morality, and the fragile scaffolding of the human mind. Each paragraph was a small act of rebellion against the silence he'd been born into.

Each idea, a light turned on in a room he'd never known existed. Sometimes, he'd fall asleep over open books, waking to the imprint of words on his cheek and the faint hum of the city beyond the glass.

Other nights, he'd walk down to the river, stand beneath the skeleton arms of the George Washington Bridge, and watch the reflection of the city ripple across the Hudson.

The water was dark, but the lights trembled on its surface like scattered constellations, unreachable but still trying.

He thought of his mother's trembling hands, his father's empty chair at dinner, the endless clock that ruled their house. And he promised himself: I'll never live small.

He began keeping notebooks; small, leather-bound volumes filled with half-legible notes and ink-stained questions. He wrote about empathy as resistance. About the beauty of imperfection. About how people weren't broken, just misheard. Sometimes he caught himself smiling at nothing, the kind of smile that comes when you've glimpsed who you might become.

He had no real plan, no mentor, no certainty. But he had momentum. And for a boy raised in quiet rooms, momentum felt like redemption. He worked part-time at a café near campus, refilling coffee for insomniac students, reading between orders, listening to their worries spill across tables. He found himself drawn to their confessions the way people softened when they were seen.

Maybe that was where it started. Not the profession, but the calling. The understanding that sometimes all a person needs is a witness to their pain. He wanted to be that witness. To hold space for what the world tried to hide. He wanted to heal what life broke, not through doctrine or discipline, but through presence.

He didn't know it then, but those late nights, the endless pages, the smell of rain on concrete, the flicker of lamplight against his notebook, were shaping him. Not into the man he already was, but into the man he would one day become. The kind who believed that listening was a form of mercy. That truth could be a salve.

That love, even the forbidden kind, was never wasted, only misplaced.

And so, in the hum of that restless city, between the heartbeat of crosswalk signals and the steady scrape of pen against paper, Michael Harris began the long, quiet work of becoming who he was meant to be.

He buried himself in Freud, Jung, and Adler, their names like passwords into secret rooms of the human mind. But what fascinated him most wasn't the theory, it was people. He'd sit for hours in cramped cafés off 8th Avenue, textbooks open but forgotten beside his coffee, watching strangers move through the theater of their ordinary lives.
A couple arguing softly over a phone, a man staring too long at the door as if waiting for someone who wouldn't come, a barista humming through exhaustion. Each face was a study in private storms. Each gesture, a story half-told. He began to recognize fragments of his own family in them.

His father's swallowed anger in the clenched jaw of a businessperson; his mother's quiet ache in the eyes of a woman reading alone by the window. Sometimes, in a reflection, he caught pieces of himself too. The boy still trying to learn what love sounded like when it wasn't silence.
NYU sharpened him further. The city was a crucible, loud, relentless, alive. Sirens cut through the night like warnings. Subway brakes screamed below the pavement. The streets pulsed with movement, bodies brushing past one another, stories colliding for a breath before parting again.

When the noise became too much, he'd cut across Washington Square Park, his sanctuary of chaos. The fountain caught sunlight in fractured arcs, tossing small rainbows into the afternoon air. Children darted between benches, their laughter cutting through the weight of the day.
A guitarist played under the arch, his song drifting and reshaping with every gust of wind. Michael loved that park because it never asked him to be still. It was proof that disorder could be beautiful, that not all noise was something to escape.

Standing beneath the marble arch, he often felt suspended between history and possibility, as if the city itself whispered: everyone is trying to become something they weren't allowed to be.

In the classrooms high above the square, he began to find his own rhythm. He discovered he had a gift for people. For drawing them out, coaxing the truth to the surface. While others rehearsed empathy from the safety of theory, Michael felt it. Raw and unfiltered.

He didn't just listen; he received. When classmates stumbled through clinical detachment, Michael would lean forward, elbows on the table, his expression open and steady. And suddenly, others would begin to speak, to really speak.

Stories would pour out of them, half-ashamed, half-relieved, as though something in his quietness gave them permission. Professors called it empathy. Michael knew better. It wasn't empathy. It was hunger. A craving to understand people because he had never been understood.

A need to make sense of human pain, to map it, to soften it, because if he could decode others, maybe he could finally decode himself. By the time he graduated, the city had carved him into something new. He was no longer just surviving silence, he was shaping it, turning it into a tool.

And it was during a seminar on trauma narratives, under the pale glow of a projector and the hum of a radiator that never stopped hissing, that he first saw Evelyn.

Her hand was raised before she spoke, voice steady but edged with something brittle beneath the confidence.

Her words caught him. Not just the meaning, but the weight of them.

It was the first time in a long time that Michael stopped analyzing and simply felt. He didn't know it then, but that single moment, the glance, the question, the shared silence afterward, would alter the entire course of his life.

She sat two rows ahead, hair pinned neatly, glasses slipping down the bridge of her nose as she scribbled notes with a furious intensity that made her pen sound alive.

Evelyn Clarke.

Sharp. Ambitious. A mind that didn't just absorb but devoured. Her questions sliced through the seminar air with the precision of a scalpel, dissecting ideas others only dared to circle.

But when she smiled: rare, sudden, it transformed everything. The hard edges softened, and in that fleeting warmth, Michael found himself believing, for the first time in years, that maybe love wasn't a myth.

Maybe it was simply hidden in plain sight, waiting for the right kind of quiet to find it.

They began with study sessions in coffee shops, hunched over journal articles and lukewarm cappuccinos that turned into refills and laughter. Her voice carried conviction, his carried calm. They fit like two halves of an unfinished sentence.

What started as theory turned into confession, hopes, fears, the futures they were both desperate to build before the world hardened them too much. They married in his late twenties, quickly, almost recklessly, as though the life they wanted might evaporate if they didn't seize it fast enough.

Their first apartment in Queens was small. A secondhand couch pressed against walls that peeled in quiet rebellion, a kitchen barely large enough to turn around in. But they filled it with laughter, with half-burned dinners, with cheap wine and whispered promises murmured between exhaustion and love.
On weekends, they'd walk the city until their feet ached, holding hands, sharing dreams too fragile to say aloud. Evelyn wanted to open her own firm one day; Michael wanted to open a clinic that could help the ones who fell through the cracks.

They believed in each other's fire. They believed belief was enough. When Eva was born, the world tilted on its axis. Michael held her in the hospital room, skin to skin, her tiny fists curled against his chest, and for the first time he understood what permanence felt like.
Her cry cracked something open in him that had been locked away since childhood. It wasn't just love, it was revelation. He would never be the same again. For a while, it was enough. For a while, they were enough. But cracks came. They always did.

At first, they were hairline, almost invisible. His long hours at the clinic. Her late nights at the firm. The quiet accumulation of missed dinners, forgotten texts, promises postponed with good intentions. They told themselves it was temporary, that love was durable.
But distance isn't loud, it's subtle, patient, relentless. Michael carried his pain the way his father had; quietly, inward, until it hardened into something that resembled composure. Evelyn hurled hers outward. Her voice sharp as glass, shattering the calm when silence failed her.

She shouted because she didn't know how else to be heard. Arguments flared in vivid color: her red lipstick bleeding against the rim of a wineglass, her heels striking the hardwood like punctuation marks, the brittle laughter at dinner parties when the tension between them grew too thick to ignore.

"You're not here, Michael," she would say. "You listen to everyone but me." And he'd answer quietly, "You don't stop long enough to see me." Each word chipped away at something they once swore was unbreakable.

There was no explosion, no grand betrayal to point to, just the slow, relentless erosion of two people who had stopped hearing each other years before they stopped speaking. It began with small fractures; forgotten dinners, unanswered texts, nights spent in separate rooms under the same roof.

Then came the colder silences, the ones that didn't ask for answers because both already knew them. Love had become a language they'd forgotten how to speak, and every attempt to remember only made them sound like strangers mimicking old lines.

When the divorce came, it was ugly in its honesty but merciful in its swiftness. No pretense, no performance. Just truth, stripped bare. The lawyers tried to make it procedural. Signatures, clauses, custody schedules, but there's no form for grief, no column for what it means to hand over half your life in the name of civility.

They both knew the exact moment the thread had snapped. It wasn't during the shouting. It wasn't during the accusations. It was that night in the kitchen when Evelyn dropped a glass, and neither of them bent down to pick up the pieces. That was the sound of something ending. Not the glass, but the years between them.

When the papers were finally signed, they didn't even look at each other. Just pens scratching against paper, a quiet violence disguised as resolution. Custody of Eva was split evenly. A sterile word, evenly, as if you could divide a child's heart into fractions without breaking something sacred.
On paper, it meant balance. In practice, it meant absence. Michael always felt he'd lost more than he'd kept. He got the weekdays; the homework, the bedtime routines, the mornings with cereal and cold coffee, while Evelyn got the weekends, all laughter and leisure, the easier version of love.

He envied her sometimes. Not for her freedom, but for the lightness in Eva's laughter when she returned, the sound of joy unburdened by routine. Every curbside exchange was a quiet ritual of grief. Evelyn would pull up, engine idling, her posture perfect behind the wheel.
Michael would be waiting on the sidewalk with Eva's overnight bag, his hands deep in his coat pockets to hide their trembling. "Did she eat breakfast?" Evelyn would ask, as if it mattered. "Yes." He sighed "And her jacket?" She asked impatiently. "In the bag." He replied. The same questions, the same hollow choreography.

Two people pretending to be polite while bleeding through their smiles. Evelyn's face carried the poise of victory, the calm of someone who'd already rehearsed her next chapter. Michael's carried surrender; not to her, but to the inevitability of loss itself. But then, Eva's hand would slip into his, small, warm, certain.
She would tilt her head, squint up at him, and say, "See you soon, Daddy." That was all it took. That single sentence, that tiny palm, that weight of innocence anchoring him to a world that still made sense.

It was enough to keep him from shattering completely. Enough to remind him that love, even fractured, could still be the thing that held you together.

He watched her climb into the car, waving until the taillights disappeared around the corner. And when the street fell silent again, when the wind picked up and the world resumed its indifferent hum, he would whisper to the empty air, "See you soon."

Because hope, even when it's foolish, has its own kind of gravity.

Now, at forty-two, Michael wore the role of therapist like a suit tailored too tightly. His office in midtown was all polish and order; mahogany desk, framed degrees, soft leather chairs angled in gentle symmetry. To his patients, he was a pillar: calm, measured, endlessly patient.

His voice had the cadence of safety. But beneath the surface, the crisp shirt, the careful posture, the neutral tone, was a man splintered by loneliness. The fissures ran deep, invisible but constant.

He felt them most in the quiet between sessions, when the hum of the city faded and his reflection in the darkened window stared back, hollow-eyed, and weary.

He could calm others. He could translate chaos into language. But when the last client left and the clock ticked toward evening, the silence in that office was deafening. The ache wasn't sharp; it was steady, grinding, a dull weight that lived behind his ribs.

Some nights, when Eva wasn't with him, he would stand in her room and smooth the corner of her pillow, tracing the indent her head had left as though the gesture could tether him to something whole.

He understood brokenness not because he studied it, but because it lived inside him, an inheritance he could never outgrow. His colleagues respected him. His patients trusted him. His daughter adored him. And still, he felt like a fraud. Every compliment, every word of praise slid off him like rain on glass.

The world saw steadiness; inside, he was still the boy from that silent New Jersey house, still waiting for someone to look up and really see him. He thought of himself as a man with two faces: The one he wore for the world, composed, articulate, safe.

And the one that surfaced in the mirror at night, eyes hollow, jaw clenched against the weight of other people's pain. He wondered if his patients ever sensed it; the tremor beneath his calm, the quiet desperation coiled behind his empathy. Michael loved fiercely, gave endlessly, but deep down he believed he was never quite enough.

Not enough for Evelyn. Not enough to keep the family whole. Not enough to silence the ache of his youth. Even Eva's love, pure and unshaken, sometimes pierced him with guilt. What if she saw it, the hollowness behind the smile? What if she realized her father's wisdom was scaffolding built over fragile beams? So he kept moving. Kept giving. Kept listening. Because to stop was to risk collapse, to face the boy inside who had never truly stopped straining for a voice in the dark.

And that was why, on a rain-heavy Thursday afternoon, when Claire Alden walked into his office six minutes late, something inside him shifted.

He felt it before he understood it. The tick of the clock, the faint scent of rain on her coat, the way the air seemed to rearrange itself around her. Her lateness should have irritated him, it usually did.

But instead, it branded itself in his mind. *4:06 p.m.* Her name on the intake form was ordinary enough. Her file unremarkable.

But when she looked up, green eyes meeting his, something moved inside him; something old, something dangerous. It wasn't attraction. Not exactly. It was recognition.

The brokenness in her gaze reached across the room and touched the fractures he thought he'd hidden. He straightened, clinging to professionalism like a life raft, his voice steady even as the air grew thin. Underneath, something raw and wordless stirred. This was no ordinary session.

This was the hinge moment, the breath before a life begins to tilt. Michael Harris didn't know it yet, but everything he had ever learned about silence, love, and control was about to unravel, one heartbeat after 4:06 p.m.

The Patient

Claire Alden had learned young that beauty was both a weapon and a curse. She was born in Savannah, Georgia, beneath a canopy of ancient live oaks draped in Spanish moss that swayed like ghosts in the humid air.
The summers there were thick enough to taste; heat heavy with magnolia and honeysuckle, the hum of cicadas filling the spaces between breath and prayer. Her father, Reverend Thomas Alden, filled the pulpit with fire and certainty. His sermons were thunder dressed as truth, his voice echoing through the small wooden church until even the rafters seemed to tremble.

He spoke of sin and salvation, of purity and obedience, his eyes alight with conviction that left no room for doubt. Her mother, Beth Alden, moved through the world as though she were afraid of making noise. Even her footsteps seemed rehearsed yet soft, deliberate, the way one might walk through a house already on the edge of breaking.
She painted porcelain plates with tiny, perfect flowers; roses, lilacs, forget-me-nots, arranging them in even rows along the kitchen wall and calling it art. Each one looked nearly identical, yet Beth treated them as sacred.

She painted in the afternoons when the light came through the lace curtains in pale ribbons, and the dust motes floated like ghosts she refused to acknowledge.
When the paint ran thin, she mixed it with water and whispered prayers that it would last until her husband's next paycheck. Sometimes she spoke to the plates as she painted, gentle murmurs Claire was never meant to hear.

Stay beautiful, she would tell them. Stay still. Her beauty was quiet, the kind that apologized for existing. Her smile was polite, practiced for church socials and grocery store aisles, but it never reached her eyes. And her hands; those delicate, tremoring hands, were always busy. Kneading dough. Wiping counters already clean.

Folding laundry that didn't need folding. They trembled, not from weakness, but from the constant effort of keeping peace. Claire used to watch her from the doorway, a little girl holding her breath so she wouldn't disrupt the rhythm.

The air in that house was fragile, a kind of invisible glass always one vibration away from shattering. Her father filled the pulpit on Sundays, his voice booming with certainty and scripture, but at home, it was Beth's silence that ruled.

A silence that said: Don't provoke. Don't contradict. Don't break the spell that keeps us standing. The kitchen was Beth's sanctuary. She filled it with the smell of lemon polish and the faint sweetness of porcelain paint, trying to scrub out the sting of sermons that turned their home into confessionals.

She rarely hugged Claire. Instead, she straightened the collar of her dress, brushed imaginary dust from her shoulders, and said softly, "Be good, baby. Good girls make life easier." It took Claire years to understand that her mother's trembling wasn't fear of her husband, it was fear of what would happen if she stopped pretending everything was fine.

And when Beth finally died; her heart giving out one quiet morning as she rinsed her brushes, the plates remained on the wall, perfectly aligned. Roses. Lilacs. Forget-me-nots. A fragile gallery of survival. Claire couldn't bring herself to take them down. She left them hanging, each one a hymn of her mother's restraint.

Each one a reminder that beauty, when built on fear, eventually cracks. From them, Claire learned contradiction: her father's booming certainty and her mother's whispered surrender.

She was the preacher's daughter. The girl who smiled too sweetly in Sunday school, whose ribbons were tied too tightly, whose posture was perfect under the watchful eyes of a congregation that believed virtue could be measured by posture alone.

The town adored her for it. "Pretty little thing," the elders would say, "with her mama's grace and her daddy's fire." But beauty came with expectations.

Men looked too long; women whispered too often. Every compliment was a cage disguised as praise. Every stare felt like ownership. She learned to smile as armor, to wield charm the way her father wielded scripture, carefully, decisively, aware of its power.

By twelve, she could read a room before she entered it. By fifteen, she could tell which kind of smile would make an adult trust her, which kind of silence would make them underestimate her.

And by eighteen, she had already mastered the art of vanishing behind poise. Yet beneath the perfection was hunger, an ache for freedom she couldn't name.

Late at night, she'd sneak onto the porch when the house fell quiet, listening to the sound of the marsh frogs and the distant creak of boats in the river. She'd imagine herself leaving. Boarding a train north, the wind in her hair, the moss falling away behind her like a memory.

Her mother once caught her staring out the window and asked softly, "What do you see out there, baby?"

Claire had answered without thinking, "Something that doesn't hurt." Beth had smiled sadly and said nothing. By the time she turned twenty-one, Savannah felt smaller than the cage she'd built inside herself.

She left on a gray morning without ceremony, her suitcase scuffed and light, the scent of magnolia still clinging to her dress. She told no one her plans, only that she needed to "breathe somewhere else." New York was chaos, loud, alive, unyielding. And for a while, which was enough.

She waitressed, studied part-time, reinvented herself in the reflection of every subway window. Men noticed her, but she'd already learned that attention was not affection. What she wanted, what she'd always wanted, was to be seen without being consumed.

But even in the city's anonymity, ghosts followed: her father's sermons ringing in her head, her mother's silence haunting her reflection. By the time she walked into Michael Harris's office, six minutes late, she'd spent a lifetime trying to understand why she could make people fall in love with her but never quite feel loved herself.

The Alden's home was small but immaculate, polished until it gleamed with a kind of forced holiness. The walls seemed to hum with expectation, every surface scrubbed until it reflected obedience.

On the mantel sat framed Bible verses cross-stitched in pastel thread, reminders stitched by her mother's trembling hands: *Honor thy father. A virtuous woman is worth far above rubies.* Even the air smelled disciplined, like lemon polish and restraint. Every Sunday morning was a performance.

Her mother's smile, delicate and brittle, stretched across the pews; her father's booming voice filled the church like thunder made righteous. Claire played her part perfectly; the preacher's daughter with the perfect bow in her hair, perfect posture, perfect silence.

But behind closed doors, silence reigned. Not the silence of peace, but of judgment. It was a silence so dense it had shape and temperature, wrapping itself around her chest until even breathing felt like an act of rebellion.

It came laced in scripture and guilt; modesty, obedience, purity. Words that sounded holy but landed heavy. She learned early that a girl's beauty was temptation, her laughter a sin if it rang too loudly, her thoughts a battlefield where goodness and shame were indistinguishable. She learned to move with grace not out of freedom, but fear. Posture straight. Steps measured.

Words chosen carefully, as though each syllable might shatter like glass if spoken wrong. Still, beauty clung to her like light through stained glass, refracted, inescapable, impossible to dim. The brunette waves of her hair refused to stay pinned. Her green eyes caught the sun and turned it into something bold.

The soft curve of her mouth; caught between sorrow and defiance, invited the world to look, even as she wished it wouldn't. Men stared. Women whispered. Their glances were verdicts: too pretty, too proud, too dangerous for her own salvation.

At fourteen, she overheard two church wives murmuring near the punch bowl: She'll be trouble one day, that one. You can see it in the way she looks at the world.

She hadn't meant to look at the world that way. It was just that curiosity had always been her first sin.

When she smiled, her father's jaw would tighten, and he'd quote scripture about vanity. When she stayed quiet, her mother's eyes filled with pity, as if silence were a punishment she'd been born to endure.

So Claire learned to wear her beauty like penance. Head high, eyes lowered, her grace precise enough to be mistaken for peace.

But inside, something wild stirred, a spark she couldn't pray away. It whispered to her in mirrors and moonlight, in the stillness after sermons. It told her that goodness wasn't the same as holiness, and holiness didn't always mean love.

And deep down, beneath the layers of guilt and lace, Claire Alden began to understand that her beauty wasn't her sin. It was her rebellion. Claire, even as a girl, understood that her appearance gave her power but invited punishment in equal measure. Compliments always came with a warning, affection always with a cost.

She learned to smile in ways that didn't provoke, to speak softly so her voice wouldn't sound like pride. In her father's eyes, beauty was a test of obedience; in her mother's, it was a burden to be managed, hidden, survived.

Her father loved his congregation more than he loved his daughter. On Sundays, his gaze swept over the pews like a searchlight, finding sinners to save but never once stopping to truly see her. When he spoke of temptation, his tone would shift almost imperceptibly, and she'd feel the weight of his words fall on her shoulders like ash.

Her mother loved appearances more than she loved herself.

Beth's hands stayed busy, polishing silver, trimming flowers, pressing dresses, as though constant movement could ward off the shame of imperfection.

Her smile was as delicate as bone China, something beautiful but easily cracked. And so, Claire learned early to raise her own heart in secret corners.

In the quiet hours between her father's sermons and her mother's sighs, she'd hide in the narrow space behind the house where the moss grew thick on the brick and imagine a different life. One where love wasn't conditional, where silence wasn't the price of survival.

By twelve, she already knew that sorrow, when bottled, turned sour. She could feel it fermenting in her, turning innocence into defiance, ache into ambition. At sixteen, she fled Savannah on a scholarship for dance, her one holy thing.

She left behind the house that smelled of lemon polish and scripture, carrying little more than a battered suitcase, a roll of tights, and a hunger for air that didn't reek of judgment. New York hit her like a tidal wave. The horns, the exhaust, the heat rising from subway grates, it all crashed against her in a dizzying symphony of freedom. Skyscrapers carved the sky into hard angles of light and shadow, but the studio became her sanctuary.

Ballet was her oxygen. In that mirrored room, she could exist without apology. The discipline sculpted her into something new, each blister hardening into callus, each ache refining her posture, her will, her form. The burn in her calves was a kind of prayer.

Pain was currency, and she paid it gladly, because each strain, each bruise, was proof she was remaking herself; one pirouette at a time. Her spine grew into grace; her breath fell into rhythm.

Her body spoke in languages her voice had never been allowed to learn. On stage, she became poetry.

Her brunette hair slicked tight into a bun, her skin gleaming under the stage lights, she was a storm disguised as elegance. Every movement was confession. Every extension, release.

She didn't dance to be adored, she danced to be understood. For a while, it was enough. The spotlight washed her clean. It erased the whispering women, the condemning eyes, the small-town ghosts who had defined her.

The applause rose like tidewater, crashing against her ribs, filling her with something dangerously close to joy. In those brief, luminous moments, Claire Alden could believe she was more than her past.

More than the preacher's daughter, more than the silence that raised her. She was breath and motion, grace, and rebellion alive in a way that frightened her. But when the lights dimmed and the curtain fell, the quiet returned.

It came creeping in with the same soft cruelty as the nights back home; thick, heavy, jealous of the light she borrowed. In her tiny dorm room, tights draped over the back of a chair, bruises blossoming violet along her shins, she'd lie on her back and stare at the cracked plaster ceiling.

The applause still echoed faintly in her ears, fading like a tide pulling away. And she'd wonder, how long could beauty keep her alive?

How long before the silence found her again?

Enter Lucian Alden.

He was older, a venture capitalist whose charm was polished like glass.

Smooth, reflective, giving back only what he wanted people to see. His suits were tailored in shades of midnight and ash; his cologne smelled faintly of cedar and money. The world bent around his confidence. Waiters moved faster when he entered a room. Investors leaned forward. Women looked twice, even when they didn't mean to. Lucian carried himself like a man who had never been told no. And when he did say it, the word cracked through the air like a whip.

When he met Claire, he saw not a young woman clawing for light but a prize. Something exquisite to display among his acquisitions: the penthouses, the artwork, the companies he collected and then forgot.

Her dancer's grace, her delicate poise, her unspoken hunger to be seen, these were proof of his power. Beauty, to him, was not something to cherish. It was something to own. Claire was twenty-two when she married him.

He was dazzling. His world was nothing like she'd ever experienced, full of chandeliers and laughter, the clink of crystal, the murmur of privilege. Town cars idled at curbs for her. Restaurants that once turned her away now held tables waiting.

Their penthouse overlooked Manhattan like a throne carved from light. Lucian called her his salvation. He said she gave him what no deal, no fortune, no lover ever had; meaning.

And Claire, starved for devotion, mistook possession for love. She didn't yet understand that Lucian's affection was never soft. It was a contract; binding, conditional, cold.

To be loved by him was to surrender in installments.
The years that followed hollowed her out.

Lucian was generous in public and cruel in private. On red carpets and at charity galas, he played the part of the devoted husband, his hand resting at the small of her back as cameras flashed.

He filled her champagne glass before the reporters, leaned close enough for microphones to catch the low hum of laughter, called her his muse, his queen, his redemption. The image was immaculate. Behind closed doors, the performance ended.

His voice turned sharp, deliberate, slicing through her composure with surgical precision. He left no bruises where the world could see, but his words carved deep. *"You're nothing without me." "You'd still be barefoot in Savannah dirt if not for me."*

The words sank like teeth. Claire learned the art of disguise. She smiled until her cheeks trembled. She sipped champagne with trembling fingers disguised as elegance. She folded herself into whatever shape Lucian required.

She wore gowns like armor and diamonds like chains, her beauty repurposed into spectacle. His trophy, his validation. And every night, when the doors locked and the city outside glittered like a world that had forgotten her name, the silence pressed harder than it ever had in Savannah.

Loneliness, in that penthouse, became a living thing. It sat with her at the vanity, watched her undress, followed her to bed. When Lucian's breathing deepened beside her, she'd stare through the floor-to-ceiling glass at the skyline. The constellations of windows flickering with other people's lives, and wonder if any of them knew what it meant to be loved wrong.

She found comfort where she could.

In the orange bottles tucked discreetly into the drawer beside her bed; prescriptions written for anxiety, sleep, grief, that promised quiet edges, merciful blur, a soft fade from consciousness. Then came the loss.
A daughter, gone before she could be held long enough to leave a sound. Sometimes Claire still saw the hospital room when she closed her eyes. The sterile walls, the smell of antiseptic and iron, the relentless hum of a machine that eventually fell silent.

She remembered the nurse's hand on her shoulder, gentle but trembling, and two words that detonated her life: *"I'm sorry."* They placed the baby near her for a moment, a swaddled bundle that already felt like memory. Claire traced her tiny face, too fragile to touch, skin cooling even as her mother's hands warmed with panic.
There was no first cry. No squirm of life. Just stillness. Lucian never spoke of it. He signed the paperwork, shook the doctor's hand, and told her they would "try again."As if this child could be replaced like a lost investment. As if grief were inefficient.

His silence that day cut deeper than any insult he'd ever thrown. It turned her mourning into exile. Claire never forgave herself. She cataloged every possible cause. Something she ate, something she did, something in her body that had failed the way love always did.
The guilt calcified. It pressed against her lungs when she tried to breathe, her ribs when she tried to laugh, her throat when she tried to pray. A mother without a child was still a mother, and Claire carried that truth everywhere, an invisible weight, unbearable and unshakable.

★ ✪ ★

By thirty-four, she had become a masterpiece of contradictions. Poised yet fractured, elegant yet exhausted, beautiful in the way ruins are beautiful; magnificent but marked. People stared and saw perfection. They envied what they mistook for peace.
But Michael Harris, when he would one day look at her across the room, saw something else entirely. He saw sorrow dressed as grace. He saw a woman holding her breath between worlds. The one she escaped and the one she still hadn't found. What he didn't know, what she never admitted, was that long before she ever crossed his threshold, she had already found him.

She had read his articles, traced his words, studied the way he spoke about healing as if it were possible. And in her quietest moments, she began to wonder if maybe he was the one man who could finally teach her how to stop apologizing for surviving.
Claire spent her nights in the half-light of her penthouse office, the glow of her laptop painting her face in blue. The city outside throbbed with motion; sirens, laughter, arguments, but she was suspended above it, searching.

Always searching. She typed Michael Harris, trauma therapist, New York into the search bar, and the results unfurled like a breadcrumb trail left by someone who had never meant to be followed.
At first, it was all credentials. Columbia graduate, postdoctoral fellowship in clinical trauma, adjunct lecturer at Fordham. The kind of accomplishments that should have felt sterile. But they didn't.

Claire read each entry like it was a letter meant for her. She found his name in journals she barely understood, Journal of Psychosocial Recovery, Clinical Perspectives on Post-Traumatic Growth, Cognitive Therapy Quarterly. Each title sounded cold, technical, distant. But within the dense, academic paragraphs, she found something else, the tremor of empathy breaking through the scientific restraint. He wrote about grief as if it were a living thing. Not a symptom to be treated, but a presence to be acknowledged.

He described trauma not as an event but as a geography, an internal landscape scarred but still capable of growing light. One phrase, buried near the end of a 2016 article, made her stop. "Healing begins not with answers, but with being heard." She read it twice, then again.

It was the kind of sentence that didn't sound written, it sounded remembered. Then she found the clip. A short interview filmed for a public mental health initiative, archived on a hospital website. The lighting was poor, fluorescent and too bright, but his voice was calm, deliberate, unhurried.

He sat with his hands folded, posture straight but unguarded, speaking with the rare stillness of someone who didn't need to prove his own goodness."People think recovery means erasing what happened," he said. "It doesn't. It means carrying it differently. Making room for it to exist without letting it devour everything else."

She played it again. And again. Not for what he said, but for how he said it. There was no performance, no practiced cadence. Just presence. The kind that speaks directly to the part of you that no one else has ever found.

She let the video run in the background as she scrolled further, the hum of his voice threading through the quiet of her apartment like a ghost that didn't haunt but steadied.

She read about his lectures at Columbia and Mount Sinai, "Ethics of Empathy," "Boundaries of Care," "The Physiology of Trust."She studied his photos from conferences. The professional headshots with the muted smile, the kind eyes behind wire-frame glasses.

In one, he stood at a podium mid-sentence, expression intent, as if he was explaining how to hold another person's pain without breaking your own hands. Colleagues described him as measured, ethical, quietly relentless. "He listens like he's cataloging the air," one former intern wrote in a forum. "Like silence itself is data."

To Claire, it felt like sorcery. She pieced him together from fragments. The abstract phrasing of his research, the kindness in his gaze, the deliberate softness of his words, and built in her mind a portrait of a man both broken and incorruptible.

Someone who had known darkness yet refused to let it define him. Someone who had not only survived his own storms but learned to guide others through theirs. The more she read, the more something dangerous began to stir. Not attraction, not yet. It was recognition.

She saw in him the gravity that mirrored her own; a person stitched together by loneliness, still reaching toward connection even after it had burned him before. He had endured, she thought. And endurance, maybe, would understand her. So she searched deeper. Every article became a thread, every podcast, a door slightly ajar.

She learned his father had been a teacher, that he'd grown up in New Jersey, that he'd lost his marriage two years before the interview. She found an old conference recording where he spoke about empathy as both medicine and risk.
"We think of empathy as light," he said. "But it's a flame. Manage it long enough, and you'll burn, too." That line lodged itself in her chest like an ember.

By the time the evening blurred into midnight, Claire's eyes were raw from the glow of her laptop. The city outside her window pulsed with life. Headlights sweeping across the rain-slick street, sirens echoing somewhere near the river.
All she could hear was his voice replaying in her head. A voice that seemed to know her before she'd ever spoken. When her friend from the charity board, a woman with kind eyes and the hollow calm of someone who'd been broken and glued back together, pressed a folded card into her hand and said, "You should try him. He's good. He'll make you talk,"

Claire only smiled faintly. She didn't tell her friend she already knew his name. That she'd already memorized it. Michael Harris. She said she'd think about it. But she already had. She didn't want to talk. Talking meant bleeding.
And bleeding, in her experience, had never saved anyone. It only made people recoil. But something deep inside her, the same quiet force that had once made her dance barefoot in the rain, that had made her believe love could still redeem whispered, Try again.

So she made the call. The phone rang twice, then a calm voice answered. "Dr. Harris's office."
And when the receptionist asked for her name, she almost said, "No one." Instead, she whispered, "Claire Alden." An appointment was set for Thursday. 4 p.m.

She didn't know why that time mattered. Only that when the moment came, she would be six minutes late. When she stepped through the glass doors of his midtown office, the world seemed to tilt, imperceptibly, inexorably.

As if everything that followed had been waiting for her all along. The clock on the wall read *4:06 p.m.*

A small, ordinary number that would haunt her later.

Michael looked up from his notes. In that brief, suspended moment, Claire felt something shift. An invisible thread snapping taut between them. His presence was quiet, not commanding, but it filled the room in a way that made her pulse stutter.

He didn't smile the way most men did. Not with hunger, not with pity, but with something steadier. A kind of recognition that made her feel, for the first time in years, seen without being sized. Her grief was not dramatic. It had never needed to be.

It was steady. Relentless. Like water wearing down stone. She sat down across from him, clutching her purse as though it were an anchor. And when he asked softly, "What brings you here today?" She opened her mouth and surprised herself.

"I just can't anymore," she said. The words fell heavy between them, unadorned, unplanned. She had been can't for years, long before this room, long before him.

But saying it aloud felt like the first crack in a dam she hadn't realized she'd built. Michael didn't interrupt.

He didn't rush to soothe or explain. He simply stayed.

Something in that stillness reached her where faith, love, and money had failed. And though she couldn't have named it then, what she wanted was not just help. She wanted rescue. What she didn't know, what neither of them yet dared to, was that in the quiet of his gaze, Michael was asking for the same thing.

Two souls, both tired of surviving, circling the possibility of salvation in each other's brokenness

The Sessions

The second time she came, she wasn't late. She arrived exactly on the hour, her knock soft, almost apologetic, as if asking permission not just to enter the room but to exist inside it.
    The hallway outside his office was cloaked in half-light. The sconces along the wall gave off a subdued amber glow, the kind that blurred edges and made sound seem to travel slower. The carpet absorbed footsteps.

Even the air felt heavy with discretion. Through the frosted glass of his door, Michael saw her silhouette before he heard her voice; a slender outline haloed by the muted light of midtown dusk.
    Her figure was motionless for a breath, as though she were steadying herself before crossing into confession. He rose from his chair and opened the door himself. It was a small, impulsive gesture; something he wasn't supposed to do.

Therapists are trained to stay seated, to let the patient make the first move, to preserve the illusion of safety through distance. But when Claire Alden stood there, her dark hair neatly tucked behind one ear, her green eyes rimmed in sleeplessness, Michael found himself forgetting procedure.
    Her perfume reached him first. Something faint, expensive, but worn too thin, as if diluted by fatigue. She smiled, the polite kind of smile people wear when they're trying not to crumble. "Right on time," he said quietly. "Trying to do better," she replied.

Her voice carried a melody of exhaustion.

A tremor under the words that didn't belong to nerves, but to someone who had lived too long on the edge of her own endurance. She stepped inside, and he noticed again how carefully she moved. Every gesture was measured, deliberate, the choreography of someone who had learned to survive scrutiny.

She set her purse down beside the chair and smoothed her skirt before sitting, as if every wrinkle might reveal something she couldn't control. Michael watched her for a moment longer than he should have, the practiced empathy of his profession giving way to something less clinical.

Her presence filled the room not with sound, but with gravity. The clock on the wall ticked faintly, its rhythm a steady metronome between them. He sat down opposite her, the same distance as before, yet the air felt closer. "Last time," he began, "you said, 'I just can't anymore.'"

She nodded, eyes fixed on her hands. He waited. Silence in therapy is a tool, but this silence was different. It wasn't empty. It was charged. Claire inhaled slowly, the breath trembling at its edges. "People think grief is... noise. Crying, screaming, falling apart. But it isn't. It's quieter than that."

She paused. "It's waking up every day and realizing you survived what you shouldn't have, and not knowing what to do with that fact." Her words struck something deep in him. He felt it, like a ripple under the skin.

He kept his tone steady. "And you feel guilty for surviving?" She lifted her gaze to meet his. The contact was electric, two wounds recognizing each other. "I feel guilty for everything," she whispered. "For leaving. For staying. For loving the wrong people. For still breathing when others don't."

Michael wanted to tell her she wasn't alone, that guilt was the shadow grief left behind. But the words stayed lodged in his throat. His training told him to remain still, to hold the silence. But something in her eyes; the tremor behind that composure, made the distance unbearable. He leaned forward slightly, elbows resting on his knees, voice low. "You don't have to earn your right to exist, Claire."

The way she blinked, once, slowly, told him no one had ever said that to her before. Her mouth opened, then closed again. For a second, he thought she might cry, but instead she gave a soft, disbelieving laugh, the kind that breaks more than it relieves. "Michael," she said softly, his name landing in the room like a confession.

He almost corrected her, asked her to call him Dr. Harris, but it felt cruel to build that wall when she had finally lowered one of her own. So he didn't. And in that small defiance, the boundary between them thinned, just slightly, but enough.

He would think about that moment for days afterward: the sound of her voice saying his name, the echo of it after she left, the faint scent of her perfume lingering long after the session ended. He would tell himself it was empathy. He would tell himself it was professional concern. But deep down, he knew better. Something in him, quiet, long-dormant, had stirred awake. And it terrified him.

The lamplight in his office spilled over her as she stepped inside, catching the pallor of her skin, softening the sharp lines of exhaustion etched across her face. The amber glow reached for her gently, as if light itself knew to tread carefully.

Outside, the city murmured faintly of horns, wind, the distant thrum of life beyond glass, but here, in this narrow room of books and quiet, time thinned to a single heartbeat.

Shadows gathered in the corners, holding their breath. The air was thick with the kind of stillness that exists only when two people are both afraid to speak and afraid not to. It felt less like the start of a session and more like the fragile beginning of something neither of them yet had language for.

"Punctual," he said finally, his voice calm but a shade lighter than he felt. She smiled, small, involuntary, and for a moment it felt like sunlight had breached the office, soft and impossible.

But it wasn't sunlight. It was the fragile flicker of someone remembering what warmth felt like after too long in the cold. She crossed to the couch, and, unlike the first time, she didn't perch on its edge like a visitor uncertain of her welcome. She sank a little deeper this time, letting the cushions take her weight.

The change was subtle but seismic. Her body wanted rest even if her mind couldn't name it. Her hands, though, betrayed her. The right one tugged lightly at the sleeve of her blouse, smoothing an invisible crease.

The left worried at her wrist as if trying to erase a memory that still burned beneath the skin. "I hate how much I care about being on time," she said quietly, eyes dropping to the rug. "I think about it all day. I plan for it. I panic over it." She exhaled shakily. "I was terrified I'd be late again."

Michael leaned forward slightly, pen balanced between his fingers. "Why terrified?" She paused. The word terrified hung in the air between them, more honest than she intended. When she finally spoke, her voice was thin, unraveling. "Because I thought you'd think less of me."

He didn't look down at his notes.
He watched her. "And if I did?"

Her head lifted, sharply like the question had struck something tender. Her gaze found his, and for a heartbeat it held. The green of her eyes was glassy, but behind it lived the storm of someone who'd spent her life reading approval like scripture.

"Then," she said softly, "I'd be another disappointment." A beat passed. "And I'm tired of being that." Silence stretched. Not the kind that awkwardly fills a space, but the kind that builds weight. The kind that means something sacred has just been said. Michael didn't rush to fill it. He simply breathed, slow and even, grounding himself.

Inside, something coiled in him; a strange ache that wasn't pity and wasn't professional concern. It was recognition. He set the pen down on his notepad, its click startlingly loud. "Who taught you that being late makes you unworthy?" He asked. She smiled bitterly. "I don't remember not knowing it."

Her fingers pressed together tightly, whitening at the knuckles. "My father used to say that lateness was disrespect, 'time is God's currency,' he'd call it. If I missed curfew, even by a minute, I'd stand outside while he locked the door for an hour. Said it would help me remember next time." Her voice didn't waver, but her eyes did. "I remember the cold more than anything.

How the porch light buzzed. How I counted minutes by the sound of the crickets." Michael's throat tightened. He wanted to say something like "you didn't deserve that," but she wasn't ready for comfort. Comfort too soon feels like disbelief. So he stayed silent, present.

When she looked up again, something fragile lived in her expression; an old pain, yes, but also a flicker of curiosity. "Do you ever… feel like the world keeps giving you the same test until you fail the right way?"

He let the question breathe. "Sometimes it's not a test," he said quietly. "Sometimes it's a memory that keeps asking to be rewritten." She blinked, eyes glinting with something wet that didn't fall. For a long moment, neither spoke. The clock ticked softly behind him. Her hands finally stilled.

And Michael, against his better judgment, felt the smallest part of himself lean toward her, toward the ache in her voice, the trembling resolve that matched his own. He reminded himself to breathe, to anchor, to stay the doctor in the room. But as the seconds passed, he realized something undeniable: whatever line existed between them, it was already shifting.

Michael had learned long ago to use silence like a scalpel, to let it carve open space for truth, to let it coax hidden things into light. But this silence wasn't surgical. It throbbed; raw, unclean, filling the room like a wound that refused to close.

The air between them seemed to pulse with something almost physical, an ache that belonged to both of them but neither dared claim. Her words, *I'm tired of being a disappointment*, echoed in him like a bell struck too close to bone. He could feel them pressing against the old, unhealed corners of himself, the places he'd built a career around never touching.

And then, unbidden, came his father's voice. "Why can't you be more like the other boys?" It arrived the way memories always did; not as sound, but sensation. The clink of ice in a glass of Jack Daniel's and Coke, that familiar fizz softening the edge of the whiskey; the smell of it rising through the years like a ghost that still knew his name.

The low hum of a television no one was really watching. The rasp of a red pen dragging across essays, drowning out everything that might have been conversation.

He saw his father hunched at the dining table, shoulders tense, eyes fixed on the page as though grading the world itself. Michael remembered wanting to speak, to tell him something; anything but the silence had already filled the room, thick and absolute.

It was his mother who broke it, not with words, but with motion: the click of knitting needles, rhythmic and detached, as if each stitch might keep the family from unraveling. She never looked up. Not once. He could still see the lamplight catching on her wedding ring, the silver glinting like restraint.

He remembered thinking that love must be a quiet thing; measured, careful, something you keep your hands busy to avoid feeling too much of. And then Evelyn's voice rose from the ruins of memory, sharp as broken glass. "You were never enough." The words sliced through him even now. He could see her as she'd been that night.

The faint tremor of rage disguised as poise, the lipstick smudged on the rim of her wineglass, the red of it too bright against the white of her teeth. Her arms had been crossed like a fortress, her eyes dry and bright, the way they get when love has already curdled into contempt. "You make everyone else whole," she'd said. "But you drain me."

He had said nothing then. What could he? He'd built his entire identity on being steady, on being the one who didn't break. But steadiness can be its own cruelty, and now, sitting across from Claire, he felt the old guilt rising again: the quiet, corrosive truth that he had always been better at healing others than saving himself.

Claire shifted slightly on the couch, her sleeve slipping back enough to reveal the faint shimmer of a scar near her wrist, not fresh but not forgotten. It caught the light for an instant before she folded her hands to hide it.

Michael's chest tightened. The therapist in him recognized it; a silent story, years old, carved into flesh. The man in him felt something deeper, something terrifyingly tender: recognition. He steadied his breath, the way to which he'd been trained. "What do you feel," he asked softly, "when someone calls you a disappointment?"

Her lips parted, but no sound came. Her eyes glistened, and for a moment, neither of them belonged entirely to the present. He wasn't looking at a patient anymore. He was looking at a mirror. And what stared back was the boy who'd grown up mistaking silence for love, and the man who still couldn't tell the difference.

Now, sitting across from Claire, the silence twisted all of it together. It wasn't just her confession about being terrified to disappoint him, it was every moment in his life when he had been weighed and quietly overlooked. Every subtle withholding that had taught him to hide the trembling parts of himself.

Every quiet room that had demanded his perfection in exchange for love, until he learned that approval was just another way to measure obedience. Her words had been simple, but they struck through years. They threaded through the sound of his father's glass clinking against the table, through his mother's clicking needles, through Evelyn's cold laughter echoing across a kitchen filled with half-packed boxes.

And yet, unlike with any of them, he didn't want to retreat. Something in him, something buried deep and starved of warmth, wanted to lean forward.

He wanted to tell her that she wasn't alone in her fear of not being enough, that he understood the private exhaustion of trying to earn your own worth.

He wanted to tell her that the ache she carried lived inside him, too. But the boundaries of his profession; those invisible lines he'd built his entire identity around, held him still. He sat anchored in his chair, hands folded neatly in his lap, the picture of restraint.

His pen hovered over the yellow legal pad, unmoving. He didn't dare write; his thoughts were too close to confession. The storm gathered quietly inside him, pressing against his ribs like thunder trapped in a sealed room. His jaw tightened. His pulse thudded at the base of his throat.

He studied her face to steady himself, the pale curve of her cheek, the delicate tremor at the corner of her mouth when she fought back emotion. The lamplight caught the faint shimmer of tears she refused to let fall. Her beauty wasn't showy; it was human. Fragile.

The kind that came from surviving too much and still showing up anyway. He drew a breath, controlled, deliberate, and when he finally spoke, the words came softer than he intended. "I don't think less of you," he said. The air shifted. She looked up at him slowly, her eyes meeting his. And something in them changed. Not a spark, but a quiet easing, like a locked door that had been left slightly ajar.

Her gaze softened, the defensiveness melting into something almost tender. For the first time, she didn't look like a woman braced for judgment. She looked like someone trying to believe she could still be safe.

"Then why do I feel like everyone does?" She asked, voice barely audible. Michael swallowed. "Because people taught you to mistake control for love." She blinked, surprised by the precision of his words. He hadn't meant to say them aloud, hadn't even realized the thought had escaped.

But there it was; hanging in the space between them, fragile and irrefutable. Claire exhaled slowly, her fingers twisting the fabric of her sleeve. "I don't even know who I'd be without trying to prove myself to someone." He wanted to tell her that she'd be free. That she'd be whole.

That she already was, somewhere underneath the fear. But that wasn't his role. He had to be the stillness, not the answer. So he simply nodded, his gaze steady. "You don't have to prove anything here." The words landed with quiet force. For a moment, neither moved. The lamp hummed faintly.

Outside, a siren wailed, distant but insistent, a reminder that the world still existed beyond this suspended hour. Claire's lips parted like she might say something, but she didn't. Instead, she drew a shuddering breath and let her eyes fall closed.

Michael watched her, the rise and fall of her chest, the fragile steadiness returning to her breathing. He felt the ache in his own chest mirror hers. And though he told himself it was empathy, that it was the practiced art of understanding, he knew. Deep down, that it was something else.

Something unprofessional. Something human.
Something that scared him more than silence ever had.

The third session, she cried. Not loud, not messy, just tears that slid down her cheeks as if gravity had finally won a battle years in the making.

They slipped soundlessly, catching the lamplight, leaving faint wet constellations on the sleeve she'd been worrying between her fingers.

She didn't move to wipe them away. She sat perfectly still, shoulders straight, as if a single gesture might scatter the fragile control, she'd fought so hard to keep. The room rearranged itself around her grief.

The hum of the air-conditioning, the faint tick of the clock, even the city's heartbeat beyond the glass. All of it dimmed until there was only the sound of her breathing and the ache of what it cost her to let go. Michael felt it press against his own chest, the air growing thick with the kind of pain that doesn't demand attention, it asks for witness.

He had seen tears before: the sobbing kind that tore through people like storms, the guttural cries that emptied a person. But this was different. This was the body refusing to keep its secrets. Sorrow stripped of language, performance, or pride. He sat still and watched the years leak out of her. And as he did, something stirred in him; not pity, but recognition.

The shape of her grief was familiar. It mirrored his own. "I don't even know what I'm crying for," she whispered, voice thin, tissue clutched tight. "I'm not supposed to cry. Lucian…" She stopped, the name escaping like smoke from a crack she couldn't seal. "Lucian?" He asked, careful. "My husband," she said, then corrected herself. "Ex-husband."

Her lips flattened to a thin line. "He used to say tears were weakness. That if I wanted to keep him, I had to be stronger." Michael's fingers tightened around his pen until the plastic creaked. "And did you believe him?" "I believed him because I loved him." Her eyes flicked upward, then fell. "Or I thought I did.

Maybe I just loved being chosen." That last sentence landed inside him like a blade turned gently. He thought of Evelyn. Her perfume, her cold precision, the way she'd said You make everyone else whole, but you drain me.

He'd loved being chosen too. And he'd never forgiven himself for what it meant when that choice was revoked. Being chosen isn't love," he said. Her eyes, still wet, lifted to his. "Then what is?" He had a hundred answers ready. Definitions, theories, citations.

He could talk about secure attachment, vulnerability, mutual regulation. He could give her the safety of distance, wrap the truth in professionalism. But the words caught in his throat. Because the truthful answer, the one pulsing just beneath his restraint, was something he could never say aloud: Love is what I feel every time you look at me like that.

The thought burned through him like a secret too hot to keep. He swallowed it down and let the silence stretch. His pen rested useless on the pad in his lap; his heartbeat filled the space where words should have been.

Across from him, she sat fragile and luminous, a ruin lit from within. He watched the faint streak of mascara trace down her cheek, the way her fingers clung to the hem of her sleeve as if it were the only thing keeping her tethered to the world. And in that moment, with a clarity that hurt, he thought: *You are not broken. You are the most beautiful proof that survival itself can shine.*

He would never say it. Not to her. Maybe not to anyone. He drew a breath. His voice, when it came, was calm, deliberate, exactly what a therapist's should be. "Love," he said, "is when you feel safe enough to be seen. All of you. Even the parts you hate."

She nodded slowly, her mouth trembling. "Safe enough to be seen," she repeated, tasting the words like something foreign. Her gaze lingered on his, longer than it should have. Something passed between them, something neither of them dared to name. It wasn't agreement.

It was understanding, or maybe recognition.

And in that lingering look, Michael felt the truth vibrating beneath his careful tone, the one she seemed to hear anyway: *Love is you. Right here. Right now.*

By the fifth session, the air between them had changed. It was no longer just the practiced quiet of a therapist's office. It carried something heavier; warmer, the kind of silence that thrums with anticipation, that hums beneath the surface like a storm building behind glass.

It was the stillness before lightning, the pause before confession, the breath before something that could ruin or redeem them both. When she entered, she wasn't the same woman who had once flinched at the sound of her own name.

She came in wearing a black dress. Simple, unadorned, but devastating in its restraint. It wasn't the kind of dress that demanded to be seen; it was the kind that expected to be.

The fabric hugged her gently, obedient to the subtle grace of her movement, and as she walked, the air seemed to fold around her. Michael felt it. The shift, the low current that pulsed in time with his heart.

He stood before he meant to, a gesture that felt instinctive rather than professional. "Claire," he greeted, and the sound of her name in his voice was softer than it should have been.

She smiled faintly, a controlled, practiced smile, yet something in it faltered, an edge of vulnerability threading through her composure. "I almost canceled," she said, sliding into her seat.

"Why didn't you?" He asked. "I don't know," she admitted. "Maybe I wanted to see if I could say something today without falling apart." Her hands smoothed the fabric of her dress.

Her eyes didn't quite meet his. He wanted to tell her she didn't have to be composed here, but he already knew that would sound like permission for something larger than either of them could contain.

Instead, he said quietly, "You can start anywhere." She exhaled, the kind of breath that shakes at the end, and then laughed softly. Too brittle to be joy. "Anywhere," she repeated. "That's the problem. I don't know where it starts, or where it ends. The marriage. The grief. Me." Michael listened, his pen still in his hand, though he hadn't written a word since she'd entered.

He couldn't bring himself to break the rhythm of her voice with the scratch of ink. "When Lucian was angry," she continued, "he didn't yell. He'd just… disappear. Days sometimes. No calls. No messages. And when he came back, I was expected to pretend nothing happened."

She paused, eyes flickering toward the window, where the city glowed like a distant constellation. "I got so used to silence that I started craving it. It was the only time I felt safe. But it's strange, when you live in silence long enough, it stops being safety and starts being a kind of death."

Michael's chest tightened. He understood that sentence more than she could know. "What do you feel now, when it's quiet?" He asked. She hesitated. "Lonely," she whispered. Then, after a beat: "And I hate that loneliness feels familiar. Like it belongs to me." He wanted to reach across the space between them; not with touch, but with something truer, something words could only imitate.

The part of him trained to observe cataloged every detail; the tremor in her voice, the way her fingers pressed into her palms, the quick swallow that came before every truth. But the man beneath the therapist felt it all instead of noting it.

"Loneliness can feel like home," he said gently, his voice low. "Especially when it's the first place we were ever safe." Her gaze lifted to his, green eyes bright but unsteady. "You talk like you've lived it."

He didn't look away. "I think everyone who sits in this chair has." For a moment, the world narrowed to the space between them. The lamplight, the faint ticking of the clock, the pulse of the city outside, all of it blurred into a single, trembling awareness. Claire's voice softened, barely audible. "Sometimes I wonder what would happen if I stopped surviving and started living." Michael's throat tightened.

He could feel the answer forming, the kind that would undo them both. He didn't say it. He couldn't. Instead, he held her gaze and said quietly, "That's what we're here to find out." She smiled then, small, fragile, and entirely real.

And for the first time since she'd walked into his office, Michael realized he was no longer guiding her through her pain. He was walking beside her in it.

And that, he knew, was the most dangerous place of all.

Her hair was pinned loosely that afternoon, the kind of careless arrangement that suggested she'd stopped trying to hide how tired she was.

A few strands had escaped, brushing against her cheek, softening the exhaustion that lived beneath her eyes.

Even the faint trace of perfume that followed her seemed to settle into the room, delicate but undeniable, a quiet insistence that she was still capable of beauty even when she didn't believe it. Michael noticed before he could stop himself. His gaze dipped, a brief, instinctive betrayal of his role, then snapped back up.

The guilt that followed was immediate and physical, a tightening behind his ribs. He knew better. He always knew better. But knowing didn't stop the wanting. When his eyes found hers again, he realized she had been watching him. Her expression didn't change, but something in her gaze shifted. No accusation, no invitation, just acknowledgment.

As if she had felt the air change too and was brave enough to name it without words. She sat down slowly, smoothing the black dress over her knees, and the motion was almost reverent, like a prayer she didn't believe in anymore. "I almost didn't come today," she said, her voice soft enough to force him to lean in. "Why not?" Michael asked.

"Because every time I leave this room," she began, fingers tracing the seam of the couch, "I feel like I've given you too much." She looked at him then, and her eyes held something raw vulnerability without apology. "Like I've left pieces of myself here with you. And I'm not sure I'll get them back." The admission hit him in the chest like a heartbeat out of rhythm.

He shifted in his chair, straightened his tie, reached for something, anything, that might sound professional. "Maybe," he said quietly, "that's not a bad thing."

Her eyes flashed, bright and pained. "You don't understand." He wanted to tell her he did, that he understood better than she could imagine, but she didn't stop.

"With Lucian," she said, "I gave everything. I mean everything. He took my laughter, my body, my sleep. He made me feel small enough to fit into the spaces he left when he walked out. And when he finally did," Her breath faltered, "there was nothing left of me to save." Michael leaned forward before he realized he was moving.

His tone was gentle, but his steadiness was a fragile thing, borrowed from instinct rather than discipline. "Claire, you're not empty," he said. "You're still here. I see you." Her lips trembled. She looked away as though the words were too bright to stare at directly. "You say that" she whispered, "like it means something." "It does." He said under his breath. The word broke inside his throat before it left his mouth.

He didn't mean for it to sound that way. Too human, too close. The silence that followed wasn't the kind prescribed by therapy textbooks. It wasn't a tool, or a pause meant to encourage reflection. It was alive. It pulsed. It trembled. It filled the space between them until it felt less like air and more like gravity.

The ticking clock on the wall became deafening. The faint hum of the city below them sounded like a tide rising fast. Claire's gaze lifted, steady now. "You shouldn't say things like that," she said, her voice neither angry nor afraid, just certain. Michael swallowed hard. "And yet," he whispered, "I did."

For a long time, neither moved. Her breath came shallow, her pulse visible at the base of her throat. His fingers tightened around the pen in his hand until the knuckles went white.

What existed in that moment wasn't love, not yet, but the terrifying recognition of it: the moment before a flame catches, when the air itself seems to wait.

He wanted to tell her that he hadn't felt this alive in years, that her presence reached into parts of him no one else had touched. He wanted to tell her that seeing her, really seeing her, made him realize how little of himself he'd been living with. But he didn't. He couldn't.

Because the moment he named it, it would become real. And reality would destroy them both. So he sat there, the words burning behind his teeth, and she looked back at him as if she already knew. The session ended in the usual way.

Calendar, time, polite nods, but when she stood to leave, she lingered near the door. Her hand hovered over the knob, trembling just slightly. "Same time next week?" She asked. "Same time," he said. When the door closed behind her, Michael exhaled the breath he hadn't realized he'd been holding.

The scent of her perfume still lingered, faint but present. And in that lingering air, he understood that the line between helping her and needing her was dissolving, slow and irreversible, like ink in water.

That night, long after the last client had left and the corridor lights dimmed to their lonely blue glow, Michael lay awake in the half-dark of his apartment. The city still breathed beyond his windows; restless, alive, indifferent.

Neon veins pulsed through the blinds, smearing red and violet against the ceiling like half-remembered dreams. Far below, traffic murmured like a distant ocean, a steady tide of motion and machinery that never slept.

Even the horns seemed muted tonight.

Less anger, more ache.

Inside, the only sound was the hiss of the radiator, an old cast-iron thing that exhaled unevenly, like an old man muttering in his sleep. It was a weary metronome, marking time that refused to move forward, as if the night itself had stalled somewhere between thought and regret.

The apartment was small, too clean, its silence the kind that belonged to people who didn't expect company. Books lined the walls in orderly stacks; case studies, journals, the anatomy of empathy printed and bound. Beside them, a few framed drawings Eva had made, stick figures with oversized smiles, a sun too big for the sky.

He stared at one now, the colors dim in the lamplight, the uneven scrawl that read me and daddy and mommy. He traced the outlines of the crayon sky with his eyes until they blurred. The couch still held the ghost of his last client, a perfume note, a crease in the cushion, evidence that people came to him to unburden their pain and then left it behind for him to hold.

That was the secret of therapy no textbook mentioned: healing others meant absorbing fragments of their hurt until your own mind began to echo. Michael rubbed his temples, the day replaying itself in fragments. The trembling of a woman's hands as she spoke about loss. A man's hollow laughter when he said he no longer dreamed.

And Claire, the newest face, the quiet one with the guarded eyes and the lateness that somehow felt deliberate. He remembered the way she'd lingered by the window, the city's gray light pooling around her like a confession she hadn't made yet.

Something in her silence had unsettled him. Not because of what it concealed, but because of what it reflected back at him.

He rolled onto his side, the sheets cool against his skin, the glow of the alarm clock slicing the dark in green numerals: 12:41 a.m. Sleep hovered somewhere beyond reach, just close enough to taunt He thought about Eva, about her laugh, her soft hair against his shoulder, the way she always fell asleep mid-sentence during bedtime stories.

He thought about Evelyn, the sharpness in her tone that still found its way into his head like a splinter, even now. And then, uninvited, he thought about Claire; the tremor in her voice, the fragility she tried to hide behind control. He hated that his mind lingered there.

He hated the pull, not desire, not yet, but recognition. That strange gravity between two damaged people who don't yet know they're circling the same wound. The radiator sighed again, metal ticking as it cooled.

He closed his eyes, but the city's glow still pressed faintly against the lids. The way it always did, as if even darkness refused to let him rest. Michael Harris, healer of others, lay there in the half-light, unable to heal himself.

And outside, New York pulsed on; indifferent, infinite, while one man tried to quiet the noise that would not stop inside him. In the next room, Eva slept. He could hear her faint, even breaths through the cracked door, the soft sigh of a child lost safely in dreams. That sound steadied him more than anything else in the world.

It was proof that he had done at least one thing right. Proof that he could still protect something pure. He thought of her small hand curling around his when they crossed the street, her voice when she whispered secrets that had no weight except that she trusted him with them. Her love was simple, absolute. It was the kind of love that never asks to be earned.

He should have fallen asleep holding on to that thought. But he didn't. Because the quiet was treacherous, and his mind went elsewhere. It went to the faint shimmer of Claire's eyes across his desk, green, sleepless, luminous even in their exhaustion. It went to her voice, low and trembling, each word drawn like thread between defiance and despair.

And it went, most dangerously, to the way she looked at him, not as a therapist, not as a stranger paid to listen, but as a man. That look lived in him now, a pulse that hadn't faded. It had reached inside, past the tidy compartments of his professionalism, past the calm he had spent years building like walls. It had found something alive under all that stillness.

He turned onto his side, pressing his hand against the cool sheet where another body might have been years ago. The guilt that followed was sharp and familiar; an old companion, but guilt was not enough to drown what had begun stirring. It wasn't just attraction; it was recognition. It was the dangerous understanding that she saw the same ache in him that he saw in her. She had looked at him like she could read the fractures he'd hidden from everyone else.

That terrified him. Because if she could see him that clearly, it meant the masks he wore; the calm, the certainty, the moral distance, were already cracking. And yet, beneath the terror, something else burned: thrill. It came quietly, like the hum before rain, and he hated how honest it felt.

For years, he had lived in the gray. Predictable, composed, numb. His life was a sequence of sessions, reports, custody weekends, sleep without rest.

But with her, in those sessions thick with silence and confession, he felt something return, a heartbeat that had been missing.

He didn't want to name it. Names made things real. Names broke worlds open. But he couldn't escape it. He felt alive. Alive in ways his profession forbade. Alive in ways that frightened him more than loneliness ever had.

Michael turned toward the faint glow leaking through the blinds, the city's reflection scattering like fractured stars across his ceiling. He imagined her somewhere in that sprawl of light; awake too, perhaps thinking of him the way he was thinking of her.

The thought both comforted and condemned him. He covered his eyes with the heel of his hand, willing sleep to come, willing the world to reset. But all he could see behind his closed lids were those eyes, green and unguarded, and all he could hear was her voice, trembling with the same question that haunted him:

What would it cost to feel whole again?

And deep in the dark, with his daughter's steady breathing just beyond the wall, Michael Harris understood the most dangerous truth of all; the thing he felt for Claire Alden was no longer something he could simply control. He lay there in the dark, caught between two worlds; two breaths.

From down the hall came the slow, rhythmic whisper of Eva's breathing, steady and safe, the small, perfect sound of everything he'd sworn to protect. It was the breath of innocence, of mornings spent making pancakes, of her tiny hand gripping his finger as they crossed busy streets.

It grounded him, reminded him of who he was supposed to be. But the other breath, the one that haunted the edges of his consciousness, belonged to Claire. He could still hear it, feel it, from memory: the faint tremor in her voice, the catch between confession and restraint, the sound she made when silence pressed too close.

That breath was wild, intoxicating, forbidden. It lingered in the hollow of his chest like an echo he couldn't quiet. He lay perfectly still, staring up at the ceiling where the city's light fractured through the blinds. Neon streaked the darkness like restless veins, painting his skin in pale blues and bruised pinks. Each flicker seemed to pulse in rhythm with his thoughts; rapid, fevered, guilty.

He had always lived by rules. Rules had saved him once, given shape to the chaos of his childhood, kept him from becoming the man his father had been. Every line, every boundary, every professional code had been built brick by brick to hold him steady.

But now those same walls felt thin, fragile, as though a single word, a single look, might shatter them completely. He turned onto his side, facing the faint glow beneath Eva's door. It should have been enough; her safety, her presence, her unbroken trust. But the truth clawed at him, shameful and electric: he didn't feel safe anymore. He felt alive. The realization was a slow, poisonous thrill.

It terrified him. And it thrilled him all the same. He saw Claire's face in the dark. Those green eyes rimmed with sleeplessness, the trembling in her voice when she said she didn't know who she was without someone else to tell her.

He'd told her she was still here, that he saw her. And he had meant it. But now he wondered if that truth had cut both ways. He saw her not as a patient but as something luminous and wounded, something that mirrored the ache inside him.

And in that reflection, he found himself again. Not the careful man with degrees and credentials, but the one who still craved connection so fiercely it scared him. The radiator hissed, a low warning. He could taste the metallic tang of guilt at the back of his throat.

He told himself that this was empathy, nothing more. That this was what good therapists did; they felt deeply, they cared. But even in the dark, he could no longer lie to himself. This wasn't empathy. This was hunger.

A hunger for the warmth in her voice when she spoke his name. For the way she looked at him like she could see the boy beneath the man; the one still desperate to be told he was enough. He pressed the heel of his hand to his eyes, as if he could blot her out, but her image only burned brighter.

The city's hum rose and fell around him, restless, relentless, like his thoughts. He knew the precipice he was standing on.

The ethical line every therapist swore never to cross. He knew what waited on the other side of it:

Ruin, shame, the collapse of everything he had built.

But as he lay there, torn between his daughter's safe, steady breath and the ghost of Claire's trembling one, the truth surfaced with terrifying clarity. He was already leaning toward the fall.

And somewhere deep inside; beneath the fear, beneath the guilt, a small, reckless part of him wanted to see how far he could go before gravity won.

Chance, Or Something Like It

The city had been rinsed clean and left glistening; a cathedral of rain and reflection. Droplets trembled along the power lines, jeweled strings suspended above streets that gleamed like obsidian. The scent of wet asphalt and iron hung heavy, mingling with the faint sweetness of roasted chestnuts from a vendor's cart that refused to close.

Rain still clung to everything it could touch. To awnings and eyelashes, to the glossy backs of taxis idling at lights that refused to turn green, to the shoulders of people who had long since surrendered their umbrellas to the wind. Jackets plastered to skin, shoes darkened with damp, faces half-hidden behind collars and steam.

The streets shimmered like black glass, fractured by veins of neon; the pink spill of a diner sign, the electric blue hum of a storefront window, the hazy red and green of traffic lights bleeding into one another across the puddles. Each color swam and trembled, an oil-slick prayer whispered by the city itself. Steam unfurled from subway grates, thick and ghostly, curling around ankles and disappearing into the night.

It made the world feel slightly unreal, as though Manhattan had slipped into one of its own dreams. One where everything was both alive and dissolving. Horns blared, but the rain muted them, softened their sharpness until they became part of the rhythm, an urban symphony of impatience. Tires hissed through puddles.

Water dripped from awnings in uneven beats.
Somewhere far off, a saxophone played under a bridge, its melody wandering and half-forgotten.

The slap of wet shoes echoed against the brick walls, a tired heartbeat marking time in a city that refused to rest. And beneath it all, there was that particular hush that only comes after rain; a pause that wasn't peace but exhaustion.

A quiet that hinted at something waiting to begin again. It was the kind of night that made people think of things they shouldn't, remember faces they'd tried to forget. The kind of night that blurred boundaries. That made every light look like a promise and every shadow like a secret.

Michael left the building later than usual, the doorman's voice following him into the drizzle before fading into the rhythm of the rain. The revolving door gave a final, sighing turn behind him, sealing him out of the warmth and into the blur of the city's damp night.

The rain met him immediately cool, insistent, and oddly intimate. It crept down the back of his collar, soaked the edges of his cuffs, and turned the pavement into a slick mirror that caught every glimmer of light. His bag felt heavier than it should have, the weight of its contents far less than the pull of what he was carrying inside himself.

Every step along the sidewalk echoed the same quiet struggle; the ache of a thousand careful knows that had kept him upright, the whisper of one reckless yes that had begun to bloom beneath his ribs. He adjusted his collar against the drizzle, breath fogging faintly in the air. The smell of wet asphalt mixed with something sweeter.

Roasted chestnuts from a cart across the street, the scent tugging at some memory of comfort he couldn't quite place. It was the kind of smell that belonged to winter markets and simpler years, but here, it mingled with the metallic bite of rain and exhaust, creating something both ordinary and hypnotic.

Above him, the sky still wept in indecision; scattered drops falling through the glow of streetlamps like bits of broken glass. The rain came steady enough to sting, soft enough to tease, as if Manhattan itself couldn't decide whether to let go or to hold everything in.

He walked east on Forty-Seventh, the traffic a low growl beside him, headlights streaking across puddles like restless ghosts. The city seemed endless, alive with light and loneliness in equal measure. Then suddenly, inexplicably, he stopped. Right there on the corner, beneath a flickering streetlamp that hummed like a failing heart.

He didn't know why. The rain gathered at his feet, silvering his shoes, and for a long moment he just stood there listening. To the hiss of tires. To the muffled music spilling from a bar down the block. To the city's pulse, thrumming faint and infinite around him. Maybe it was exhaustion. Maybe it was the residue of Claire's voice still clinging to the walls of his mind.

Maybe it was the quiet admission that he had already crossed the line between professional concern and longing. There was no pretending otherwise. He looked up. In the reflection of a storefront window, the city stretched behind him; blurred, glowing, alive.

But in the glass, he didn't see the calm, controlled man his patients knew. He saw a man tilting, standing on the narrow edge between duty and desire, waiting for something unnamed to tip him over.

And for the first time in years, Michael Harris didn't turn away from the fall.

★ ✪ ★

In the bookstore window, beneath a string of delicate paper cranes swaying gently in the draft and a fat orange cat asleep atop a stack of staff picks, Claire Alden stood with a book open in her hands. The sight stopped Michael mid-step.

The shop itself was small, one of those rare holdouts wedged between a dry cleaner and a nail salon, a relic from another decade that still smelled faintly of paper, binder's glue, and rain-soaked wool coats.

Its front window was crowded with displays: dog-eared classics, handwritten recommendations on index cards, and the soft amber glow of a single lamp that made everything inside look warm and half-dreamed.

And there she was, framed perfectly by that light. Her black dress, still damp at the hem from the rain, caught the glow in subtle ripples of shadow. Her polished shoes looked almost too formal for the place, as though she'd stepped out of a ballroom and accidentally wandered into a forgotten story. But the moment she smiled, just slightly, eyes tracing something on the page, the incongruity disappeared.

She belonged there. She belonged anywhere she forgot to be careful. It was that. More than her beauty, more than the sharp ache of recognition, that undid him. The ease. The unguarded curve of her lips. The way her shoulders had relaxed, just barely, as if the weight she carried had loosened its hold for the briefest instant.

Through the glass, Michael could see her thumb resting in the crease of the book, her fingers trembling slightly as she turned a page. The rain had darkened her hair, a few strands clinging to her cheek, and in the lamplight, it gleamed like ink still drying.

He stood there in the drizzle, hands buried in his coat pockets, watching her; not like a voyeur, but like a man who had stumbled into a dream he wasn't meant to find. The city moved around him, impatient and loud.

She seemed to exist in another tempo entirely. A car horn blared; the cat lifted its head, blinked once, and resettled. Claire didn't look up. Michael thought of walking away. He told himself to. Every rational thought he'd ever had screamed at him to turn, to vanish into the crowd, to erase this chance encounter before it became something he couldn't undo. But his feet stayed rooted to the wet pavement.

He didn't know what he wanted. To speak, to listen, to stand there forever in that quiet bubble of rain and lamplight. He only knew he couldn't look away. Because in that single unguarded smile, he saw the woman she might have been before the hurt, before the silence, before Lucian. And something in him; tired, lonely, breaking, wanted to believe that version still existed.

That it wasn't too late for either of them to be seen without the armor. Michael could have walked past. He could have pretended not to see her, could have let the rain and the city swallow the moment whole. He could have remembered the ethics. Those tidy bullet points he'd memorized like scripture, the ones that promised to keep feeling at bay.

But he didn't. He pushed open the door. The bell above it gave a soft, brittle chime, like a secret being spoken aloud. The air inside was warmer, laced with the smell of paper and rain-damp wool. The cat didn't stir.

Its tail flicked once in lazy acknowledgment, but its eyes stayed closed, as if even it knew not to disturb whatever had just entered. Claire looked up. And for a heartbeat, neither of them spoke.

"Dr. Harris," she said at last, her tone delicate, almost teasing. Then, softer, "Michael." The sound of his name in her voice loosened something deep in him. It felt like an unbuttoned collar, like a door he shouldn't open but already had. "I didn't expect.." He began, fumbling for steadiness.

"To run into me?" Her mouth curved faintly. "Me either." There was humor there, but it trembled. Like glass thin enough to crack if pressed too hard. He nodded, unsure what to do with his hands, then stepped closer, pretending interest in the display table between them.

The sign above it read, Essays & Other Arguments, letters curling slightly at the edges from humidity. She still held the book. It was small, its corners softened from being loved by strangers. The title was handwritten across the spine in faded ink. "What is it?" He asked.

Her thumb brushed the edge of a page as she answered, "Letters. A poet writing to someone younger telling them to be patient with their pain. That it'll open you if you let it." Her voice faltered at the last line, as though the words themselves might break her open if she said them too completely.

He looked at her. "Does it?" She met his gaze. "It hasn't yet." The quiet that followed was dense, fragile. Rain tapped softly against the windows, running in thin silver veins down the glass. Somewhere toward the back of the store, a radio played faint jazz, the notes bending slow and blue.

Michael should have said something measured, something safe healing takes time, trust the process, pain can be transformative. The stock phrases waited on his tongue, polished and sterile. But looking at her; at the rain tangled in her hair, the defiance trembling at the corners of her mouth, none of those words felt big enough.

"Maybe," he said, voice low, "pain doesn't always open us. Maybe sometimes it just sits inside us until someone else notices." Her eyes softened, but the muscle in her jaw tightened, as if fighting the instinct to believe him. " And then what?" He hesitated. "Then it starts to move."She laughed quietly, the sound small but unguarded. "You don't stop, do you?"

"Stop what?" He asked. "Turning everything into hope." She sighed. Michael exhaled a breath he didn't realize he'd been holding. "It's a bad habit, a dangerous one." They stood there, side by side, the world outside blurring into water and color. The bookshop smelled of dust and ink and the faintest hint of her perfume.

For a long moment, there was nothing clinical between them. No patient. No therapist. Just two people standing in the wreckage of their own restraint, pretending the ground beneath them wasn't already giving way. She closed the book gently, fingers resting on its cover. "You should go," she said, but she didn't move.

"I know." He said with trepidation. "And yet," she murmured, looking up at him, "you haven't." His pulse stuttered. "Neither have you." Something flickered between them. Half a spark, half a warning. The bell over the door chimed again as a breeze rushed in from the street. The cat stirred, stretching lazily before settling back down.

Neither of them moved. Because for the first time, both of them knew this wasn't an accident anymore. It was the beginning of the fall.

Around them, the shop moved in gentle, bookish rhythms; the soft rip of a receipt, the muted creak of floorboards under the cashier's slow steps, the rustle of pages turning somewhere in the poetry section.

Rain tapped against the window in patient intervals, like a clock with soft hands marking the seconds of their restraint. Michael reached for the book in Claire's hand, meaning only to steady it, to have something to do with his hands. Their fingers nearly brushed. And then didn't. The almost was deafening. Louder than contact, sharper than touch.

It lived in the space between them like a held breath, a suspended possibility that neither dared name. He drew his hand back slowly, the air between them charged and trembling. "This is not..." he began, voice low, deliberate, "appropriate." It was the kind of sentence designed by policy manuals and ethics committees, a brittle thing that crumbled the moment it met emotion.

Her lips curved, just barely. "No," she said, almost gently. "It isn't." Neither of them moved. The cat stretched in its sleep, a soft yawn echoing between them, as if even the animal sensed the tension and refused to intervene. Claire's fingers lingered on the book's spine before she closed it with careful grace, like a fragile thing that might not survive sudden motion.

"There's a coffee shop next door," she said, voice even, though her eyes betrayed her. "If we were other people, we could go sit somewhere public and talk about absolutely nothing for twenty minutes." Michael's heart stuttered. "If we were other people," he echoed, the words almost tasting like regret.

Claire turned the book over, studying the blurb though she wasn't reading. Her thumb grazed the corner of the cover in small circles; a nervous habit he'd seen before in session, though never this close.

"You once told me," She said, her tone softening, "that love is when you feel safe enough to be seen. All of you."

"I said that" he admitted, a rueful smile tugging at the edge of his mouth. She nodded. "It sounded like something you believed... before you learned to be careful." That landed between them like a spark hitting dry kindling.

The rain outside grew heavier, tapping against the glass with sudden insistence, as though the city itself had leaned in to listen. He didn't know what to say. She didn't ask for an answer. The bell over the door tinkled again. A gust of wet air swept through as two strangers entered, laughter spilling briefly into the quiet before the door closed behind them.

The world, it seemed, had just tried to decide for him. To remind him that he was supposed to turn away, to step back into the safe, dull rhythm of rules and distance. But Michael didn't let it. He looked at her, really looked. The faint sheen of rain still clinging to her hair, the pulse fluttering just below her throat, the fragile bravery in the way she stood her ground.

"I can walk you to the corner," he said, his voice steady, though the steadiness cost him something. "Umbrella. Crowd. City. We'll be two people among a thousand." Her breath caught, then left her in a shaky exhale, relief and fear braided together. "Twenty yards," she said. "Nothing more." He nodded.

But when their eyes met again, both of them knew that those twenty yards could hold an entire lifetime of consequences. The bell tinkled once more as they stepped out into the rain, and for a brief, impossible moment, the city seemed to hold its breath with them.

They stepped back out into the night, into a city still trembling from rain. The streets steamed faintly, heat rising from the asphalt in thin ribbons that caught the streetlight and turned it spectral.

Somewhere nearby, tires hissed through puddles. A siren wailed and faded. The air smelled of ozone and exhaust; alive, damp, electric. The umbrella was small, too small. The kind you buy in a hurry, not meant for sharing. Its black canopy bowed slightly under the weight of lingering drizzle, and the closeness beneath it felt like a confession neither of them had spoken aloud.

Their shoulders brushed, a fleeting touch that hummed through the narrow space between them, then broke as they adjusted, pretending it hadn't happened. Then it happened again. The rhythm; touch, retreat, touch again, made the block feel impossibly long, the air charged with things better left unsaid.

Michael cleared his throat, searching for something safe, something that could occupy the space without exposing the quiet war inside him. "What did you read as a child?" He asked finally. It was a harmless question, or it should have been.

But even harmless things had teeth in moments like this. "Library sales," she said, her voice thoughtful, drifting. "Whatever was cheap and smelled like other people's houses." She smiled, that small, crooked smile that always arrived half a second after her sadness. "Fairy tales, mostly. The darker ones. Girls cutting off their toes to fit into shoes that weren't meant for them."

Michael looked at her from the corner of his eye. "Did you think that's what love was?" "Not then." Her tone softened, the words fragile enough to fog the air between them.

"Then I thought love was a staircase I could climb if I were good enough." A pause remained. "Later, I learned it was a trapdoor." He wanted to tell her that wasn't true, that love could be something gentler, steadier.

But the protest died before it reached his lips. Because he wasn't sure he believed it anymore. Not with her so close and the air between them so fragile it might break from the weight of honesty. They reached the crosswalk.

Steam rose from a maintenance hole cover like the street was exhaling, the city sighing through its own exhaustion. The traffic light flicked from red to green, painting their faces first with blood, then with permission.

Across the avenue, a black SUV idled at the curb, its windows tinted to a glossy, unreadable black. Michael wouldn't have noticed it, but she did. Something in her posture changed, subtle but sharp. Her hand twitched at her side; her breath faltered.

It was there and gone again, a tremor swallowed by poise, but he felt it like a temperature drop. "Claire?" He asked quietly as the light changed. "Nothing." She shook her head, forcing her voice steady. "Just ghosts with engines." The phrasing lodged in him.

He didn't press, and she didn't explain. They crossed in silence; an unspoken agreement, a boundary kept not because it should be, but because the words inside it were sharp enough to draw blood. The rain had thinned to a mist by the time they reached the coffee shop.

The windows glowed amber, fogged from the warmth inside. The scent of espresso drifted out as a couple laughed softly over two untouched mugs. They didn't go in. Instead, they stood beneath the awning, umbrella closed, watching the rain smear the world into watercolor. The street behind them bled into hues of gray and gold; the headlights blurred into slow-moving stars.

Claire tucked a wet strand of hair behind her ear.

Her hand trembled slightly, and when she looked at him, there was no performance left; just fatigue and longing wearing the same face. "If I tell you I came to that bookstore hoping I'd see you," she said, voice breaking into quiet bravery, "does that make me a bad person or just a desperate one?"

The honesty of it hit him harder than he expected. There was no manipulation in her tone, no seduction, just the raw ache of someone who had forgotten how to want without apology. He searched her face, the faint freckles on her cheek, the curve of her mouth when it hovered between confession and regret. "It makes you someone who wants," he said gently.

Her breath caught; she let out a shaky laugh that sounded like surrender. "That's the problem," she whispered. "Wanting has never been kind to me." He could have said a dozen things then; that wanting wasn't wrong, that desire didn't always end in ruin, that maybe kindness wasn't the point at all. But he didn't. Because she was right. Wanting wasn't kind.

It was the most dangerous, beautiful cruelty they had left. And standing there in the rain, shoulder to shoulder, two silhouettes under a leaking awning, Michael realized that every rule, every promise, every line he had ever drawn around his heart had already been washed away.

He could have said all the things he was supposed to say. He could have summoned the professional tone, the careful cadence of a man reciting policy by heart.

He could have offered referrals and guardrails, a tidy handoff to a colleague without his particular cracks. He could have built a wall out of procedure and hidden safely behind it. But he didn't.

Instead, Michael asked, quietly, "What do you want right now?" Claire didn't look away. The rain blurred the windows behind her, the city moving like watercolor. "To sit somewhere that isn't my head."

He gestured toward the café door, toward the hum of voices and the smell of espresso thick in the air. "Ten minutes. We talk about the book. Nothing else." Her lips curved, faintly, the smile caught somewhere between disbelief and hope. "And then we pretend it didn't happen?" He nodded. "And then we try." They stepped inside.

The warmth of the café folded around them; coffee, cinnamon, wet coats steaming by the door. They chose a small table by the window, two cups, no pastries, as if sugar would have been too much to bear. The rain outside streaked the glass in long, trembling lines.

Steam curled between them. Claire wrapped both hands around her cup like she needed the heat to keep from disappearing. For a while, neither spoke. Their silence wasn't awkward; it was delicate, the kind that asks to be left untouched. Then Claire said softly, "You have a tell."

He looked up, startled. "A what?" "A tell," she repeated, mouth curving into the smallest smile. "Like poker. When you're about to say something, you mean, you touch your tie, like there's a microphone hidden in it." Michael froze, hand halfway to his throat.

Then, realizing she was right, he laughed, really laughed. The sound startled him; it wanted to shake dust off a rug that hadn't been touched in years. "And you?" He asked, still smiling. "What's yours?" She tilted her head, thinking. "When I don't want to cry, I pick a word and stare at it until everything else blurs." "What's the word now?" He questioned.

Her gaze flicked to the chalkboard menu behind the counter. "Cardamom," she said, quick and sure, as if choosing it fast would keep the tears from coming. They said it together, evaluating the weight of it, the syllables soft and strange. "Cardamom."

The absurdity of it, two people sitting in the half-light, whispering a spice like a secret, broke something loose in both of them. They smiled. The tension softened. The air lightened just enough for breathing. He watched the color return to her cheeks, the way light returns to a room when you open the door slowly.

"Do you ever miss who you were," she asked, voice barely above a whisper, "before you learned to be careful?" Michael turned the cup slowly in his hands, watching the swirl of foam on its surface. "Every day," he said. Then, after a pause, "And sometimes not at all. Sometimes I'm grateful for every careful choice that kept the people I love intact."

Her eyes flickered, curiosity, softness. "Your daughter." It wasn't a question. "Yes." He said without question. "What's she like?" She inquired. He hesitated, searching for words that didn't exist in clinical vocabulary. "A small lunar body," he said finally. "She changes the tides without trying." The sentence hung between them, too beautiful to dismiss.

Claire smiled into her cup, and something in her eyes glimmered that wasn't sadness for once. "I used to dance," she said after a while. "Not well enough to be anything. But long enough to speak with parts of myself that never learned English."

"Do you miss it?" He asked. She looked out the window, where the rain still painted the streets in motion. "Every day," she said. Then added softly, "And sometimes not at all."

Their eyes met over the table, over the rising steam, and for a long, fragile moment, the entire world was reduced to that exchange. Two people admitting that the things they'd loved most still haunted them. And beneath the hum of the café, beneath the rules and the rain, something began to shift; quietly, dangerously. Like the earth deciding to move.

Outside, the SUV eased away from the curb and slipped into traffic; black, silent, and predatory. Its taillights smeared red across the wet asphalt like the aftermath of something that hadn't yet happened but already felt inevitable. Claire's gaze followed it until it vanished. When she turned back, her expression had changed, resolve and ruin braided behind her eyes.

"We should leave here," she said softly. "Before we turn talking into something it can't afford to be." Michael nodded. His throat felt raw, his pulse an uneven metronome in his wrists. The check sat between them. A thin, useless scrap of paper, damp at one corner where a drop of rain or sweat had landed.

It wasn't the cost of coffee he was paying for, and both of them knew it. He reached for it just as she did. Their fingers brushed, and the contact was barely anything; skin against skin for the briefest instant, but it sparked through him like a live wire, a sudden, electric reminder that touch is the first language we ever learn.

They both froze. The air went taut. Time thinned. There was too much silence for two people trying to behave. "Michael," she said at last.

The name came out softer than she intended, an invocation, a plea. The sound of it in her mouth undid him. His name had never sounded like that before; half prayer, half warning.

"I don't trust myself," she confessed, her eyes still fixed on where their hands had been. He could have told her to stop, to pull back, to remember everything they stood to lose. But instead... "Then trust me," he said. It was the most dangerous sentence of his life.

They stepped out into the night, the city's breath wrapping around them. The rain had gentled to a mist that softened every edge, made the streetlamps glow like secrets. Cars hissed by, throwing light across their faces and then taking it back.

He walked her toward the subway, where the grates exhaled waves of warm, metallic air. Steam ghosted around their feet, and the smell of iron and ozone made the moment feel suspended, halfway between confession and consequence. "This is where we pretend?" She asked quietly, the question trembling like glass about to break.

He looked down the dark stairs, where light and shadow coiled together. "This is where we practice," he said. "Practice what?" She asked. "Leaving," he said. "Before we can't." Claire's lips parted, but no sound came. She only nodded, eyes bright with something that wasn't quite tears and wasn't quite surrender. She reached into her bag and pulled out a scarf; pale gray, soft as a secret, and looped it once around her neck.

The wool clung to her damp skin, then slipped. It fell soundlessly to the step between them. Michael bent at the same moment she did. Their foreheads almost touched.

A heartbeat's distance, close enough that he could feel the warmth of her breath, smell the rain still caught in her hair. Below, a train traveresed through the tunnels, its echo rumbling like weather trapped underground.

"This cannot happen," he said, the words harsh with effort, holding the scarf between them like proof of his restraint. She took it from him, fingers grazing his once more, softer this time but somehow worse.

"Then why," she asked, "does it feel like it already has?" He didn't answer. Because every truth that lived inside him would ruin them both. She turned then, the scarf gripped in her hand and descended the stairs.

At the landing, she looked back, rain light glinting off her hair, her expression unreadable, suspended somewhere between goodbye and the start of something too late to stop.

He lifted his hand before he could think better of it. It was an instinct, a reach without reason, and when she disappeared into the dark, he let it fall. Slowly, helplessly, like the rest of his carefully arranged life. For a long moment, he stood there as the city breathed with him, every light reflecting his undoing.

He told himself the same old lie, that he was still in control, that one careful choice could hold back a tide that had already swallowed him whole. Then his phone buzzed. A message from Evelyn.

A photo of Eva at the kitchen table, pencil clenched in her small fist, tongue pressed between her teeth, surrounded by a fortress of markers and open notebooks. The caption: *She asked if you want to FaceTime before bed.*

Michael typed back: *Yes. Ten minutes.* His thumb hovered. Then, without thinking, he added: *Thank you.* He didn't know which of them the gratitude was for.

The woman who'd left him long ago, or the one who'd just walked away.

When he finally started home, the sky had opened into a slow unfurl of cloud, the city steaming under it like something alive. Each step felt like practice. Practice for the leaving he'd promised, practice for the ending he already knew he'd fail to make permanent.

And somewhere deep inside, beneath the steady hum of rain and guilt, Michael Harris understood the truth he'd been avoiding all along:

He hadn't just crossed the line. He'd built a home on the other side.

The Line Breaks

It happened on a Thursday again. The city had fallen into that strange, forgiving hour when the day forgets itself with amber light spilling like warm honey over glass and steel, softening everything it touched.

Even the cracked brick of the buildings across the avenue seemed briefly divine, the edges gilded, the grime turned to gold. It was the kind of light that lied beautifully. The kind that made even exhaustion look holy.

Office windows glowed like stained glass, each pane a little confession box, holding fragments of other lives; a woman watering a dying plant, a man loosening his tie and staring at nothing, the faint silhouette of someone laughing into a phone.

For a fleeting moment, the whole city looked redeemed, caught between fatigue and forgiveness. Traffic slowed to a low hum. Taxis idling, buses sighing as they braked, the faint hiss of steam escaping from a grate. A violin somewhere on the corner played a tune no one knew, the melody swallowed and reborn in echoes against the concrete canyons.

The air smelled faintly of rain that hadn't yet fallen; that clean, electric scent that comes before surrender. Michael stood at his office window, watching the light shift across the glass towers opposite.

He loved this time of day, the in-between. When the world didn't quite belong to the living or the sleeping. When things that were usually hidden could almost be seen.

The clock on his desk read *5:26 p.m.*.

The final session of the day was supposed to have ended twenty minutes ago, but Claire hadn't moved. She sat across from him, her posture looser now, her hair slipping free of its clip, a small strand resting against her cheek.

The light caught in it, turning brown to bronze, and for a moment she looked unreal; like a painting left unfinished, the artist unsure whether to ruin it with another stroke or let it remain perfect in its incompleteness. Outside, the city kept breathing that long, collective exhale of millions heading home.

Inside, the air between them thickened, fragile as spun glass. "Do you ever notice," Claire said finally, her voice soft, as if speaking too loudly might scare the moment away, "how quiet everything feels right before the city lights up? Like it's holding its breath?"

Michael looked at her, startled by the way her words aligned perfectly with what he'd just been thinking. "Yes," he said. "It's the pause before the world remembers itself." She smiled faintly, though it didn't reach her eyes. "Maybe I like it better like this, before everything remembers what it's supposed to be."

Her words settled between them like dust in sunlight; slow, inevitable, impossible to ignore. From the street below came the sound of a horn, a shout, a burst of laughter. The spell wavered. Michael leaned back slightly, forcing his tone into something neutral.

"You said last week that Thursdays are difficult for you." She nodded, eyes on the floor. "It's the day everything seems to repeat. No matter what I do, no matter how far I get, Thursdays always find me." Her laugh was small, but it trembled at the edges. "It's ridiculous, right? Being haunted by a day?"

He shook his head. "No. Some memories are smart enough to keep their own calendar." She looked up then; really looked, and something in her gaze shifted, sharpened. For the briefest moment, it wasn't the look of a patient to her therapist.

It was something else. Recognition. Understanding. Hunger. The light through the window dimmed another shade deeper, amber sliding into copper. It painted her face in molten color, her green eyes catching it like glass catching flame.

Outside, the first streetlights flickered on. Inside, silence deepened. Not empty, but full, weighted with things neither of them could name.

Michael glanced at the clock again. *6:06 p.m.*

Always a Thursday. Always six minutes late.

And somewhere in the city, a storm began to gather.

Inside Michael's office, the world felt sealed off from all that motion. The glass panes dulled the city's roar to a hush, and the air system hummed its careful monotone, filling the room with a manufactured calm.

It was a room built for composure; muted walls, symmetrical lamps, books aligned in spines of neutral color. A sanctuary for other people's pain.

He sat in his chair; his safe chair, hands folded loosely on his lap. But the quiet didn't feel safe tonight. It pressed against him instead, heavy, and deliberate, as though the walls themselves were listening. He shifted.

The leather creaked, an ordinary sound, but in that stillness, it cracked through the air like guilt made audible. The clock on the wall ticked. 3:56 *p.m.* The time caught his eye like a splinter.

He looked away, but his pulse had already begun to synchronize with it. The soft, mechanical rhythm that had come to mean something it shouldn't. Thursday again. The day she always came.

The day restraint became a ritual and desire a discipline. He tried to focus on his notes instead; columns of tidy handwriting that had once been his defense. *Clinical observations. Emotional assessments.* But her name, Claire Alden, was written at the top of the page, and that was enough to unravel him.

He told himself that the anticipation was professional. That he only wanted her to find progress, closure. But the truth pulsed underneath, undeniable: he missed her before she even arrived. He reached for his tie, adjusted it, caught himself mid-motion.

Her voice from that café whispered back to him, teasing: You touch your tie when you mean something. He dropped his hand. The air felt denser now, charged. The faint smell of rain from the morning lingered on his cuffs, mixing with the faint hint of coffee grounds from his desk.

Outside, the traffic lights blinked through the blinds, casting slow stripes of red and green across the carpet. The door would open any minute. He knew the rhythm of her arrival by heart now. The way her footsteps softened near the threshold, the moment of hesitation before her knock.

He told himself to breathe. To remember who he was, what he'd sworn never to compromise.

But his pulse betrayed him, steady and traitorous. The truth was simple and devastating: every boundary he'd built to keep her at a distance had already been breached. Not by touch, not by words, but by recognition.

Because when she walked through that door, he knew, the quiet world he'd built around himself would tilt again; slowly, beautifully, and beyond repair. He had promised himself after the bookstore, after the coffee shop, that it wouldn't go further.

It couldn't. Each encounter had already felt like a trespass, each glance held too long a step closer to the edge. He'd drawn invisible lines after everyone; quiet vows to himself made in the dim glow of streetlamps or the solitude of his apartment. And yet here he was again, waiting for her, pulse betraying him.

He told himself boundaries mattered. That they were not just professional, but moral foundations that kept the world from collapsing in on itself. He told himself that Eva deserved a father who kept his word, a man who didn't live in the shadow of his own hypocrisy. He reminded himself, too, that a man with his history; his cracks, his hungers, his inherited silence, had no business courting temptation.

He had seen what desire could destroy: his marriage, his faith in his own restraint, the fragile trust of a child who looked at him like he was unbreakable. But desire didn't care about vows. It didn't respect the architecture of his discipline.

Desire slipped in quietly, like light through a keyhole, seeping into the places he thought he'd sealed. It wore her voice, her laugh, the memory of her fingers brushing the edge of his hand in a bookstore, the sound of her saying his name like it belonged somewhere deeper than the surface.

He had tried to bury it under reason. He had told himself it was empathy, projection, transference. Clinical words that dressed longing in rational clothes. But when the clock struck 4:06, none of those words mattered. The ache was human.

The lie was professional. He could feel the duality tearing at him, therapist and man, discipline and need, father, and failure. Every part of him that knew better was at war with the part that simply wanted to feel alive.

He stared down at the notes on his desk, her name written at the top of the page, the date beneath it. The ink had bled slightly, smudged by the drag of his hand earlier that morning. A small imperfection, but it unsettled him.

Because that's what this was becoming, a smudge spreading through everything he thought he'd written cleanly. The memory of her words from the subway drifted back to him: "Why does it feel like it already has?" He had no answer then. He had less of one now. He rubbed a hand over his face, exhaling through his teeth.

The room felt smaller than it had minutes ago. The air conditioner hummed too loud. The blinds cut stripes of dying sunlight across the floor like bars. He told himself to stop thinking of her. To focus on the work. To remember that want and worth were not the same. But even as he made the promise again; another small lie meant to keep him whole, he knew that if she walked through that door.

If she said his name in that low, careful way she had...he would forget every reason he'd ever given himself to resist. And yet, sitting in that amber light, he felt the promises bending. Slowly, silently, until he wasn't sure what strength he had left to keep them from breaking. The air seemed too still, too expectant.

Every sound, the hum of the vent, the faint tick of the clock, felt amplified, like the world was holding its breath with him. But Claire sat differently today. Not perched at the edge of the couch like before. Not folded in on herself, waiting for the pain to pass. Not fragile.

She sat like a woman who had decided to stop running from her own voice. Her posture was composed, but her hands betrayed her, clutching the hem of her sleeve, then releasing it, then clutching again. Michael watched her, felt the quiet stretch between them.

Then she spoke. "I dream about this room." Her voice barely rose above a whisper, but it cut through him like glass. He lifted his eyes from his notes, from the illusion of distance they offered. "About what in it?" He asked, trying for steady, trying for professional. "Not the furniture. Not the books." Her gaze didn't waver.

It lingered on him, heavy and knowing. "About being here. With you." The words landed softly, but their weight was enormous. He swallowed, the motion tight, audible even to himself. His pen hesitated mid-sentence and bled ink onto the page, a small black wound spreading into the paper. He didn't blot it.

He couldn't move. Every ethical alarm in his head began to scream; the words drilled into him by professors, mentors, the ethics board itself. Countertransference. Maintain boundaries. Protect the therapeutic frame. His eyes darted to the framed license on the wall.

His name etched in serif letters, the thin line between legitimacy and ruin. But none of it stopped the truth of what was happening inside him. The heat climbed up his throat, a slow, traitorous burn. His chest tightened, not in panic but in hunger.

The kind of ache that had nothing to do with lust and everything to do with recognition. His pulse pressed hard at his wrist. His body remembered what his mind had outlawed. "Claire..." Her name left his mouth like a confession. She cut him off, her tone both defiant and trembling.

"I know what you're going to say. That this is transference. That I'm confusing safety with desire." She drew a breath that trembled on the edge of breaking. "Maybe I am." Then, quieter: "But maybe... maybe you feel it too." The words struck him like a match against dry tinder. He didn't answer.

He couldn't. Because to deny it would be a lie. And to admit it would be the end. The silence that followed wasn't the careful kind he'd learned to use in therapy. It wasn't space for her to think. It was charge. It was gravity. It was the sound of two people standing too close to the edge, pretending they didn't already know which way they'd fall.

He tried to shape the air into something safe, something clinical, something detached. But when he opened his mouth, no words came. Her voice broke first. "Michael." Not Dr. Harris. Not the title that kept him safe. Just Michael.

Soft. Bare. Dangerous. "Please don't pretend." She whispered. And then, finally, fatally, she cried. Not the restrained tears of earlier sessions, but something rawer, older. The kind that doesn't ask permission. Her shoulders trembled, her breath caught. The tears slid down her cheeks, carving through the thin powder on her skin, catching in the corners of her mouth. He felt it all.

The instinct to comfort, the training that forbade it, the electric pull of empathy turned to ache. For a moment, he saw his own reflection in her grief; how close compassion could sit to longing, how minor difference there was between wanting to heal someone and wanting to be healed by them.

He wanted to reach for her hand. He wanted to stop himself. He did neither. The only sound in the room was the small, stifled rhythm of her crying, and the slow, doomed realization that something had already crossed over, quietly, invisibly, and there would be no turning back.

Not the steady tears of earlier sessions, but broken sobs, the kind that cracked her ribs and bent her shoulders forward as if grief itself were trying to fold her into nothing. Her body shook. Her breath came in ragged bursts, each one sounding like something torn loose from deep inside.

Michael didn't think. He moved. Across the room. Across the boundary. Across the line that had defined everything he thought he was. He sat beside her on the couch, careful at first, the way a man approaches a wounded animal; slow, open, palms visible. He told himself he would only steady her breathing.

Only help her find the ground again. That was all. But when she leaned into him, when her forehead brushed his shoulder, her hair damp with tears and perfume that smelled faintly of lavender and rain, the air itself seemed to tilt. Her body trembled. He hesitated for a heartbeat, then wrapped an arm around her, a motion both instinct and betrayal.

His hand rested against her back, feeling each trembling inhale, each fracture in the rhythm of her body. "You're not alone," he murmured. The words left his mouth before he could censor them, soft but certain. "I've always been alone," she whispered into his shirt. "Even when I wasn't."

The confession vibrated against his chest. He closed his eyes, felt the wet warmth of her tears seeping through the cotton, marking him. He should have pulled away. Should have stood, created distance, summoned the authority that once came so easily.

But something in her voice, something in that word always broke him open. Instead of retreating, his hand moved a small, tender motion at first, tracing slow, steady circles against her back. Comfort, he told himself. Steadiness.

A rhythm to calm her breathing. But it wasn't just that anymore. The circles became softer, slower. His palm slid upward, felt the shape of her shoulder beneath the thin fabric, the tremor of her breath against his collarbone.

Her fingers, small, cold, curled into his sleeve, anchoring herself. He should have stopped. He didn't. She tilted her face upward, and for a single suspended moment, he saw every contradiction in her eyes: fear and need, apology, and dare. The distance between them wasn't distance at all.

It was a thread; thin, trembling, pulled too tight to survive another second. The kiss was tentative, almost hesitant, born not from desire but from exhaustion, grief, and the human ache to be understood. Their lips met softly, like a secret assessing its own weight.

For an instant, it was pure stillness, two people suspended in the impossible mercy of touch. Then the world rushed back in. The taste of salt. The hum of the vent. The sound of rain on the window, steady as a heartbeat. He tried to tell himself it was just comfort. But grief, he realized, can be the fiercest hunger of all, because it doesn't crave pleasure.

It craves proof that you're still alive. And in that moment, with her breath catching against his mouth, he felt frighteningly alive. It deepened. Her lips trembled against his at first; hesitant, uncertain, but then steadied, pressing harder, the tremor giving way to something that felt like surrender.

Michael's breath caught; his thoughts scattered like startled birds.

He broke the kiss first, pulling back just enough to speak. "This is wrong," he said, voice shaking. Claire's reply came fractured, raw. "Yes," she whispered. "And I don't care." Her hand rose to his jaw, fingers trembling but resolute.

She touched him like someone memorizing the shape of a forbidden truth, her thumb tracing the faint stubble along his chin. The touch stole his breath. He had spent years teaching people how to name their impulses, how to contain them.

Yet here he was, unlearning everything in the space of a heartbeat. Then she pulled him back. Their mouths met again, not gently this time, but with the urgency of two people who had run out of ways to speak. The sound of it; soft, desperate, alive, filled the small room like a confession neither could retract.

It was fire, yes, but not the kind that destroys all at once. It was the slow burn that starts in the chest and spreads, pulling at everything it touches. Every thought he'd locked away; every lonely night, every quiet ache he'd disguised as Professionalism, rushed to the surface.

He could taste salt and heat, the faint trace of her perfume, the rain still drying in her hair. His hands betrayed him next. They moved instinctively, uncertain whether they meant to comfort or to hold.

One found her waist, feeling the tremor beneath her ribs, the other pressed lightly at her back, as though anchoring himself to something solid while the rest of him dissolved. "Claire…" he breathed, her name breaking apart between his teeth. But she was already there, closer, her body leaning into his, the lines between them erased by need.

For a moment, time ceased to exist; no patients, no ethics board, no fragile balance of right and wrong.

Michael began to unstrap the back of Claire's black bra. As she started to stroke the outer lining of Michael's suit pants. She could feel his length as she continued. They both moved slowly toward the couch. Clumsy knocking over a few stacks of Michael's papers on his desk.

As they reached the couch. Michael began to reach around and cup Claire's curves and pull down her black panties sliding them down with his right foot as she pushed him down gentle. Her hair a mess, and lipstick smeared she began to straddle him.

Clarie could experience every inch of Michael as it eased in, and out of her. Her whimpers were like music of soft symphonies. Her breath was as warm as tea on skin. Micheal could feel them as every breath moved seamlessly across his neck and ear. They both moved together as in unison.

She whispered into Michael's ear. "I'm coming" as they both succumbed to their desires. Only the sound of rain against the glass, and the terrifying beauty of two people remembering what it meant to feel.

Then came the stillness. The kind that follows lightning. He drew back just enough to look at her eyes wide, wet, luminous with guilt and something more dangerous: recognition. "What have we done?" He whispered.

Claire shook her head, a single tear sliding down her cheek. "Something we've both been doing for a long time," she said quietly. "We just stopped pretending." The words hung between them, trembling, alive. Neither spoke again. The room pulsed with what couldn't be undone.

Outside, the storm had stopped.
But the air still crackled like it remembered.

The hum of the office faded; the clock, the city beyond the window, even the echo of his conscience, all swallowed by the fire of her mouth on his. It wasn't careful, it wasn't measured. It was the language of everything they had denied, spoken in heat and urgency.

For the first time in years, Michael wasn't thinking about rules or consequences. For the first time, he was simply burning. The damage was done. They made love; not with innocence, but with the desperate, shattering tenderness of two people who had run out of ways to keep pretending.

When he touched her, it wasn't desire he felt first, but recognition, a desperate, burning need to be seen and to disappear all at once. Her body trembled. Not from fear, but from the fragile, fevered joy that comes when pain and want to become indistinguishable.

Claire moved against him, her rhythm desperate and deliberate, each motion drawing his length deeper into the heat of her. Their bodies moved together like fire chasing the wind; wild, consuming, unstoppable. When it was over, the room seemed altered. Air heavier, time slower, everything too quiet to be safe.

Claire dressed in silence, her movements careful, almost reverent, as if sound itself could break the fragile truce between guilt and longing. She didn't look at him when she reached for her bag, didn't meet his eyes when she whispered, *"Goodbye."* The word lingered in the air, soft but final.

When the door clicked shut, she was gone. Her scarf forgotten again on the couch, pale gray against the dark leather, folded like a ghost of her presence. Michael sat with his head in his hands, his fingers digging into his scalp. He was trembling, his breath uneven, chest rising in a rhythm that felt closer to panic than relief.

He told himself he could still fix this. That it was one moment, one mistake, one lapse in a life built on restraint. But the lie wouldn't hold. He could still smell her perfume on his shirt. Still feel the warmth where she had been. His phone buzzed. The sound made him flinch. He turned it over in his palm, thumb hesitating before pressing play.

Eva's laughter filled the room; bright, unfiltered, spilling through the tiny speaker like sunlight into a tomb. *"Daddy, look! I made a moon out of markers!"* Her voice cracked with joy, pure and careless. Michael's eyes stung. The sound of her small voice split him in two.

The father she believed him to be and the man he had just become. He lowered the phone, staring at the darkened screen until his own reflection looked like a stranger. The guilt came in waves. Sharp, physical, like something crawling up from inside his ribs.

    He silenced the lights one after another, until the darkness felt earned. But even in darkness, he felt watched. He crossed to the window, hesitated before touching the blinds. Outside, the street was slick and glinting, rainwater catching the orange glow of passing headlights.

And there, across the street, a black SUV idled at the curb. The motor hummed softly, smoke unwinding toward the streetlights in delicate spirals. The glass was tinted so dark he couldn't see inside, but the sight of it made his stomach twist. He turned away, telling himself it was nothing. Just another city car waiting for someone else. But it wasn't.

Inside, in the back seat, Lucian Alden sat motionless. His eyes were fixed on the darkened third-floor window; the one he knew too well. The one where his wife, his property, had just been. The faint reflection of his own face stared back at him in the glass, cold and immaculate.

He didn't blink. Didn't move. His driver shifted in the front seat, breaking the silence. "Home, sir?" Lucian's jaw tightened, the muscle at his temple twitching once. His gaze never left the building. "No," he said finally, voice low, even. "Not yet."

And then, just barely, the corners of his mouth lifted. Not in amusement. Not in surprise. But in the quiet, precise smile of a man who had just confirmed what he already suspected. The kind of smile that promised retribution.

Outside, the light turned red, bathing the SUV in color like a warning neither of them could hear. Inside his darkened office, Michael Harris sat in silence, unaware that the moment he'd broken his own rules, he'd also opened a door that someone else had been waiting for years to step through.

And across the street, Lucian Alden waited.

Patient. Certain.

Already planning where to strike first.

The Night We Couldn't Leave

It should have ended with the kiss. A single mistake, sealed by silence. A line crossed, regretted, then tucked beneath the rug of professionalism where all the dangerous things go to hide. But some moments are not content to be buried. They breathe under the floorboards. They whisper through walls. They wait.

Michael told himself he had drawn the line again. That one lapse did not have to become a pattern, that the body could be disciplined the way the mind pretended to be. He returned to work the next morning wrapped in his usual armor; the pressed shirt, the steady voice, the clinical detachment polished to glass. Yet everything looked slightly off, as though the world itself knew.

The office seemed dimmer, the air heavier, the ticking clock louder, each second an accusation. Even the photographs on the wall, those meaningless black-and-white prints of bridges and rain-soaked streets, seemed to lean closer, watching. The faint hum of the fluorescent light overhead had a pulse to it now, a slow and mocking rhythm.

He could still feel her, the press of Claire's hand at the back of his neck, the tremor of her breath against his lips, the heat that had felt less like passion and more like confession. It clung to him, invisible but undeniable, a ghost that refused to be exorcised. That night, he washed his hands until the skin reddened, as though guilt could be scrubbed out like dirt. But the memory stayed. It lived in the veins, not the skin.

Outside, the city had shifted too.

The skyline wore its dusk like a bruise; violet fading to black, windows glowing like watchful eye. The rain that came later was soft, deliberate, the kind that seemed to wash everything except what needed cleansing most.

Michael sat in his chair, the same chair where she had sat the day before, her scent still faint in the air, not perfume, but something subtler, human, raw. He stared at the couch opposite him, the indentation of where she had once rested her hands, and tried to pretend it was just furniture again.

But it wasn't. It was an altar now, to a transgression neither of them could take back. He thought of his daughter, Eva; her laughter, her drawings taped crookedly to his refrigerator, her small voice asking why he always worked late.

He thought of Evelyn; cold, measured, her disappointment sharpened into something almost elegant. And then he thought of Claire, the way her pain had felt like recognition, like standing at the edge of a mirror and finally finding a reflection that looked back. The mind makes its bargains with the heart, but the heart has no sense of ethics.

Only rhythm. Only pulse. Only want. He told himself he would fix it, that he would apologize, that he would redefine the boundary before it dissolved completely. But every time he rehearsed the words, they sounded false. How do you apologize for a gravity you never meant to create?

Outside his window, the rain had turned to mist. Steam curled from the vents in the street, rising in thin white ribbons like ghosts released from the city's skin. He imagined her somewhere out there; walking, perhaps, head bowed beneath an umbrella, carrying the same ache he did, pretending it could be folded into something as simple as guilt.

In another life, in another story, the kiss would have been a beginning. But in this one, it was an ending. The kind that leaves fingerprints long after the lights go out.

He poured himself a drink; whiskey, neat, and watched the amber liquid catch the lamplight. The glass trembled slightly in his hand, not from fear but from recognition. He wasn't sure what frightened him more. The mistake itself, or how much of him wanted to make it again.

A draft moved through the apartment, though no window was open. It brushed against his skin like breath. Somewhere, far off, thunder rolled; low, steady, promising rain again before morning.

Michael closed his eyes. The city held its breath. And in the hollow between lightning and thunder, he could almost hear it, her voice, soft and broken, whispering his name.

The sound was not memory. It was haunting.

And the worst part of all was that he welcomed it. Michael told himself that the next morning he would make it right, he'd apologize, redraw the boundary, bury the temptation before it learned to speak. He would become Dr. Harris again, measured, and unshakable, a man who knew where to stop.

But temptation does not bury. It waits. Patient. Breathing just beneath the surface, like an ember pretending to die. He made it through Friday on muscle memory; his sessions mechanical, his tone steady, his smile practiced. But everything underneath felt off-kilter, like the world had shifted half an inch to the left.

Every voice he listened to blurred into hers. Every confession from a patient echoed fragments of her words.

By evening, he'd stopped trying to pretend he wasn't waiting for her name to appear on his phone.

It came on Saturday, at dusk. The city was quieting, the light outside his window thinning into amber, gray. He was grading intake reports at the kitchen table, Eva's crayons still scattered across its surface like small, forgotten constellations. His phone buzzed once, face down beside a half-drunk cup of coffee.

He didn't look at first. He already knew. When he turned it over, the message was there. Just one word. *Please.* No punctuation. No explanation. Just the word itself; bare, trembling, enough to undo him. He stared at it for a long time. He should have ignored it.

He should have thought of Eva, of her laughter, of how she still called his apartment home even when she spent half her nights elsewhere. He should have thought of the trust his patients placed in him, the years of restraint that had built the fragile scaffolding of a life that finally looked steady from the outside.

He should have remembered the faces of the mentors who taught him that compassion, unchecked, can rot into ruin. He didn't. Instead, his thumbs moved before reason could catch up. A heartbeat, a pause, and then the message appeared on her screen. My address.

When he hit send, the sound was almost imperceptible; a soft click, but it felt like the world tilting. Like a door opening that would never close again. Outside, the city had gone still. Somewhere, a siren wailed far off and then faded, swallowed by distance.

Michael sat there, phone still in his hand, staring at the last thing he would ever be able to undo. She arrived in rain again. Always the rain, as if the city itself conspired to blur their outlines, to wash away the edges of what they were about to do.

It fell soft but steady, a whisper against the windows, the kind of rain that makes everything shimmer and nothing clear. Claire stood beneath it, her hair damp, her dress clinging to her like memory, creased where the fabric met her skin, darkened at the shoulders where the water had found her first.

When Michael opened the door, she didn't speak. Neither of them did. For a long, impossible heartbeat, they just stood there, two shapes framed in the glow of the hallway light, breathing each other in like oxygen they'd been denied. He should have said no.

He should have said "Why are you here?" "Or we can't." But words felt useless against what was already happening inside him. "You shouldn't have come," he managed, though his voice was soft, not reprimand but surrender. "I know," she whispered. *"But I didn't know where else to go."*

He took one step closer, rain still gleaming on her skin. "You could have gone anywhere." "No," she said, eyes shining. "I couldn't." The door shut. And the world broke open. The first touch wasn't graceful. It was desperate, almost clumsy; two people reaching for something they couldn't name, each afraid the other might vanish if they hesitated.

Her fingers found the front of his shirt, fisted the fabric like she was holding herself together by it. He caught her wrists, meaning to still her, to reason, but reason didn't live here anymore. "Claire…" he began. "Don't," she said, breath trembling against his jaw. "If you say my name, I'll stop pretending this isn't real." Her lips found his before he could answer. The kiss was hunger and grief tangled into one.

It wasn't the softness of romance; it was the gasp of two people trying to remember what it felt like to be alive. She tasted of rain and salt, of the ocean just before a storm. He felt her breath against his cheek, sharp and uneven.

Her hands moved to his collar, fingers shaking as they loosened his tie, not seduction, but release. "Tell me this is wrong," she whispered, half plea, half dare. "It is," he said. "Then why are you shaking?" She added mischievously. He didn't answer. He couldn't.

His tie slipped free, falling to the floor with the sound of surrender. Her hand lingered at his throat for a moment, pulse meeting pulse. Outside, the rain deepened, a steady percussion against the glass, the city's heartbeat keeping time with theirs. It wasn't gentleness that moved them, it was recognition.

The kind that strips a person to their truth. Two haunted people, finding each other in the wreckage. And in that small, dim room, they stopped running. For the first time in years, neither of them felt alone. His hands found her back, her waist, the curve of her hip. The map of a body that felt both foreign and inevitable beneath his touch. The room held its breath, the air thick with rain and want.

"Tell me this is wrong," she whispered against his mouth, the words trembling, almost lost between heartbeats. "It is," he breathed. And then he kissed her harder. They stumbled toward the couch, the rhythm of their steps uneven, frantic, as if they were being pulled by something larger than themselves.

Clothes gave way to skin, one piece at a time, until the world around them narrowed to heat and breath and the faint creak of the leather beneath them. Each gasp felt like confession. Each touch, a vow broken quietly between them.

Claire dropped to her knees. Micheal laid his head back, as she began to suck and stroke. The passion was intense as two storms colliding in a single sky.

Every boundary, every ethic, every oath he had sworn dissolved in the press of her against him; the careful life he'd built splintering under the weight of something primal, something human. It wasn't lust alone; it was loneliness, the kind that eats at the edges of the soul until even ruin starts to look like mercy.

It was grief and hunger and the need to be seen, all colliding until they could no longer tell which was which. Her sobs became sound without name, his whispers turned to pleas that weren't words. They clung to each other like survivors of the same wreck, desperate to believe that touch could undo what time had done to them.

Michael led Claire to his room in silence, every step measured, every breath careful. The curtains hung motionless, and the moonlight slipping through them was the only light. Michael eased in his length and began to thrust without making a sound though holding back he couldn't help but whisper in Claire's ear *"It's my turn"* as Michael came.

For a while, the world outside ceased to exist. No patients. No oaths. No Lucian waiting in the dark. Even Eva, her laughter, her crayons, her small orbit of innocence, vanished from his mind like a light switched off. There was only this. The woman who looked at him as though he might save her, and the man who wanted, for once, to believe he could.

When it was over, silence rushed back in, heavy and absolute. Rain tapped at the window, steady as breath, as if the sky itself were trying to wash the room clean. Claire's head rested on his chest, her hair damp against his skin, her breathing slowly synchronizing with his.

Michael lay still, one arm curved around her shoulders, the other hand stroking through her hair in slow, dazed motions.

His heart beat hard, too loud in his ears, not from triumph, not from passion, but from terror. "What now?" She asked, her voice small, almost childlike in its exhaustion. He closed his eyes. The question hung there, impossible, too fragile to answer.

He could still taste rain on her lips, still feel her pulse under his hand. And in the quiet that followed, a single truth lodged itself in his chest.

Now I lose everything.
He didn't say it aloud. He didn't need to.
The silence between them already knew.

The fallout began the next morning. The rain had stopped sometime before dawn, but the air still carried its weight; heavy, metallic, alive with the scent of something ended. The city outside his window glimmered under a thin film of water, every reflection sharp, unforgiving.

Michael sat at the edge of his bed, shirt half-buttoned, the quiet hum of the refrigerator in the next room his only company. He hadn't slept. Every time he closed his eyes, he saw her. Hair damp against his chest, the gray scarf abandoned on the couch like an accusation.

When his phone vibrated on the nightstand, the sound sliced through the silence. He didn't move at first.
He knew before he looked that it wouldn't be good.
Finally, he reached for it.
Subject: URGENT, Immediate Attention Required
From: Dr. Lillian Cohen, Clinical Director

Dr. Harris, a concern has been raised regarding potential boundary violations with a patient.
Please arrange a meeting Monday morning. Confidential and serious.

Michael read it twice, then again, the words blurring until they stopped making sense. Boundary violations. Patient. Serious. His stomach hollowed, a slow, sinking dread pooling in his chest. His hand went cold around the phone.

His first thought, of course, was Claire. He tried to swallow, but his throat was dry. He reread the message again, as though it might change if he stared hard enough. It didn't. He thought of the security cameras in the hallway outside his office. Of the after-hours cleaning staff.

Of Lucian's black SUV idling across the street. "No," he whispered aloud, voice cracking. "No, no, no." He set the phone down carefully on the nightstand, as if dropping it too hard might make the truth more real.

The clock beside it read *7:12 a.m.* In less than two hours, he was supposed to meet another patient, sit across from them with his steady voice and careful empathy, pretending he wasn't coming apart. He stood and crossed to the window. The glass was cool against his palm.

Outside, the world looked too bright for what it was holding. He thought of Claire, how she had whispered please two nights before, how her eyes had held equal parts hunger and apology. He remembered the way she'd left, without looking back, without a word.

He wanted to believe it wasn't her. That someone else had said something, that this was some bureaucratic misunderstanding. But deep down, he already knew.

It was never if. It was when. And when had come.

His second was, who saw? Meanwhile, Lucian Alden already knew. The black SUV hadn't just been surveillance, it had been patience made visible. Lucian didn't believe in guessing. He believed in proof.

Weeks earlier, he'd hired a man named Daryl Finch, a former police officer turned private investigator, the kind of man who understood that truth was negotiable, but evidence was currency. Finch had a camera, a good lens, and no moral compass to speak of.

He worked quickly and without conscience. Now, there were photographs. Not perfectly focused but damning in their suggestion. Claire stepping into Michael's building after dark, raincoat buttoned but hair loose.

Another, later, her leaving just before dawn, head down, face half hidden, but the flush in her cheeks unmistakable even through grain and blur. One frame caught her silhouette behind the glass of the lobby, Michael's shadow just beyond. Proof enough for a man like Lucian.

He studied them with a kind of clinical detachment, seated in his private office surrounded by dark mahogany and silence. A tumbler of whiskey turned slowly in his hand, amber light catching the crystal edges as he swirled it in deliberate circles. He didn't rage. He didn't shout.

Lucian didn't need to. He planned. "This will ruin him," he murmured, his tone almost affectionate. "And when it does…" He smiled small, controlled, the smile of a man who thought love and ownership were the same thing. "…She'll come crawling back." He took a slow drink, the ice clinking softly.

Outside, the city lights shimmered against the rain-streaked glass, and in their reflections, Lucian's smile remained sharp, satisfied, certain.

★ ☼ ★

Across the city, Michael Harris spent Sunday split cleanly between guilt and dread. The morning came with the sound of laughter, Eva's, high and bright as birdsong.

She was sitting cross-legged on his couch, her hair in uneven braids she'd made herself, syrup smeared on her sleeve, proud of the pancakes she'd flipped with her father.

He smiled, because she deserved a father who smiled. He laughed, because she laughed first. He listened when she told him about the picture she drew of the moon with purple crayons. But his mind wasn't there.

Every time his phone buzzed, his chest clenched; half-hoping, half-dreading that it might be Claire. It never was. He kept glancing toward the couch. Her scarf was still there, draped over the armrest, the faintest trace of her perfume woven into the fabric of lavender and rain. He should have thrown it away. He couldn't.

After Eva left, after her small arms wrapped around his neck, after she said "*I love you, Daddy*" with the kind of faith he no longer felt he deserved, the silence in the apartment was unbearable. He sat on the couch where Claire had been, elbows on his knees, staring at the scarf like it might explain how everything had gone so wrong so quickly.

The clock ticked. The light dimmed. Outside, the rain began again, quiet, and relentless, as if the city itself refused to let anything stay clean for long. Michael pressed the scarf to his face and closed his eyes. He could still feel her there, the warmth of her breath, the weight of her head against his chest. He told himself it was over.

He told himself he would face whatever came.

But the truth was already waiting for him in photographs, in emails, in the cold, deliberate smile of a man watching from across the city, plotting the precise moment to strike.

What had he done? The question echoed through him, merciless as the ticking clock on his wall. He was a father, a therapist, a man trusted with the softest, most fragile parts of other people's lives. He had built his career on listening, on helping others resist the very kinds of impulses to which he had just surrendered.

Now, because of one night, one moment of heat and weakness, everything he was, everything he'd spent decades constructing, balanced on the edge of collapse. He pressed his palms against his eyes until colors bloomed behind the darkness.

Guilt roared in his chest, not as shame but as grief. Grief for the version of himself that had existed yesterday, before the line was crossed and the silence that followed became unbearable. And yet, when his phone vibrated again, it felt like a pulse that didn't belong to him.

He turned it over, his thumb hovering above the screen. One word. *Tonight?* No punctuation, no hesitation. Just that word, sharp and simple, radiating through him like voltage. He stared at it for too long. His rational mind screamed delete it, don't respond, end this before it ends you.

But reason had lost its voice. His body betrayed him first. An ache rising from somewhere deep and helpless, an ache that had nothing to do with lust and everything to do with the hunger for connection, for absolution, for something that could quiet the noise inside him.

He wanted to tell himself it wasn't about her. That it was about feeling alive again, if only for a moment.

But when he typed back, the truth was simpler, uglier, and more human: *Yes.* His reflection in the dark window looked hollowed, unfamiliar eyes that once belonged to someone steady now clouded with want.

He set the phone down on the table beside Eva's forgotten crayons, the colors bright and innocent against the grain of the wood. The contrast nearly undid him. Because for Michael Harris, the night he and Claire came together was not an ending. It wasn't even a mistake contained in the past tense.

It was the fuse.

And the fire, quiet, patient, merciless, had already been lit.

Fractures

The apartment felt smaller each day; walls bending inward as if the building itself were conspiring to compress every secret into one hot, impossible point. The air thickened, dense and metallic, until each breath felt like an act of theft. Even sound had weight here.

The hum of the refrigerator, the faint tick of the radiator cooling, the distant moan of a siren below, each one pressed against his ribs like proof that the world outside still existed, though he was no longer sure he belonged to it. Silence had a texture now. It wasn't the simple absence of noise; it was alive, breathing, a thing that crept through the cracks between words and waited there, listening.

It sharpened like a blade that promised to cut if anyone so much as breathed wrong. The air smelled faintly of coffee gone cold and rain-soaked wool of the scarf Claire had left draped over the chair by the window, its threads still holding her scent. He should have folded it away. Hidden it. But he couldn't. He told himself he kept it there as a reminder of everything he'd risked, everything he still had to lose.

The truth was simpler, darker: he kept it because it made the silence less lonely. At night, the walls seemed to breathe. Old pipes groaned like voices rehearsing confessions in another room. Shadows stretched and rearranged themselves across the floor, slipping over the worn carpet like liquid dusk. Sometimes, he thought he heard her; a sigh from the hallway, the soft drag of a hand against plaster.

He would sit up suddenly, pulse hammering, but the space would remain empty, filled only with the ghost of movement.

He began to avoid mirrors. There was something in his reflection he didn't recognize anymore, not just the exhaustion, the sleepless hollows beneath his eyes, but the expression of a man who had crossed some unseen threshold and couldn't find his way back.

He looked like someone waiting for a verdict. The city beyond the window carried on as it always did. Neon bleeding through fog, tires hissing on wet pavement, a million lives unspooling without him. He envied their noise, their blindness, their freedom to forget.

Inside his apartment, time had become circular; a loop of memory and regret, each hour indistinguishable from the last. Sometimes, when the loneliness became unbearable, he'd whisper her name just to feel the room respond. Claire. It always did. The syllable seemed to echo in the air, low and familiar, as if the walls themselves remembered her.

And maybe they did. He would sit at his desk, staring at the faint imprint of her fingertips still visible on a sheet of paper, the one she had touched absentmindedly during their last session.

It wasn't visible to anyone else, but he could see it.

He could feel it.

The apartment had become a reliquary of their trespass; every object a relic, every shadow a sermon. He told himself it would fade, that guilt would eventually dull into memory.

But it didn't. It grew. It bloomed in the quiet hours like mold beneath wallpaper, invisible until it took shape, until it became the air he breathed, the pulse beneath his skin, the whisper in his ear telling him the truth he didn't want to hear.

That what had begun as comfort had become hunger. And hunger, once awakened, does not sleep. Michael paced, the pattern of his steps a staccato metronome that kept time with his panic. Claire sat, hands folded in her lap, fingers wearying at the hem of her dress until the fabric threaded under her nails.

They moved around one another like strangers trapped in the same cage: the same space, the same pulse, various kinds of damage. "Why won't you just tell me everything?" Michael's voice cracked across the room, brittle with the part of him that still wanted order.

His words tried to make a wall of sound; they only trembled. Claire's eyes never left her hands. When she spoke, her voice was small and careful, as if the truth might shatter if released wrong. "Because I don't know everything. And because if I say it wrong, you'll never believe me."

He stopped pacing and looked at her like a man trying to read a map printed in an unknown language. His fists closed, then opened uselessly, as if that motion might wring sense from the air. "You should have told me about Evelyn," he said, each name a stone he didn't know what to do with.

Claire's face folded inward for a moment, less a show of shame than the physical ache of memory, but she didn't let the tears come. "And you should have trusted me enough to ask sooner," she answered. Her words landed soft and certain, a rebuke wrapped in exhaustion.

The exchange hung there, fragile, and dangerous. They were naming old ghosts and fresh betrayals in the same breath, trying to stitch together a logic for two people who had already undone themselves. Outside, rain kept time on the windowsill; soft, indifferent percussion that made the room feel smaller, closer, more merciless.

Across town, in a room of low light and expensive veneers, Lucian Alden watched the scene unfold the way a chess player studies a board. The screen grain hid details but not intention; movement blurred into meaning. He swirled his whiskey in a slow, polished arc and didn't bother to hide how pleased the tableau made him.

"See how they claw at each other?" Lucian said, amusement threading his voice like a deliberate rasp. The words were not loud, but they had the weight of something that had already been decided. Evelyn stood behind him, arms folded tight, a statue of contained contempt. Her posture was austerely defensive, history's armor worn like a second skin. "You're enjoying this," she said.

Lucian didn't bother to deny it. His pleasure was a cool, clinical thing. "It's not enjoyment," he corrected, every syllable measured. "It's strategy. Break their bond, and they have nothing left." Evelyn's lips pressed thin.

For a half-second her gaze slid across the grainy screen to Claire, and something unreadable flickered. A sliver of pity, perhaps, or the reluctant recognition of a woman who knows the private language of being betrayed.

It was almost, horribly, human.

Back in the apartment, Michael's hands found the nearest stable thing, a bookshelf, the spine of a book. He inhaled as if the air itself might clarify things. "Do you realize what this is?" He asked, not accusing so much as cataloging the ache. "If anyone finds out, my practice, Eva, the people who trust me. I could lose everything."

Claire met his eyes then, and for the first time the same panic that had hollowed his chest shone in hers. "I know." Her voice was flat, the word a stone dropped into a dark pool. "I know what you are risking."

He laughed then, a sound short and ugly. "You don't know, Claire. You don't know how small the world gets when everyone starts whispering."

She flinched. "I don't want whispers. I don't want pity. I didn't come to ruin you." Her hands came up then, palms spread like a plea. "I came because I couldn't breathe. I needed someone who would see me." "You should have come before," he said. "Before any of this." The regret cut him more than anger did.

Outside the halo of streetlight, the rain seemed to fall harder as if the city itself were outraged by their trespass.

Inside, the lamp threw a small island of light over the couch where Claire sat like a confession.

Lucian's voice punctured the quiet across miles. In his office, the whiskey glinted as he set the glass down with purposeful finality. "Get me everything Finch has," he told the man on the other end of the line. "Every frame, every time stamp, the car registration, the cleaner's schedule. I want names. I want leverage." His words were a machine being wound. "And keep it quiet. For now."

Evelyn watched him, jaw working. "You really think she'll come back to you?" She asked, less incredulous than tired. The question floated between them; Lucian's smile was an answering slash. "She will." He didn't need to convince her, only himself. "They break, Evelyn, people always come back to the shape that held them first."

Back in the apartment, Michael sank onto a chair, finally letting the exhaustion of pretense bear him down.

He put his face in his hands as if he could smother the sound of his own pulse. The possibility, the certainty, of destruction pressed at him like a physical force. He envisioned his license number in a file, his name beside the cold phrase "boundary violation."

He imagined Eva's bright face somewhere else, the spaces he had inhabited paper thin. Claire rose and paced once, then stopped in the middle of the room and let herself be small. "If he does this," she said, voice gone raw, "I will tell them everything. I will tell them how he watched, how he hired a man, how he… how he waits." Michael looked up as if struck. "You can't…" He broke off.

The words were useless. Evidence didn't care about pronouncements or promises. She stepped closer. "No more pretending we're private," she said. "If you love Eva, if you want to keep your life, then you must let them see what is real. We can't rewrite what happened. But we can decide how it's told."

He wanted to refuse, to wrap himself in some last scrap of control, but his throat closed. He pictured Lucian's slow smile, the way he had looked at the photographs as though savoring their hurt. He heard Evelyn's tempered voice say strategy and realized how many arms the plan had.

Lucian tuned the feed on his screen, watching the two of them in their cramped playpen of regret. He liked the way the tension wound them like cord. "Let them speak," he said. "Let them scramble. When they tear at each other, that's where we move." Evelyn's expression was not wholly unkind.

She had learned, in her own life's curriculum, that pity doesn't change the calculus; power does. Still, her eyes lingered on Claire a beat longer, an involuntary ache for what people lose on the battlefield of adult love.

★ ☉ ★

In the apartment, rain carved slow rivers down the windowpane. Michael's phone lay on the coffee table like a landmine. He could feel its quiet weight. He imagined every possible headline; his face in black type, his daughter's name dragged through the gossip mire.

The walls seemed to crowd closer. Claire knelt then, sudden, decisive, and picked up the scarf from the couch. She held it like evidence or amulet, and for a pulse they were both the same kind of survivor, people who had answered a private hunger and paid with the currency of risk.

Outside, Lucian's driver closed the door of an SUV and let the night swallow him. Inside, two lives tilted on an axis that had been shifted forever. "Do you want to call him?" Michael asked finally, the plea half hope, half threat. He did not mean Lucian. She considered the question as if it were a wound. "No," she said. "We call when we have to. Not before."

They stood in the quiet left, listening to the rain and the small sounds of a life about to be dismantled. Neither spoke for a long time. Each had cataloged the cost in his or her own way. When at last Michael moved, it was to the window. He looked down at the street where puddles reflected sodium light, where nothing seemed permanent enough to trust.

He felt, perhaps, finally, the full extent of what he had done. Across town, a man with a glass in his hand and images on a screen folded his plans into the night like a precise, merciless geometry. He had lit the fuse. He would wait for it to burn.

At night, Michael and Claire still reached for each other. Not out of trust anymore. Not out of comfort. But out of the simple, animal fear of being left alone with what they'd done.

Their bodies found each other like habit. Muscle memory in the dark, need disguised as forgiveness. His breath tangled in her hair; her nails dragged small crescents down his back, as though trying to hold him in place, to stop time from carrying them further into the ruin they'd created.

Their whispers were not tender. They were confessions spoken against skin; half-formed, gasped into the spaces between heartbeats. "I didn't mean for this to happen," she murmured once, her words dissolving before they reached his ear. "I know," he whispered back, though he didn't. There were no promises anymore, no soft declarations. Just the ragged sound of two people trying to drown the guilt before morning.

When it ended, the silence came back heavier, like the air had learned the weight of what they refused to say. Michael lay on his back, eyes open, staring at the ceiling where the light from the street slipped in through the blinds; thin, sharp stripes that looked like bars.

He listened to the soft tick of the radiator, to her breathing beside him, to the hollow echo of his own heart. Claire turned away, facing the wall, one arm curled protectively over her ribs. The curve of her shoulder rose and fell with uneven breaths. She didn't cry. She hadn't for days. He watched her back and wanted to reach out, to smooth his palm down her spine, to say I'm sorry, I'll fix this, we'll be okay.

But every word felt false before it even reached his lips. "You're awake," she said quietly, her voice flat. "I can't sleep." He whispered. "Because of me?" She asked with a twinge of ache in her heart. He hesitated. "Because of everything."

A bitter laugh caught in her throat. "That's not an answer." "It's the only one I have." He sighed.

She turned then, just enough for him to see her profile in the dim light. Her face looked older somehow tired in ways makeup could never hide. "Do you think they know?" She asked, eyes flicking toward the window. He followed her gaze, the same window he'd once thought he saw movement beyond. "Who?"

"Everyone," she said simply. "The world. Him." Lucian. The name didn't have to be spoken for it to fill the room. Michael exhaled slowly. "If he knew, we'd already be bleeding for it. You think he hasn't started?" The words landed like a warning.

She turned back toward the wall before he could answer, the motion small but final. The distance between them grew, not measured in inches, but in the things unsaid. He reached out anyway, his hand hovering for a moment above her shoulder before he let it fall uselessly to the mattress.

"Claire," he said softly. "Don't." She said bitterly. "I just…" He started. "Don't," she repeated. Her voice cracked on the second word. He withdrew his hand. The air between them pulsed with the ache of something that had once felt like salvation and now felt like sentence.

The moonlight through the blinds traced pale lines across the sheets, dividing them neatly; his side, hers, a gulf of shadow between. He turned onto his back again, staring at the ceiling until the shapes blurred.

The silence pressed down harder with every minute, as though the room itself wanted to erase them. "This can't keep happening," he said finally, voice low, almost swallowed by the dark. "I know." She said without hesitation. "Then why does it?" Michael questioned. She didn't answer. Her breathing steadied, whether sleep or pretense he couldn't tell.

He lay awake long after, counting each slow rise and fall of her chest, memorizing the rhythm he knew he would one day lose.

And when the first light of dawn crept through the blinds, he realized what terrified him most wasn't that they might be caught, but that this quiet, unbearable distance between them had already begun to feel like punishment enough.

The distance grew. And still, neither of them moved.

The Collapse

The hearing room smelled of old wood and older judgment, like every mistake ever made in that place still lingered in the grain. It was the kind of room built to remember sin. The walls were paneled in dark oak, polished to a dull sheen that reflected no light, only shadow.

The air tasted faintly of dust, coffee gone bitter, and something else. The dry tang of anxiety that clung to bureaucratic spaces where fates were quietly decided. The ceiling fan above clicked softly with each rotation, the blades stirring nothing but tension.

It was too slow to be comforting, too rhythmic to ignore; a mechanical metronome marking the pace of dread. Each click was a reminder. The moment was still coming, and there would be no pause between accusation and answer.

Light slanted through the half-drawn blinds, striping the long mahogany table with harsh gold lines that made the papers scattered across it look less like documentation and more like evidence.Every folder seemed to hum with implication, with the weight of things that could not be unsaid or undone.

Michael sat at one end, his posture rigid, his hands clasped together so tightly his knuckles had gone white. The chair beneath him creaked with every shift of his weight, each sound echoing through the stillness like a confession he hadn't yet spoken aloud. He could feel eyes on him.

Steady, unblinking, though no one in the room had spoken since he entered. Behind him, the faint scent of rain drifted in through a cracked window, mingling with the room's stale air.

Outside, thunder rumbled somewhere far away, the kind of low, patient sound that promised a storm still gathering. Across from him, Dr. Evelyn Stone presided over the proceedings like an executioner dressed in empathy.

Her hands were folded neatly atop a leather-bound folder, her expression carved from composure. Years of shared history and professional respect meant nothing now; they were relics of a world that had already turned to ash.

The fluorescent light above her crown caught the edge of her glasses, making her eyes momentarily opaque, unreadable. To her left sat three colleagues; doctors, peers, once-friends, their faces as still as portraits, their pens poised like scalpels over legal pads. They would not meet his gaze. Cowardice, or mercy, he couldn't tell. Maybe both.

Somewhere in the hallway beyond, a phone rang and stopped, as if the world outside had remembered itself for a moment before falling back into silence. Michael's pulse filled the space that followed, steady, loud, too human.

He had walked into rooms like this countless times before; panels, reviews, assessments, where he'd been the calm one, the voice of reason, the advocate for second chances. But this was different. This was personal. This was punishment dressed in procedure.

His lawyer sat beside him, gray suit, gray tie, gray eyes; the embodiment of neutrality. He whispered something that sounded like reassurance, but Michael didn't hear it. All he could see was the folder in front of Evelyn. The one stamped *CONFIDENTIAL*, the one that held his ruin in black ink and glossy photos.

He could almost smell the paper; sharp and clean, as though judgment itself had a scent.

Somewhere deep in the wood, a floorboard cracked. No one moved. The sound lingered in the air, long enough for Michael to think absurdly of Claire, of the way her laughter had sounded against his shoulder, fragile, human, alive.

And here, surrounded by protocol and pretense, the memory of that sound felt like the only real thing left in the world. The fan clicked again. A page turned. Evelyn lifted her pen. "Dr. Harris," she said finally, her voice smooth, deliberate like a surgeon preparing the first cut. "Let's begin."

Michael sat at the long table, hands clasped to stop them from trembling. His license, his livelihood, his dignity; all of it hung by threads thinner than the paper files stacked before him. The faint hum of the fluorescent lights above seemed to buzz directly inside his skull.

Across from him, Dr. Evelyn Stone presided like a surgeon about to cut, precise, unsentimental, the embodiment of procedural mercy. Her glasses caught the light, obscuring her eyes, but her posture left no doubt: she was not there to console him. Three colleagues flanked her, faces familiar but cold. People who had once laughed with him at conferences, traded case notes over coffee, spoken his name with respect.

Today, their expressions were carved from stone, the kind reserved for those who'd come to watch a man fall. The chair creaked beneath him as he shifted, the sound far too loud in the hollow quiet. "Dr. Harris," Evelyn began, her tone measured, devoid of warmth. "You understand why you've been called here today." He nodded once. "I do."

"A formal complaint has been filed," she continued, tapping the top page of the folder before her. "Alleging serious boundary violations with a patient, Claire Alden. Do you deny that she was under your care at the time the alleged misconduct took place?"

Michael's mouth was dry. "No." "And do you deny that a personal relationship developed during or immediately following treatment?" She added questioning. He hesitated. Every cell in his body screamed to say yes, to fight for the last intact piece of himself.

But the silence that followed his pause answered for him. Evelyn's jaw tightened. She didn't look angry, only tired. "Michael," she said, and for a flicker of a moment, it was the voice of an old friend, not an investigator. "You've worked in this field for over fifteen years. You know what this means."

"I know," he whispered. His voice came out raw, the sound of someone already half-buried. One of the board members, Dr. Patel, adjusted his glasses. "This isn't just about your career, Dr. Harris. It's about the patients who trusted you. The integrity of the practice. You were a mentor to younger clinicians." Michael's stomach turned.

He wanted to argue, to explain "You don't understand. She wasn't like the others. She needed someone. I needed..." But even in his head, the words sounded like excuses. Evelyn opened a second folder, its edges sharp, deliberate. "We've received corroborating materials, photographs, timestamps, surveillance footage." The world seemed to tilt. Photographs. Timestamps. Surveillance. Lucian.

Of course it was Lucian. Michael's vision tunneled, his pulse roaring in his ears. "These images," Evelyn said carefully, "appear to show you meeting with Ms. Alden outside of scheduled sessions. On multiple occasions. In locations that would suggest... Personal involvement."

She slid the photos across the table, face down. He couldn't bring himself to turn them over. "Do you have anything you wish to say for the record?" She finished.

He stared at the polished wood, his reflection fractured by scratches and stains left by others who'd sat where he sat now, others who had fallen, too.

Finally, he said, barely audible, "It wasn't manipulation. It was... Two broken people trying to survive."The words hung there, fragile, and useless. Dr. Patel sighed, his tone clinical. "That may be true. But survival doesn't exempt responsibility. Compassion isn't an excuse for misconduct."

Evelyn leaned forward, her hands folding over the file. "You're a good man, Michael. But good men still make choices. And some choices don't get to be forgiven."The room went quiet again, the kind of silence that feels like judgment taking form. He wanted to plead, to ask for one more chance, but the weight of his own guilt pressed down too heavily.

The truth was, he couldn't even tell them they were wrong. Through the slats of the blinds, the city glowed;indifferent, endless. Somewhere out there, Claire was breathing the same air. Somewhere else, Eva was probably coloring at the kitchen table, blissfully unaware that her father's name was being stripped from the wall of his profession.

Michael sat perfectly still, the echo of Evelyn's last words hollowing through him. Some choices don't get to be forgiven. He finally turned the photos over. And when he saw them; grainy, intimate, inarguable, his throat closed.

There was no denying it now. The fall had begun. The hearing room was a crucible of light and law. Every panel, every breath, every word carried the weight of precedent. "Dr. Harris," Evelyn began, her voice steady as a metronome, the rhythm of procedure, not compassion. "You are here to respond to formal allegations of boundary violations with a patient under your care, Ms. Claire Alden."

She didn't look at him when she said the name. Instead, she opened the folder before her and slid a smaller one across the polished table. The manila edges rasped softly against the wood. "Photographs and testimony suggest a relationship of an intimate nature," she continued. Her pause was deliberate, surgical. "Outside the therapeutic setting." Michael's throat closed as the folder stopped before him.

He didn't want to open it. He didn't have to. He already knew what was inside. Still, his hand moved, almost automatically. The photographs stared up like open wounds. Claire leaving his apartment in the rain. Her scarf folded neatly beside his office couch.

His own silhouette at the window, two figures behind the glass, one of them unmistakably him. "Do you deny the relationship?" Asked Dr. Howard from the end of the table. His tone was clipped, legal, impersonal; a man who'd practiced detachment so long it had calcified into his bones.

The question landed with the weight of ritual. Michael's throat worked soundlessly before any words could form. His tongue felt thick, metallic, like it had forgotten how to shape language. The air tasted of dust and old coffee, of something too sterile to breathe.

"I acknowledge…" he began, voice roughened from sleeplessness. "Mistakes." The word trembled on the air; too small, too human for what they were discussing. Dr. Howard's chair creaked as he leaned forward, fingers laced, knuckles white. "Mistakes, Michael?" He repeated, the syllables clipped like a scalpel. "Or misconduct?"

The word misconduct hit like a slap. Michael flinched before he could stop himself. Even the fluorescent hum overhead seemed to pause, the silence swelling in its absence like a held breath.

Across the table, Evelyn looked up, the faint gleam of her glasses catching the light, sharp as a blade. Her expression was unreadable, but her tone cut cleanly.

"You're aware of Section Seven, Subpart C of the Ethical Code for licensed therapists in this state?" The phrasing was bureaucratic, but her voice carried something personal beneath it. An echo of betrayal, a cold satisfaction at finally being the one asking the questions.

Michael nodded once. He couldn't trust his voice. Evelyn continued. "It prohibits any romantic or sexual involvement with a current patient. Under Statute 45.3-110, that extends to a minimum of two years following the termination of treatment. Do you dispute that?"

The room felt smaller with each sentence, the walls drawing closer, the table longer, the faces across from him harder. Michael shook his head. "No." Dr. Patel shifted beside Evelyn, his expression weary but resolute. He'd been a friend once; they had shared coffee after seminars, traded patient theories, even laughed once about the futility of bureaucracy.

Now, his voice was low and deliberate, as if mourning the need to speak at all. "Then explain," he said. "Explain how a man who's lectured on countertransference and boundary ethics ends up in bed with someone who trusted him to keep her safe."

Michael's lips parted, but no words came. Every answer he might have given "I loved her. She needed me. I needed her." Sounded obscene inside this room. The truth, stripped of its humanity, was just a confession waiting to be used against him. He stared down at the grain of the table, at the fine lines that branched like veins through the wood.

His reflection shimmered faintly on the polished surface, tired eyes, sunken cheeks, the ghost of a man who'd once believed in his own goodness. "I never meant to harm her," he managed, his voice little more than a breath. "I only wanted to help."

Dr. Patel's pen clicked once. "And that's what makes it worse," he said quietly. Evelyn leaned forward then, her elbows resting on the table, hands folded neatly together, the same posture she used when she was trying to steady a patient on the brink.

Her voice, however, carried no steadiness now. "You understand," she said, "that help, and desire is not the same thing?" Each word was slow, deliberate; an incision meant to expose, not heal. Michael looked up finally, and for a fleeting second, their eyes met.

Behind her precision, he saw a flicker of something raw. Anger, yes, but also sorrow. Maybe it was pity. Maybe it was memory. He couldn't answer. His throat locked, his breath came shallow, and the silence rushed back in, heavy, sentient, almost alive. Not the neutral silence of professionalism. The condemning kind. The kind that filled every corner of the room, pressing inward like water in a sealed tank, suffocating slowly.

His lawyer shifted beside him but said nothing. The movement was small; a careful realignment of papers, a quiet sigh through his nose, but in the stillness, it sounded thunderous.

His name was Samuel Grayson, though everyone called him Sam. He was a man built for endurance, not glory, gray suit, gray tie, gray around the temples. The kind of lawyer who didn't believe in miracles, only margins.

His briefcase, weathered leather with a broken latch, sat open beside his chair, spilling over with legal pads and highlighted case codes. He'd been doing this too long, defending people who had already half-convicted themselves before the gavel ever fell.

Sam's face was calm, but his fingers betrayed him, tapping once against the edge of the table, a rhythm that might have been meant to steady them both. He didn't look at Michael when he spoke, didn't need to. They had already exchanged every possible argument in the days leading up to this moment. Every strategy. Every warning.

All that was left now was survival. He cleared his throat, voice low, even. "Let's stick to the facts, Michael," he murmured under his breath, not for the board, but for the man beside him who looked like he might unravel at the sound of his own name.

"Keep your tone measured. No emotion, no justification. They want remorse, not reason." He reminded him quietly. Michael nodded faintly, though he wasn't sure if he could manage either. Sam leaned back, exhaling through his nose. The weight of a man who'd seen too many lives crumble behind conference tables and fluorescent lights.

He looked tired, not just physically, but in that way people look when they've spent their lives arguing with the inevitable. There were dark crescents beneath his eyes, his tie loosened just enough to suggest resignation rather than rebellion. At his wrist, a wedding ring gleamed faintly when the light caught it; worn, scratched, but still there.

What could he say? Every defense sounded like denial. Every truth like guilt. Sam knew it. He'd seen it before. He'd watched good men twist themselves into knots trying to make their hearts legible to systems that only recognized violations.

And he knew, just by looking at Michael, that no amount of logic would make this right again. Still, he straightened the folder before him, the movement precise, deliberate. It was all performance now, the illusion of control, the ritual of process.

He smoothed his sleeve, adjusted his pen, then placed a hand flat on the table, steady, solid, as if to remind his client that something in this room still stood upright. But the look he gave Michael, brief and wordless, said what professionalism wouldn't allow: "I can't save you from this. All I can do is help you survive the fall."

Michael's palms were slick now, his pulse hammering against the inside of his wrist. He imagined Claire's face, not the woman in those photographs, not the proof in Evelyn's folder, but the one who had cried in his office, trembling and brave.

He wanted to say her name aloud, to tell them she was not a case file but a person, that what happened between them was not calculation but collision. But the board didn't deal in collisions. It dealt in codes. In consequences. Dr. Howard cleared his throat. "Dr. Harris," he said, "this isn't about whether you intended harm. It's about what you did."

Michael looked up then, hollow-eyed, and whispered, mostly to himself. "I know." The words seemed to fall somewhere between confession and prayer. For a long moment, no one spoke. The only sound was the soft buzz of the lights above and the scratching of a pen against paper.

The quiet, bureaucratic sound of a life being rewritten. And when Evelyn finally looked at him again, her expression was unreadable. But her voice, low, level, trembling just slightly, carried the truth neither of them could escape.

"Michael," she said. "You didn't just break the rules. You broke her." When it ended, he signed the temporary suspension notice with a shaking hand. The pen slipped once, leaving a smear of blue ink that looked almost like blood before it hits the air.

The words pending investigation floated at the bottom of the page, sharp and sterile. A sentence all on their own. No one spoke. Not when he rose. Not when he gathered the scattered copies of his life's work; the notes, the credentials, the remnants of belief.

Even the hallway outside the hearing room felt hostile. The hum of the fluorescent lights followed him like an accusation. He passed a mirror near the elevator and almost didn't recognize himself.

The suit, the one he'd bought years ago for conferences and lectures, looked suddenly borrowed, too formal for a man stripped bare. His reflection stared back hollow-eyed, lips pale, collar undone, the outline of someone who'd tried to do right and failed at it spectacularly.

That night, shame clung to him like smoke. It followed him home, seeping into the seams of his jacket, into the hollow of his throat, into the quiet of his apartment where everything still pretended to belong to the man he used to be.

The city murmured beyond the glass, traffic hissing like waves, a siren wailing somewhere far enough away to sound mournful instead of urgent. Inside, the silence was merciless. The letter from the board lay open on the table beside an untouched glass of whiskey.

Its condensation had pooled into a small, perfect circle; the mark of something waiting to be consumed but never dared. He stared at it for hours. At the black typeface that reduced his whole career to administrative phrases. At the signature line where his name sat obediently below his undoing.

At the date in the corner, proof that the world still moved forward even when he didn't. He'd lost his composure. His work. The trust of everyone who mattered. He sat there until the room began to tilt, not from drink, but from exhaustion so deep it blurred the edges of thought. He didn't turn on the lights. Darkness was kinder. It didn't judge.

And still, when the knock came, soft, deliberate, familiar, he didn't move. He didn't have to. He already knew. The door creaked open, slow, tentative. Claire stood framed in the weak spill of the hallway light, her body taut like something hunted. Her hair clung damp to her face, rainwater tracing black lines down her cheeks where mascara had run.

She looked less like a woman and more like a memory that hadn't decided whether to stay or vanish. "Michael," she whispered. Just his name. Nothing else. The sound of it undid him. She crossed the threshold, shutting the door behind her with the quiet finality of someone sealing off the world. She didn't ask about the hearing.

She didn't need to. The collapse was already written across his face. The slack in his posture, the tremor in his hands, the vacancy in his eyes where purpose had once lived. She moved toward him slowly, her footsteps barely a whisper on the floorboards.

When she reached him, she lifted a trembling hand and brushed the side of his jaw, her touch light enough to break him."Let me take it away," she murmured. Her voice cracked.

Her words landed like a knife's slow turn. He didn't answer. He didn't have to. Outside, thunder rolled somewhere deep above the city; low, distant, inevitable. And in the brief flash of lightning that followed, he saw the truth reflected in her eyes. They had not escaped Lucian Alden.

They had only given him another way to win. And when it was over, the rain had stopped. The city beyond the window was still, waiting. Claire's head rested against his chest. Her breath slowed. She pressed her lips to his shoulder and murmured, "They can take your license. Your reputation. They can't take this." Michael stared at the ceiling.

The hum of the refrigerator filled the space between heartbeats. He wanted to tell her the truth, that this was exactly what they could take. That love, when built on the ashes of ethics, becomes evidence.

But he only said, "I know," and kissed her hair.

Knowing the lie would cost him the rest of his life.

On the other side of town, the night had teeth. Lucian Alden moved through it like someone born to the dark; measured, deliberate, the kind of man who didn't need to raise his voice to make the world bend.

Rain slicked the pavement, catching the glare of passing headlights in fractured reflections. The city's pulse thudded beneath his feet. Subway rumble, distant sirens, laughter spilling from the kind of bars where desperation and desire blurred after midnight.

To most, it was chaos. To Lucian, it was rhythm.

He slipped his hands into the pockets of his black coat, collar up against the wind, and cut through the noise like a man moving through his own domain. Even the air seemed to part for him, as though it understood instinctively that this was not someone to inconvenience.

The photographs had done their job. The complaint was filed. The ethics board stirred. The whisper networks, that invisible bloodstream of academia and psychology circles, were already alive with gossip.

Dr. Michael Harris. A name once spoken with respect now carried with it a subtle curl of contempt. A rumor here, a headline draft there. The kind of slow erosion that destroyed not with scandal, but with suggestion. Lucian smiled faintly as he walked, the corner of his mouth lifting in satisfaction.

He could almost taste the rot beginning to spread. But Lucian Alden had never been a man satisfied with reputation. Reputation was fragile. Too easy. Too public. Control that was the marrow of his hunger. Control meant ownership. Control meant silence. Control meant fear.

And fear, in his hands, was an art form. He turned into a narrow alley between two shuttered shops, the kind of place most men avoided. The puddles there reflected nothing but black, and the air smelled faintly of iron and rain-soaked brick. Halfway down the alley, a rusted door waited, unmarked, featureless, except for the faint indent of fingerprints along the edge. He pressed his palm to the steel.

The door recognized him with a click. Inside, the world shifted. The space was large but windowless, lit by the cold blue hum of screens. Dozens of them; some mounted to the walls, others propped on steel tables, flickered with feeds from cameras scattered across the city. Hotel lobbies. Corridors. Apartment exteriors.

Even a subway platform or two. The hum of machinery filled the silence. It was a low, constant purr, like the breath of something alive. Lucian shrugged off his coat and draped it neatly across the back of a leather chair. His movements were meticulous, almost reverent. There was ceremony in the way he lived, precision in every gesture.

He poured a glass of whiskey, no ice, and swirled it once, watching the amber liquid catch the light. The scent was peat and smoke, old as rot, familiar as sin. On one of the screens, Michael Harris's face froze mid-sentence; a grainy capture from the hearing that afternoon.

His eyes looked sunken, his mouth tight, every inch the image of a man who'd begun to realize just how far he could fall. Lucian stepped closer, glass in hand. "Almost there," he murmured. On another monitor, Claire's building glowed under streetlights, a single window still lit. Her silhouette moved faintly, pacing, maybe, or weeping. Lucian's smile widened.

He spoke to the empty air as though it were an audience that adored him."You see, the trick isn't to destroy them all at once. It's to make them participate in their own undoing." He sipped the whiskey. The burn pleased him. He placed the glass down beside a spread of photographs. Glossy prints of Michael and Claire in half-light. Her head against his shoulder, their fingers brushing, an embrace blurred by rain.

His fingertip traced the outline of her jaw in one of the images. "Pretty, but predictable," he whispered. "The good ones always think they're immune."

He moved to a desk in the corner, littered with tools; flash drives, burner phones, a recorder, a stack of sealed envelopes labeled with dates. Each one was a moment waiting to detonate.

He picked one up ~ *Harris, Phase II* ~ and turned it over in his hand. He didn't open it. Just smiled, content with the weight of it. Control, to Lucian, wasn't about chaos.

It was about choreography. Every reaction measured. Every scream rehearsed. He leaned against the desk, the light from the monitors painting his face in alternating stripes of blue and shadow.

His reflection flickered across the glass; half-human, half-phantom. He raised his glass one final time, a toast to no one."To fear," he said softly. "The only truth people never lie about."

Then he drained the whiskey and set the empty glass beside the photographs. On the screen behind him, Michael Harris's office camera blinked once, faint, almost imperceptible.

Lucian Alden, the man who didn't need to shout to make the world bend, smiled into the dark.

He stood in the shadows of Claire's apartment that night, the soft hum of the city muffled by drawn curtains. The place still smelled faintly of her perfume, coffee, rain, and underneath it all, the trace of a life she'd built without him. He hated it. The independence. The defiance.

The illusion of freedom. He'd told her once, half-drunk, and entirely sincere, "You don't walk away from me. You orbit me." He hadn't been wrong. Not yet. The locks hadn't stopped him; they never did. He knew her passcodes, her patterns, her habits. He'd helped her set them up.

A cruel irony. She had always trusted him to keep her safe, never realizing she'd given him the map to her cage. So he waited. He poured himself a drink and sat in her favorite chair, the one by the window, legs crossed, posture relaxed, as though he'd been invited.

Outside, dawn began to gray the skyline, the world quietly resetting. When she returned, hair tousled, clothes creased from the night in Michael's bed, she froze in the doorway. Her keys slipped from her hand and clattered to the floor.

"Lucian." Her voice barely found shape. He smiled without warmth. "Claire." He raised the glass, the ice clicking softly. "You've traded down." Her throat worked as she swallowed. "Get out." He ignored her, letting his gaze drag across her like a verdict. "A therapist with no practice. No title. No future. A man clinging to his daughter like she's the last thing keeping him upright."

He tilted his head. "You always did have a talent for finding the weak ones." "Get. Out." Her voice cracked on the last word, but she didn't back away. Lucian rose slowly, a cat stretching after a kill. The glass in his hand caught the first light of morning, amber flickering across his knuckles. He set it down on the counter, deliberately, so close to the edge it wobbled.

He closed the distance between them. His voice softened, and that softness was worse than a shout. "Do you really think he'll keep you when it costs him everything?" She met his eyes, her breath shallow. "I don't care what it costs."

Lucian leaned in, close enough for her to smell the whiskey, to feel the faint tremor of control barely leashed beneath his calm. "Oh, but you should," he whispered. "Because men like him, they break clean. Men like me…"

He let the words hang, his smile tightening. "…We leave pieces behind." Her hands clenched into fists, nails digging into her palms until blood rose beneath the skin.

"Get out, or I'll scream." He chuckled, low. "And tell them what? That your ex-husband came to check on you? That you were alone after ruining another man's life?" He brushed a strand of hair from her face, almost tender.

"You'll never be free of me, Claire. Because even broken things are mine." He leaned close enough that his whisper grazed her ear. "Especially broken things." For a moment, she didn't move. Then something in her shifted; a stillness, sharp and certain, like the moment before a glass shatters. Her voice came low, steady. "Then maybe," she said, "I'll learn how to break you first."

Lucian stilled, studying her. The defiance sparked something dark in him, amusement, admiration, rage, all braided together. He smiled, slow, cold, promising. "We'll see." He took his coat from the back of her chair, the fabric brushing her arm as he passed.

At the door, he paused just long enough to say, "Tell your therapist I said thank you. For making this easier." Then he was gone. The door clicked shut. Claire's knees gave way, her body folding against the wall. Her pulse thundered in her ears, the echo of his cologne still thick in the air.

For a long moment, she just breathed shallow, trembling breaths that felt borrowed. Then she rose, crossed to the window, and stared down at the street.

The black SUV idled at the curb, headlights cutting through the dawn haze. Then it rolled forward, vanishing into the city like a shadow retreating from light.

★ ✪ ★

When she came back to Michael later that day, her knock was softer than before, almost a question instead of a sound. He opened the door and saw it instantly. Something fractured in her eyes, something she was trying to bury under a careful calm. She didn't tell him everything. She didn't have to. Her hands shook when he reached for them. Her breath came shallow, as though the air itself had turned treacherous.

And when he pulled her close, she pressed her face into his chest like she could hide inside his heartbeat. "You're safe," he whispered. "Don't say that" she breathed against him. "You don't know what safe means anymore." He didn't ask what she meant. Some part of him already knew. Lucian had found her. Or maybe she had found him.

Either way, something had shifted in the dark, the air heavier, the world suddenly smaller. That night, their love wasn't frantic. It was slower, deeper, an ache stretched thin over longing and fear. The silence between them pulsed like a wound. Her fingers traced the outline of his jaw, the scar on his chin from childhood, the fragile veins at his throat.

"If we disappear," she said quietly, "would anyone notice?" "Eva would," he answered, his voice raw. "That's why I can't." She nodded, tears sliding down without sound. When he kissed her, it was gentler than before; a plea, a prayer, and a promise he knew he couldn't keep.

He tasted salt and fear, the ghost of whiskey on her tongue, and something else, something electric, doomed, alive. Their bodies moved in slow rhythm, not with hunger this time, but with grief, the kind of grief that tries to make sense through touch.

Every breath felt like confession. Every kiss, apology.

Every whisper, a prayer for mercy neither believed in. "Tell me you won't leave," she murmured into the dark. "I can't," he whispered back. "But I'll try."

The words hung between them, heavy and insufficient, yet she kissed him anyway, as if to fill the space where truth had failed. When it was over, they stayed tangled in the half-light, her head on his shoulder, his hand lost in her hair.

Outside, thunder rolled somewhere far away, low, and restless. The city never truly slept, but it felt like it was holding its breath. Michael's gaze drifted toward the ceiling, to the shadows that trembled in the faint glow of the streetlamp.
He could feel the unraveling; the job, the board, the walls of the life he'd built, all collapsing inward, one choice at a time. And yet, as he listened to her heartbeat against his ribs, slow and uncertain, he knew with terrifying clarity.

Losing her would be his worst ruin.

Because some disasters don't destroy, they define.

Relocation

The ethics board reconvened on a Wednesday; the kind of cold, colorless day that made everything feel fated. The sky outside was a bruised gray, too pale to be called overcast, too lifeless to be called winter. The city below trudged on in shades of concrete and chrome, the kind of weather that refused to commit to rain but still left everything damp.

Inside, the same heavy room waited. The same table; long, lacquered, polished to an almost blinding sheen, stood like an altar to bureaucracy. The same folders lay in place, their corners sharp, their contents damning, spread open like autopsy reports waiting to be read aloud. The faint smell of varnish and old carpet lingered, a scent that mixed uneasily with the bitterness of burnt coffee cooling in paper cups.

But this time, the air carried something different. The quiet wasn't tense, it was resigned. The storm had already passed. What remained was aftermath. It was the kind of silence that follows an accident, when everyone has already seen the damage and can do nothing but count the pieces.

The fluorescent lights hummed softly, indifferent witnesses to the collapse of a man's life. The blinds were drawn, but daylight pressed thinly through, turning everything a sickly shade of gold. Michael sat at the end of the table again, but this time there was no defiance in his posture. His tie was knotted perfectly, too perfectly, the way people dress for punishment. His hands were clasped on the tabletop, steady only because they had no strength left to tremble.

Across from him, Dr. Howard shuffled his papers without looking up.

Dr. Patel rubbed the bridge of his nose, as if weary of the ritual. Evelyn sat composed, pen aligned precisely with her notepad, her face as unreadable as porcelain. Only the faint tapping of her heel under the table betrayed her restlessness, or her anticipation.

Sam Grayson, his lawyer, sat beside him once more, shoulders drawn tight. His briefcase rested open but untouched, its contents irrelevant now. His hand hovered near his client's elbow, ready to steady, to intervene, but knowing there was nothing left to salvage.

No one spoke at first. The clock on the wall ticked with quiet cruelty. Finally, Dr. Howard cleared his throat, the sound brittle in the still air. "This board reconvenes today to deliver its decision regarding the conduct of Dr. Michael Harris."

His voice was measured, rehearsed, like a man reading the same verdict for the hundredth time. The word conduct hung in the air, too soft for accusation, too hard for mercy. Michael's eyes stayed on the table. He could see his own reflection in the lacquer, distorted, ghostlike.

"Following review of the submitted evidence," Howard continued, "and in consideration of Dr. Harris's prior record, the board has reached a unanimous conclusion." The pause that followed was not for suspense, but for ceremony. Everyone already knew. Dr. Patel looked away. Evelyn didn't.

Her gaze lingered on Michael's bowed head, a study in quiet ruin. "Effective immediately," Howard said, "Dr. Harris's license is revoked pending appeal. He is hereby prohibited from clinical practice or client contact in any therapeutic capacity." The words fell with a finality that no gavel could improve upon. Michael blinked once, not surprise, not even grief.

Just the physical reflex of a man confirming reality. Beside him, Sam exhaled through his nose, slow and deliberate. He closed the folder in front of him, the soft click of its clasp echoing through the room. It sounded like the end of something sacred. No one reached for the coffee now. No one spoke condolences.

The board members rose, gathering their papers, their expressions carefully neutral, professional empathy, polished and hollow. Evelyn remained seated the longest. When she finally stood, she smoothed the sleeves of her blazer, leaned forward, and said softly, "I told you, Michael. We can't save those who don't want saving." Then she turned and walked out, her heels marking the floor like punctuation.

Michael stayed seated long after the room emptied. The clock ticked. The blinds rattled faintly in the draft. Somewhere far below, a siren wailed, rising, then fading, swallowed by the city's endless hum. He sat there until the sound of the world came back to him, and with it the single truth that would not leave his mind. He had not been destroyed by madness, lust, or betrayal.

He had been destroyed by trust, and the illusion that good men were immune to ruin. Michael sat straighter than before, though his face was drawn, his eyes hollow from sleepless nights. The sharp suit he'd chosen for the first hearing had been replaced by something simpler. The tie was gone. His hands were clasped, steady only because he willed them to be.

Beside him, his lawyer, a middle-aged man with the weary posture of someone who had seen too many people ruin themselves, adjusted his papers without looking at him.

His gray suit matched the mood of the room, the color of surrender dressed as civility. Dr. Evelyn Stone cleared her throat, her voice even, deliberate.

"Dr. Harris," she began, "the evidence against you is substantial." Her tone was not cruel, but clinical, mercy measured out in syllables.

"The board has reviewed the photographs, the testimony, and your previous admission. Based on this, we could move to revoke your license permanently under Statute 45.3-110, subsection A, breach of therapeutic boundaries resulting in dual relationship misconduct. Do you understand the gravity of this proceeding?" "I do," Michael said quietly.

His voice didn't shake. That almost frightened him more. Evelyn exchanged a brief glance with Dr. Patel. "You have the right to contest the findings, to request a review or appeal under subsection D," she continued, "though, given the evidence, I advise you to consider resolution through voluntary surrender. It will look better on record, both for reinstatement petitions and future employment in non-clinical fields."

Her words were careful, restrained, an execution disguised as advice. Michael nodded once, lips pressed thin. "I'm not contesting," he said. "I made choices. I'll live with them." The lawyer shifted, whispering under his breath, "We can still…" "No," Michael interrupted softly. "We can't." The words hung there, final as a closing door.

Dr. Howard leaned back in his chair, the faint creak punctuating the stillness. "Then for the record," he said, "you are accepting full responsibility for the violation?"

"Yes." He answered quietly. "And you understand that, by doing so, your license will be suspended indefinitely, with recommendation for revocation to the state licensing board?" Michael hesitated, then nodded. "I do." Dr. Patel sighed through his nose, a small, human sound.

"Michael," he said, and for a moment, he wasn't a board member but a man who once admired another. "You were one of the good ones. You taught my interns that empathy could coexist with discipline. What happened?" Michael looked down at his hands. "Empathy became hunger," he said. "And I mistook it for love."

Evelyn's gaze flickered, but she stayed composed. "There's no shame in being human," she said quietly. "But there is consequence." "I know." He acknowledged. Silence settled again, heavier this time. Someone turned a page. Someone else coughed.

Outside, faint thunder rolled, the kind that stays too far away to be a warning. Finally, Evelyn spoke again, the words like a gavel falling. "By vote of this board, effective immediately, your license to practice psychotherapy within the state is revoked pending appeal. You are prohibited from representing yourself as a licensed therapist in any capacity."

The lawyer reached for his papers. Michael didn't. He only whispered, "Thank you," to no one in particular. Dr. Patel frowned. "For what?" "For not making it cruel." He answered. He stood, straightened his jacket out of habit, and left his ID badge on the table, the photo of a younger man looking up at him like a stranger.

When he reached the door, Evelyn said quietly, "Michael." He paused, half-turned. "Take care of yourself," she said. He nodded, but the look in his eyes said what they both knew, that kind of care doesn't exist anymore.

Outside, the rain had started again. The courthouse steps were slick, the city unbothered by the ruin of one man. Michael stopped at the bottom, the letter of revocation folded in his pocket, and for the first time in years, he had nowhere to go.

He looked up at the gray sky and thought, so this is what it feels like when the world stops listening. The fluorescent lights buzzed faintly overhead, cold, and merciless. Every flicker seemed to count down the seconds of what remained of his life's work. Michael's voice was steady, but his hands betrayed him, trembling beneath the table where no one could see.

"I do," he said. His lawyer leaned forward, clearing his throat, his tone somewhere between diplomacy and damage control. "My client acknowledges serious lapses in judgment," he began carefully, "but no pattern of exploitation exists. This was not predatory behavior. It was a boundary collapse with one individual, under extraordinary emotional strain and mutual vulnerability."

The phrasing was rehearsed, bloodless. It sounded like something written to fit neatly in a legal transcript. Dr. Stone's brow lifted just slightly, the faintest expression of disbelief."Mutual vulnerability," she repeated, her tone cutting through the pretense, "is not an excuse." Michael met her eyes.

His throat tightened, but his voice didn't waver. "No," he said. "But it's the truth. And the truth should matter here."The words echoed in the stillness. For a moment, no one spoke. Even the usual rustle of papers, the clicking pens, the quiet bureaucratic movements of a hearing room, all fell away. Then came the shuffling.

Pages turned. Pens tapped. No one looked directly at him. Each of them was already deciding how much of his ruin they were willing to own.

Finally, Dr. Howard cleared his throat. His voice, usually warm, sounded brittle now, like glass under strain. "We've deliberated," he said.

"The board has discussed this at length. A full revocation is still on the table. However…" He glanced down at his notes, unwilling to meet Michael's eyes. "There is… a compromise. Dr. Harris may retain his license provisionally on the condition he does not resume practice in Manhattan or its surrounding boroughs. A relocation would be mandatory. A clean start. Under new supervision. A probationary period of three years, with quarterly evaluations and oversight from an appointed ethics liaison."

The words hung in the air like a verdict disguised as mercy. Michael's chest tightened. The lawyer's pen scratched quietly beside him, but Michael wasn't listening anymore. Three years of oversight. Three years of scrutiny. Three years of being a name whispered in hallways, a case study on what happens when good men forget the rules.

He nodded once, slow, and mechanical. "Understood." Dr. Patel leaned forward slightly, his tone softer than the rest. "You can rebuild, Michael," he said. "You've done clever work for years. This doesn't have to define the rest of your life." Michael managed a faint, humorless smile. "It already has." Dr. Stone watched him for a long moment, her expression unreadable.

When she finally spoke, her voice had lost its edge. "The board will send you formal documentation within the week. You're suspended effective immediately. You may reapply for provisional clearance once relocation terms are verified. Until then, no clients. No sessions. No contact with Ms. Alden, directly or otherwise. Is that understood?"

He hesitated, just long enough for her to see it. Then: "Yes." That hesitation sealed what she already suspected.

Evelyn closed the file. The sound of the clasp snapping shut was final. "Then this hearing is adjourned."

Chairs scraped the floor. People rose, collecting their papers, their pens, their moral certainty. Michael stayed seated until the room was nearly empty.

The lawyer packed his briefcase in silence. "You got off lighter than most," he muttered. Michael stared at the empty chair across from him, where Evelyn had sat moments ago. "Then why does it feel like I'm already gone?" The lawyer had no answer.

Outside, rain streaked the courthouse windows. The city blurred behind the glass, restless and uncaring. Michael pressed a hand to his chest, not because it hurt, but because he wanted to make sure there was still something left beating beneath the ruin. His career wasn't over, not officially.

But everything that had once made it matter was gone. He was, for all intents and purposes, a man without a compass, still licensed to heal, but too broken to trust his own hands.

Not gone. Not erased. Just displaced. "Where?" Michael asked, his voice quieter than the rain tapping the courthouse window. "Anywhere outside the five boroughs,"

Evelyn Stone replied, her tone clipped but not cruel. "Boston has openings. Their trauma clinics are understaffed. You could reapply there under supervision. It's a chance to start again."

Boston.

A city not too far to sever, not too near to haunt. A lifeline disguised as exile. Michael nodded once. "I'll take it." The gavel came down, not on his ruin, but on his relocation.

It sounded like mercy, but it felt like burial.

★ ✪ ★

That night, he told Claire. They sat on his couch, the same couch where confession had turned to sin, where love had learned how to burn. Her legs were tucked beneath her, hands wrapped around a mug of tea gone cold, steam long vanished.

"Boston," she repeated, voice low, almost reverent, almost broken. "You'd really go?" "I don't have a choice," he said. "It's that or lose everything." Her eyes found his and held them. There was fear there, yes, but underneath it, something fierce and shining. Devotion, or defiance.

Maybe both. "Then I'm going with you." He froze. "Claire…" "No," she cut him off, firm for the first time in weeks. "Don't tell me it's too much. Don't tell me I'll ruin your life more than I already have." Her breath hitched. "My life here is ashes. Lucian sees to that every day. If you leave without me, I'll be nothing but his ghost again. I can't do that. I won't."

Michael's throat tightened. "Boston isn't a clean slate. It's just another city. We'll still be…" "Together," she finished, eyes glinting. "That's all that matters." She reached for his hand. Her fingers trembled, but her grip was sure. For a long time, they just sat there, two fugitives bound by love and ruin, their shadows merging on the wall.

When they finally made love that night, it was slow, aching, reverent. A prayer whispered into skin. Every touch felt deliberate, as if they were trying to memorize each other before the world tour them apart again.

Michael kissed the scars no one else could see, the invisible fractures left by Lucian's cruelty, and whispered promises he wasn't sure he believed in. "I'll keep you safe," he said. "Just get me out," she breathed.

Her taste lingered on his lips; wild and bright, like the first breath of sunlight after too long in the dark. As they moved together, her breath broke into soft sounds that blurred the line between pleasure and sorrow.

Her touch lingered on his stones, kneading them with a delicious tenderness that made him ache. Each slow press and gentle roll sent a pulse of heat racing up his spine, his body tightening under her rhythm. The deeper she worked him, the more his breath broke into low groans, every nerve alight with aching pleasure he could no longer contain.

Afterward, in the quiet, Claire pressed her lips against his chest and whispered, "For the first time in years, I believe in tomorrow." Michael stroked her hair, though guilt gnawed deep at his ribs. "Tomorrow will be hard," he murmured. "I don't need easy," she said. "I just need away." But Lucian learned fast. Information came to him the way it always did; quietly, efficiently, dripping with betrayal disguised as loyalty.

A call from a friend on the ethics board. A file slipped across a mahogany bar by someone who owed him favors. The words relocation and Boston leapt off the page like a threat. He stood by the vast glass wall of his penthouse, Manhattan glittering at his feet, the skyline humming with power that belonged to men like him.

He gripped his whiskey glass so hard he thought it might splinter. "They think they can just leave," he said to the empty room.

"Walk away. Start again." His reflection in the glass smirked back at him, cold, patient, amused.

"No," he whispered. "If she goes, she goes in pieces."

★ ☼ ★

Michael began packing slowly. Books into boxes. Files into folders. The photograph of Eva went into his briefcase first, her bright smile now a haunting reminder of everything he was about to lose. He hadn't told her yet. How do you tell a ten-year-old that her father's mistakes cost her city, her friends, her school? How do you explain that love could destroy more than it saves? Claire arrived later that night to help.

Her laughter, fragile but genuine, broke the quiet. "You own too many books," she teased softly. "I'm a therapist," he said. "We hoard other people's stories." For a few moments, it almost felt domestic. Almost normal. But beneath the laughter, the tension pulsed, a quiet dread neither of them could name. Michael broke it first.

"What if it doesn't work in Boston?" He asked suddenly, voice sharp, desperate. "What if I lose you too?" Claire froze, one of his shirts clutched to her chest like a shield. "Is that what you think?" She asked quietly. "That I'll run?" He shook his head, exhaling. "I don't know what I think anymore. Every choice I've made has cost me something I couldn't afford to lose."

She crossed the room, her steps slow, deliberate. When she reached him, her palms cupped his face, her thumbs tracing the edges of his jaw. "Then let this be the one you don't lose." She kissed him, fire meeting water, defiance meeting despair. The kiss deepened, desperate, their bodies colliding against half-packed boxes, clothes spilling like confessions onto the floor.

It wasn't just love.

It was surrender, and defiance, and grief made flesh. The sound of a packing tape roll clattered to the ground like a gunshot. When it was over, they lay among the wreckage, books toppled, shirts tangled, their breathing rough and uneven.

Claire's hair clung to her face; her voice came in a whisper. "You're mine now," she said. "Not his. Not theirs. Mine." Michael closed his eyes, his hand still tangled in hers. He wanted to believe her. He wanted to believe in them.

But deep down, he knew the truth: *Lucian would never let that be true.*

A Shadow in the Walls

In every city, there are rooms where secrets rot. Lucian Alden had built one for himself. It wasn't a prison, though the air held the same metallic tang. A faint, damp scent of iron and mildew that clung to the back of the throat and reminded anyone foolish enough to breathe deeply that nothing pure survived here for long.

It wasn't a study either, though the walls were lined with books. Each spine gleamed under dim amber light; immaculate, goldstamped, dustless, the kind of collection that might have impressed a visitor had any been permitted to enter.

But inside, there were no words. He'd gutted them. A library of obsessions masquerading as literature. Each hollowed volume hid a photograph, a fragment, a trophy of possession.

Claire in the glow of a streetlamp, her coat caught mid-motion by a wind she hadn't noticed. Claire's reflection in Michael's window, the glass trembling faintly with rain as she turned toward a silhouette that wasn't meant to be hers. Claire's lips parted mid-breath as she left a doorway six minutes too late, the same delay, the same omen.

Even a single strand of her hair, taped to the inside cover of one of his favorite books, Madame Bovary, naturally, preserved like a saint's relic. The lighting in the room was low, almost reverent.

A single bulb swayed faintly from its cord, its glow filtered through the haze of cigarette smoke that had long since stained the ceiling.

Shadows pooled in corners like waiting sentinels. The walls were concrete painted to look like wood; a deception, like everything Lucian touched.

In the center stood a desk of black marble, veins of gray coiling through it like old scars. On it, a tumbler of whiskey sat beside an open file. Inside, news clippings chronicled the slow, procedural destruction of Michael Harris's life.

Each headline was underlined in precise red ink:
Therapist Under Investigation, Patient Boundary Breach, Hearing Set for Review.
He had annotated the margins, notes written in a hand so clean it might have belonged to a surgeon.

"Predictable," he murmured, eyes tracing the columns of print. "He still thinks guilt will save him." He closed the folder and leaned back in his chair. The leather creaked, a weary sigh. Music played faintly from a turntable near the wall, something classical, strings slow and mournful, the kind of composition that could make cruelty sound elegant.

A monitor flickered on the far wall, security feeds from across the city. Claire's building. Michael's street. The coffee shop where she sometimes sat pretending to read. Lucian's gaze lingered on one frame. Claire by her window, eyes distant, her fingers absently tracing the rim of a glass.

He smiled, not with joy, but with possession. "She still dreams of being unseen," he whispered. "How quaint." He rose and approached the shelves, fingertips gliding along the spines as one might along the keys of a piano.

"Every saint needs a shrine," he murmured, stopping at a volume of Wuthering Heights. Inside, another photograph, Claire in profile, the city reflected in her eyes. "Every ghost," he continued softly, "needs a haunting."

On the far wall hung a map of Manhattan, black paper marked with thin silver pins. Red string connected locations, her apartment, Michael's office, the café, the library, the clinic where the hearing had taken place. It wasn't a web. It was a wound, meticulously diagrammed.

He stood before it like a general before a battlefield. The clock above the door ticked, its sound soft but precise, like a heartbeat with nowhere left to go. Lucian glanced at it, amused. "*4:06*," he noted aloud. "Always the same minute. Always the delay."

He poured another glass of whiskey, the liquid catching the lamplight like molten amber. "Time," he whispered, raising the glass in a mock toast, "is the cruelest accomplice." When he drank, the silence thickened again, not empty but listening.

He set the glass down carefully, his reflection shivering in the marble surface, two versions of himself staring back: one human, one shadow. And behind him, in the flicker of the monitor's light, Claire's image moved again her lips forming a word no sound carried. Lucian didn't need to hear it. He already knew. Love. Always love.

The most efficient weapon ever made. He smiled again, slow, deliberate, cruel. "Let's see how much she still believes in it." Then he reached for the switch beside the desk. Every monitor flared to life at once, Michael, Claire, their rooms, their worlds.

The night filled with light and ghosts. And Lucian Alden, standing in his cathedral of rot, began to plan the next act of his masterpiece. Lucian sat among them like a priest surrounded by holy remains, the flicker of a candle painting shadows across his sharp cheekbones.

His whiskey sat untouched, condensation pooling around the base, a ring on the wood that looked like a wound. He spoke aloud, though no one listened. That had never stopped him. "They think distance is salvation," he murmured, running a finger along the edge of one photo.

"Boston, Boston, Boston. As though miles were walls, and oceans were absolution."He smiled, slow and deliberate, a serpent uncoiling beneath silk. "Fools," he whispered. "Walls are meant to be broken. Oceans are meant to drown." The laughter that followed was low, measured, the kind that doesn't echo because it doesn't need to.

On a nearby desk, his phone buzzed once. A single text. *'They're moving tomorrow.'* Lucian didn't pick it up immediately. He simply leaned back, let the words hang in the air, savoring them.

Then, at last, he lifted the glass, the ice clinking against the rim, and said softly, "Then tomorrow, we begin again."He drained the whiskey in one motion, the burn chasing the chill down his spine.

Somewhere across the city, Michael slept for the first time in days, the hum of packed boxes around him, Claire's breathing steady against his shoulder. He dreamed of quiet streets and clean slates, of Boston mornings untouched by guilt. He dreamed of peace.

But in another room, where secrets festered and glass eyes watched from hollow books, Lucian Alden dreamed of punishment.

And in his dreams, peace was just another word for surrender.

★ ✪ ★

He and Claire walked the dim streets of Manhattan for the last time, hand in hand, bound not by hope, but by secrecy and defiance. The city lay half-asleep, its pulse slower now, glistening in the aftermath of rain. Pavement slick. Windows weeping.

Steam rose from the grates like restless ghosts. Every gutter whispered the same warning: nothing stays buried here for long. Streetlights flickered in uneven intervals, their halos bleeding into the wet air. The wind moved in low sighs between the buildings, stirring paper cups and wilted leaves.

Somewhere far off, a cab hissed through a puddle; the sound echoed like memory. Claire's coat hung loose around her frame, the belt knotted carelessly, one button missing. The hem brushed the tops of her boots, already soaked dark.

Her face was pale beneath the sodium glow, almost spectral, as if the city itself were trying to erase her. Raindrops clung to her lashes, catching the faint orange light, turning tears into small, glittering lies. She leaned close, her breath shivering in the cold. "When I'm with you," she murmured, "I almost believe I can start again."

Michael's hand tightened around hers, his thumb tracing absent circles against her skin, a habit formed from anxiety and affection alike. "Almost?" He asked quietly.

Claire gave a short, broken laugh that died in her throat. "When I'm alone, I hear him," she said. Her voice cracked on him. "Always him. In the creak of the floorboards, in the hum of the refrigerator, in the sound of my own footsteps. I can't scrub him out." Michael stopped walking.

The street around them seemed to hold its breath, a flickering neon sign buzzing faintly above a boarded storefront, water dripping rhythmically from a bent awning. "He can't touch you anymore," he said, though the words trembled at the edges. Her eyes lifted to his. "You don't know him."

And in that moment, Michael saw it, not just fear but understanding. The knowledge of a cruelty that never slept. The kind that didn't end with distance or time. The kind that waited. They started walking again.

Their reflections moved beside them in the dark shopfronts. Two broken figures stitched together by desperation. The only color came from the red of a passing taillight, slashing briefly across Claire's face before disappearing into shadow.

Overhead, the clouds pressed low, bruised, and heavy. The city smelled of ozone and something else, metallic, faintly sweet, like old blood washed away by rain. At the corner, Michael paused, looking up toward a half-lit billboard advertising perfume. The model's eyes stared down at him through the mist; perfect, indifferent, untouchable.

He wondered, absurdly, if this was what Lucian saw when he looked at the world: people as images, meant only to be framed, kept, possessed. Claire shivered beside him. "He'll never stop," she said.

Michael turned to her, brushing a damp strand of hair from her cheek. "Then we'll make him tired trying." Her eyes softened, though exhaustion dulled the spark behind them. "You sound like a man who still believes in winning."

"I sound like a man who refuses to lose you."

He responded back. She smiled faintly, and for a heartbeat, the world shrank to that, the space between them.

The mingled fog of their breath, the ache of two people clinging to the illusion that love could outlast ruin. When she kissed him, it wasn't tender. It was raw, urgent, a promise and a plea wrapped into one trembling act of rebellion.

The streetlight flickered overhead, throwing them in and out of shadow as if the world itself couldn't decide whether to bless or condemn them. They didn't see the car parked half a block away. Didn't notice the man inside, motionless, watching. A cigarette glowed once in the darkness, a small, burning eye.

Lucian Alden watched them from behind the glass, his reflection superimposed over theirs. The rain traced lines down the windshield, distorting their shapes, merging them into one. He exhaled smoke slowly, almost reverently. "Run if you must," he whispered. "It makes the capture sweeter."

Then he flicked the cigarette into the gutter, the ember hissing out in the chilly rain, and the car pulled quietly into the street, following.

"When I'm with you, I believe I can start again," she said. "But when I'm alone, I hear him. Always him." Michael squeezed her hand harder, his own trembling. "He can't touch you anymore." Her laugh cracked, sharp and small. "You don't know him," she said. "Lucian doesn't need to touch. He devours."

And in her eyes, Michael saw it, the thing he'd never utterly understood until now: not just fear, but knowledge. Knowledge of cruelty that never sleeps. Lucian's plan began, as all his cruelties did, in silence. Not with blood. Not with confrontation. But with whispers. He didn't hire killers. Not yet.

He hired debtors, men who would slit a throat for a debt erased.

Men who could slip through locks as easily as air. They came at night, ghosts in black gloves, eyes dull with obedience. They planted his devices where love would not think to look, inside lamps, beneath vents, within the hollow of a smoke alarm.

Tiny eyes. Tiny ears. Each one pulsing red when the world grew dark. Now, every breath Michael and Claire shared was no longer theirs. Every confession. Every sigh. Every desperate promise. That night, in the dim glow of his apartment, Claire whispered his name as they came together again, her voice raw, a mix of grief and devotion.

Michael kissed her with reverence, tracing her scars like scripture, as if he could write her a new story on her skin. They moved with the slow desperation of two people trying to prove that love could still exist after shame. But above them, unseen, a red light blinked.
Recording. Archiving. Waiting.

In his sanctum of steel and shadow, Lucian Alden watched. His face glowed ghostly in the pale wash of monitors. Dozens of feeds, each flickering with stolen intimacy. Claire's gasps, Michael's murmured reassurances, the trembling pulse of bodies seeking forgiveness in each other's arms.

Lucian did not watch with lust. Lust was a human thing, and he had long since grown beyond that. His desire had curdled into something colder, more enduring possession. He leaned forward, elbows on his knees, eyes glinting.

"They think love redeems," he whispered to no one. "But love only reveals what was always rotten." He rewound a frame, slow motion, Claire's face tilted back in ecstasy, her mouth forming Michael's name. Lucian smiled, faint and cruel. "They offer themselves to each other," he murmured. "But what they give is mine."

Michael thought the ethics hearing had been his humiliation. He had no idea that the true degradation was yet to come, his body, his tenderness, his transgression turned to spectacle.

Lucian had already begun the unveiling. An anonymous email. A carefully edited file of clips; intimate enough to destroy, ambiguous enough to deny. Whispers sent to journalists who feasted on scandal.

Michael Harris, the fallen therapist. Claire Alden, the patient who tempted him into ruin. Their love rebranded as evidence. Their survival recast as sin. Lucian poured his whiskey finally, the liquid catching candlelight like blood.

He raised it toward the faces frozen mid-motion on his screen. "To Boston," he said softly. "May your journey begin in fire." He drank, slow and deliberate, savoring the burn.

That night, miles away, Michael woke to the sound of sobbing. Claire sat at the edge of the bed, naked, trembling, her hands knotted in her hair. "I can't," she whispered, her voice breaking. "I can't outrun him."

Michael rose, his heart splintering. He knelt before her, palms cradling her tear-streaked face. "Yes, you can," he whispered. "With me. We'll go. We'll start over. Boston isn't salvation, but it's distance. And distance is enough."

She shook her head, voice small as a child's. "He'll follow. He always follows." Michael pressed his lips to her tears, tasting salt and despair. "Then let him. Let him come. I won't lose you."

Her body fell into his, shaking. Their mouths found each other, not for pleasure but for proof, for warmth, for life. They clung together again, their movements frantic, wordless, a final prayer whispered against the dark.

And above them, the red light blinked. Recording. Waiting. Lucian smiled at the footage. His reflection rippled faintly across the monitor, almost spectral. He no longer looked like a man. He looked like something born from obsession and hunger, an echo of vengeance given flesh.

"No," he whispered to the screen. "Not death. Not yet." The most diabolical plan was not to kill them. It was to expose them. To strip them of privacy, dignity, and meaning, to make their love rot in daylight.

For Michael Harris and Claire Alden, Boston would not be a new beginning. It would be the stage of their public execution.

And Lucian Alden, the ghost in their machines, the architect of their downfall, would be the conductor.

Whispers in the Walls

It began with whispers. Not the kind that lived in mouths or traveled across phone lines, but the kind that slipped in like drafts through unseen cracks. Felt before they were heard, chilling the skin of the soul. They carried no words, only weight. The kind of sound that lived in the edges of hearing. Which made you turn your head even when you knew no one was there.

At first, they were easy to dismiss. The hum of the refrigerator. The creak of an old radiator. The wind threading itself through the window frame. Background noise, nothing more. Until it wasn't.

They began to take shape; faint, indistinct murmurs, as if someone were speaking in the next room, their voice wrapped in gauze. Sometimes a single word would slip through the static: Claire. Other times, just the echo of breath, close enough that Michael could feel it stir the hairs at the nape of his neck.

He tried to explain it away as stress, exhaustion, guilt manifesting in sound. But late at night, when he stood at the sink with the tap running and the city lights bleeding through the blinds, the whispers grew bolder. Louder.

They seemed to pulse in rhythm with his heartbeat, as though something unseen had learned his internal clock and decided to keep time with it.

They moved through the apartment like smoke, threading under doors, curling into corners. He'd catch them most often near the walls, where the paint had begun to crack.

The thin fractures that stretched like veins, the kind that made him wonder what lay beneath the plaster, whispering to get out. And Claire heard them too. She never said it outright, but Michael saw it in her, the way she froze when the air changed, the way her eyes darted to the ceiling as if expecting it to speak.

Once, in the middle of the night, he woke to find her sitting upright in bed, her hand gripping his arm, her skin cold. "What is it?" He whispered. Her voice was small, almost childlike. "I thought I heard him."

Lucian's name was never spoken aloud in that apartment, not since the night she'd fled to it. But she didn't need to say it, the silence filled in what her mouth refused. Michael tried to soothe her. "It's nothing. Just the pipes, the street." But he knew better. The city had a thousand noises, and this wasn't one of them.

This was something else, the sound of surveillance, the ghost of attention. It moved like intelligence, like malice wearing patience as a mask. The whispers became part of their lives threaded through routine, steady and unrelenting.

They followed Claire in the shower, in the kitchen, in the moments between words when she tried to convince herself she was safe. Sometimes they came through the vents, sometimes the power outlets.

Once, she swore she heard it breathing inside the radio, just beneath the static, as if waiting for her to listen. Michael unplugged it that night and threw it into the alley. The whisper didn't stop. He started checking everything; smoke detectors, light fixtures, even the hollow behind picture frames.

He found nothing, and that was worse than finding something.

It meant Lucian's reach was invisible, his presence intangible. It meant the fear had become its own kind of architecture. By the end of the week, even silence wasn't silence anymore.

It had been replaced by the faint, constant murmur of something that didn't belong to the world of the living, or perhaps worse, something that did.

And somewhere far away, in a darkened room lined with hollow books and quiet machinery, Lucian Alden smiled. Because whispers, after all, were where the breaking always began.

Michael sensed them first. In the clinic's final weeks, when his name still appeared on the door but no one knocked without hesitation. When colleagues' smiles grew brittle and their voices dropped mid-sentence as he entered the breakroom.

When even the air of the place, a place that had once smelled of paper, sanitizer, and hope, now tasted faintly of pity. He felt the shift in the smallest things. A nurse's conversation dying as he passed. A clipboard handed to him without eye contact. The pause, always that too-long pause, before a simple greeting.

In the elevator, a woman he didn't recognize looked him over once, then muttered just loud enough to be heard."Shame." The word stuck.

He wanted to snap at her, to say, you don't know me.

You don't know the weight I carry, the years I spent keeping others whole while breaking quietly myself. Instead, he muttered under his breath, "You couldn't understand."

Across the street at the café, the barista smirked as she handed him his coffee, her tone too polite to be genuine. "You're kind of famous lately." And on the subway, a man stared too long from across the aisle, his phone angled slightly, a grin playing on his mouth like he already knew something Michael didn't.

The city itself seemed to turn against him. Walls leaned closer. Windows reflected faces that whispered when he wasn't looking. Claire felt it differently.

Her world had always been one of tremors and fractures. But now, the fractures deepened. Every message she received carried poison. An email with no sender: We see you. A note slipped under her door: Whore.

A photograph in her mailbox: her face mid-ecstasy, blurred but unmistakable, caught in the half-light of betrayal. She tore it apart, paper slicing her palms, but no amount of shredding could tear away the dread coiled tight in her chest. Each piece of the image fluttered to the floor like a wing torn from something once alive.

The world was narrowing again, Lucian's voice without Lucian's presence, a haunting with fingerprints she could still feel. Their nights became prayers dressed as passion. They moved against each other with desperation, their bodies pleading for erasure. Each touch said, let it stop.

Each gasp said, make it go quiet. Michael kissed her until bruises bloomed.

Until his name on her lips sounded like salvation, not scandal.

Until exhaustion left them trembling, their hearts pounding in the dark like trapped things. But sleep was no mercy. Claire woke gasping, convinced Lucian's shadow stood in the corner. Michael would gather her close, his hands trembling, whispering, "It's just us. Only us."

Yet long after she fell asleep again, he lay awake, staring at the red digits of the clock glowing faintly on the wall. Sometimes he thought they blinked. Sometimes he was sure of it. Lucian's plan unfolded not in chaos, but in rhythm, each move deliberate, echoing with quiet inevitability. A steady tap-tap-tap, the sound of inevitability.

It didn't announce itself. It crept. He didn't send the full recordings. Not yet. He sent fragments. A moan stripped of context. A silhouette caught through frosted glass. A hand clutching a bedsheet in shadow. Enough to ruin. Not enough to prove. The genius of his cruelty was in the precision of its timing.

He waited. He let the whispers grow. He let doubt become reputation, reputation become evidence. And then, he struck. The package came on a Wednesday. Unmarked. No return address. Just his name scrawled across the front, block letters carved by intent.

Inside: a single USB drive. Plain black. Scuffed. Harmless at a glance. It was the ordinariness that made it monstrous. Michael stared at it for a long time before plugging it in. He told himself it could be anything. A client's file, a lawyer's update, some bureaucratic aftershock of the board hearing.

But when the screen flickered to life, it wasn't bureaucracy. It was Claire. Her face filled the frame, soft in lamplight, her lips parted. Her voice whispered his name. Her body moved in rhythm he knew by heart. Michael slammed the laptop shut, bile rising.

The sound echoed through the apartment, and for a heartbeat, he thought it laughed. He yanked the cord from the wall, ripped the USB free.

The plastic edge sliced his finger, a single bead of blood welling up. He stared at it, trembling. Once seen, it could never be unseen.

He sat in the dark for hours, the unplugged laptop on the floor, the drive still in his hand like a live thing. Claire found him there near dawn, motionless, eyes hollow. "What happened?" His voice broke. "He's watching us."

She froze. Her breath hitched. And then, a flicker of something else: fury. "Then let him choke on it," she said, and before he could stop her, she straddled him on the couch. Her mouth met his with violence.

Her hands tangled in his hair. "If he wants to watch," she gasped, "then let him see everything he lost. Every part of me that's not his anymore." Her hips moved against him, wild and defiant, and Michael's own rage rose to meet hers. He gripped her as if the act itself could tear Lucian's eyes from wherever they watched.

Each thrust became rebellion. Each cry became revenge. They came together, sobbing, moaning, clawing at each other as if trying to rewrite the laws of shame. When it was done, Claire collapsed against him, trembling. He held her, but neither spoke. And above them, in the hollow dark, the red light blinked

Recording. Judging. Waiting. Lucian watched. Not with lust. Not even with satisfaction. But with cold purpose.

He leaned forward in his chair, eyes catching the reflection of their bodies in motion, two broken things clinging to each other while the world sharpened its knives.

He rewound the clip once, studying Michael's face frozen mid-plea. Then he smiled, slow and mirthless. "No," he whispered. "Not death. Not yet."

The most perfect punishment was not murder. It was exposure. He would strip them bare, not in secret, but under the light. He would turn their intimacy into spectacle, their defiance into evidence, their love into the very instrument of their destruction. "Boston," he murmured, almost tenderly. "They think they'll start again. Let's give them a proper welcome."

He poured a drink, the ice cracking in the glass. Outside, Manhattan glimmered. Inside, the room smelled of smoke, whiskey, and something colder triumph.

And on the screen, the red light blinked again, steady, patient, waiting for the next act.

Eva came home from school with questions Michael wasn't ready for. The front door swung open with its familiar creak, letting in the smell of damp pavement and cafeteria spaghetti. Her curls were wild from the wind, her backpack slipping off one shoulder, a smear of glitter still clinging to her sleeve.

She kicked off her sneakers in the hallway, leaving a trail of muddy prints like breadcrumbs back to a childhood that should have been safe. "Daddy," she said, tugging at his sleeve, her voice singsong and uncertain, "why did Mrs. Kline look at me funny? And why did she say I should be proud of you anyway?" Michael froze.

The mug in his hand hovered halfway to his lips, coffee trembling against the rim. For a heartbeat, he couldn't breathe. The room seemed to tilt, sound collapsing into that one word , anyway. Such a small word, harmless on its own, but in a child's mouth, it became a blade.

He looked at her, seven years old, still in her blue school sweater, knees scuffed, eyes wide and honest, and felt his stomach hollow. "Anyway." It was the language of adults who whispered when they thought children couldn't hear. The way pity disguised itself as kindness. He crouched down, forcing his face into a smile that felt like paper stretched too thin."People say strange things when they don't understand," he said softly.

His voice was steady, but his hands shook where she couldn't see them. "How about we talk about something better? Did you learn about Saturn today?"

Her eyes lit up instantly, trusting, as if his words could mend the strange fracture she had brought into the house "We built the rings out of glitter and glue!" She said, spinning once, her backpack bouncing. "Mine was the biggest, even bigger than Ryan's!"

He smiled or tried to. Kissed her forehead, breathed in the faint scent of rain and crayons. "That's my girl," he whispered. "Biggest rings in the whole galaxy." She giggled, proud, and launched into a story about glue spills and the war over who got the last silver sparkle packet.

He listened. Laughed where he was supposed to. Pretended not to notice how his throat kept tightening. When she was done, they ate pasta from the night before, her legs swinging beneath the table as she hummed a song from music class. For a little while, it almost felt normal again.

The hum of the refrigerator, the soft clink of forks, the sound of her laughter filling in the empty corners of the room. Later, when the dishes were washed and her hair brushed and the lights dimmed to their warm bedtime glow, Michael read to her from Goodnight Moon.

Her eyelids grew heavy halfway through. He tucked the blanket under her chin, kissed the top of her head, and whispered, "Dream big, moonbeam."Her door clicked softly shut. The silence that followed was unbearable.

It wasn't peace, it was presence. The kind of silence that hummed. The kind that listened. He sat in the living room, the glow of the streetlight painting stripes across the carpet. The walls seemed closer than before. Every sound, the tick of the clock, the low groan of pipes, felt too deliberate, too intentional. The coffee mug from earlier still sat on the table, half-drunk, cold.

He hadn't noticed the faint tremor in his hands until now. He rubbed his temples, trying to breathe through the pressure in his chest. But the air itself felt wrong; thick, humming, alive. He swore he heard movement, a soft scrape, like fabric against plaster. He looked toward the hallway. Nothing. Still, the dread didn't fade. It had shape now. Breath. Teeth.

He tried the television, the radio, anything to drown it out. But when the static hit the speakers, the sound wasn't random, it pulsed, faintly rhythmic, almost like a voice caught between frequencies. He turned it off. The darkness seemed to lean in.

He could feel it beside him, not close enough to see, but near enough to know. Something was watching. And somewhere far beyond the walls of that apartment, Lucian Alden smiled at the monitor's dim glow, listening to the soft static of Michael's fear.

The next morning, the walls of the clinic seemed to hum with it. Every footstep echoed a second too long, every door closed a shade too fast. Dr. Evelyn Stone called him into her office, blinds half-drawn, her tone as cold as the steel frames around her glasses.

"Michael," she began, each syllable weighed with precision, "anonymous reports are circulating." Her fingers brushed a folder but didn't open it. "Not to the board this time. To the press. If it breaks publicly…" She let the pause hang. "…The compromise, we gave you may vanish."

Michael felt his throat dry out. "Do you know who's behind it?" Stone's gaze didn't waver. "Do you?"

He didn't answer. Because there was no need. They both already knew.

Across the city, Claire faced her own message. She came home late, her key trembling in the lock, shoulders hunched from another night of too little sleep. The air felt wrong before she even turned on the light. The faint scent of smoke, something acrid, chemical. On the bed, laid neatly across her pillow, was a zip tie.

Not the kind you'd find bundled in a drawer for fixing cables or hanging lights. This one was industrial black plastic thick as a finger, threaded with a thin, red stripe that caught the lamplight like a wound. The locking head had been melted, scorched until the plastic bubbled and curled inward, still faintly smelling of flame.

No note. No sign of forced entry.

Just the zip tie, a symbol of ownership, a warning dressed as restraint. Her scream shattered the silence. It wasn't a sound born of fear alone, but of recognition.

She tore at the thing, nails scraping, breaking it into pieces that flew across the room like shrapnel. Each fragment clattered against the hardwood floor, sharp, final, and yet the sound didn't bring relief. It only echoed.

By the time she reached Michael's apartment, she was shaking so violently she could barely speak. "He's here," she gasped between sobs. "He's here, he's here, he's always here."

Michael pulled her in, his own fear masked by the instinct to protect. He wrapped her in his arms, held her through the night as she cried into his chest until her tears soaked through his shirt. "Boston," he whispered into her hair. "We'll leave soon. He won't follow." But even as he said it, he felt the lie cling to his tongue.

Because shadows don't stop at borders. And Lucian Alden wasn't a man anymore. He was a persistence, a disease that lived in wires, whispers, and memory. In the glow of a dozen monitors, Lucian watched. His sanctuary of screens was quiet except for the hum of machinery and the faint rattle of rain against the windows. Every flickering image of Michael and Claire.

Each kiss, each tear, each desperate whisper reflected in his eyes like devotions in a dark church. He sat perfectly still, his breath even, his focus absolute. "Let them cling," he said softly, almost tender. "Let them sweat, and bleed, and hope. The tighter they hold each other, the more exquisite the breaking will be."

He swirled his glass of whiskey once, watched the amber light catch the ice.

Then, with one finger, he tapped a single key. All the screens froze at once. Michael and Claire mid-motion, caught in a moment that should have been private, sacred.

Lucian leaned forward, the light carving hollows beneath his cheekbones. Not yet," he murmured. "Not yet. But soon." He smiled then, slow, deliberate, sharp as bone. The smile of a man who didn't need to chase vengeance, because vengeance would walk to him on trembling feet.

Outside, the storm gathered again. In a small apartment across the city, Michael and Claire slept tangled in exhaustion, unaware that even their dreams had become part of Lucian's design.

Above them, in the ceiling vent, a red light pulsed faintly; steady, patient, unblinking. Recording. Waiting. Promising that what was coming next would not be silence.

A Labyrinth of Shadows

The city no longer felt like his. It had once been alive; chaotic, electric, impossible, a living, breathing organism that pulsed in rhythm with his own heartbeat. It used to speak to him in the language of movement and light: the hiss of buses, the shudder of subway rails, the pulse of neon signs flickering through fog. Manhattan had been his cathedral, his classroom, his escape.

Now it felt hollow. The same streets that once carried him felt narrower, more predatory. The glow of traffic lights seemed colder, artificial, casting colors that belonged more to fever dreams than to safety. Every block reflected something hunted. Every pane of glass shimmered with accusation. Even the air had changed.

It carried a static edge, like the moment before lightning strikes. Conversations around him seemed rehearsed. Laughter on street corners had a cruel, mechanical rhythm. He no longer walked through the city, he moved beneath it, as if everything above were watching.

The deli owner who used to greet him with warmth now barely met his eyes. The barista at the corner shop whispered something to a coworker when he ordered his coffee. A man on the subway caught his reflection in the window and smiled, a slow, knowing smile that never reached his eyes.

Manhattan had become a house of mirrors, and Michael Harris could no longer tell whether he was the reflection, or the thing reflected.

Every face he passed seemed to hold a trace of familiarity; a look too lingering, a movement too intentional.

Like a hundred Lucian's hiding in plain sight. Hunter and hunted, shadow and man, it was all blurring. He'd catch his reflection in the glass doors of high-rises and feel certain that it blinked a half-second uncoordinated. He began to walk faster, shoulders drawn tight, keys clenched between his fingers like a weapon.

He told himself it was stress. That this was what guilt did. It rewired perception, made ghosts out of gestures. But deep down, he knew better. The paranoia wasn't imagined. It was orchestrated. He could feel the precision of it now. The way every glance, every whisper, every misplaced object in his apartment seemed too deliberate.

Someone was composing this, note by note. It wasn't chaos. It was a symphony, and he was the melody. The streetlamps hummed as he passed beneath them, buzzing like insects drawn to blood. Cameras turned with faint clicks that shouldn't have been audible.

A taxi slowed beside him though he hadn't raised a hand. Even sound betrayed him. Footsteps behind him stopped when he stopped. The echo came too late, too human. The rhythm of the city no longer matched his. It moved to a different pulse, one that stalked, that waited.

He turned corners at random now, doubling back, ducking into crowded places, and slipping out the rear exits. But paranoia offered no relief. It only widened the sense of being enclosed, of the invisible perimeter tightening.

He began to feel it even in his sleep, the sense of being seen. Sometimes he would wake in the middle of the night certain that someone had just spoken his name. Close enough for breath to touch his ear. Michael Harris, the man who had once studied fear for a living, was now its specimen.

And somewhere in a room lit by the blue glow of monitors, Lucian Alden watched him, smiling faintly. His voice low and deliberate as he spoke to the empty air, "Good. He's learning what it means to be mine."

He felt it in the way headlights lingered too long behind him on Lexington. That narrow stretch between 54th and 59th where the streetlamps burned pale amber, where steam rose from the grates in ghostly columns, and puddles held reflections too sharp to be trusted.

Engines idled at the red lights, throaty and patient, the sound of metal breathing. The slick pavement shimmered with oil rainbows, each hue a warning. Violet bleeding into rust, green into gold, a city pretending to be alive while it quietly watched him.

He passed a bus stop where advertisements peeled at the corners, their faces distorted by water and time. Behind the glass, a homeless man slept upright, his reflection warping into Michael's as the light changed. For a moment, Michael couldn't tell which one of them was trapped inside.

He felt it, too, in the bodega on 3rd and 56th. The kind of place that smelled of burnt coffee, bleach, and cheap tobacco, where the fluorescent light hummed like an insect dying slow. The cashier, a young woman in a Mets cap, smiled politely, but the man near the freezer aisle didn't.

He was built thick through the shoulders, his knuckles scarred, his coat hanging open to reveal a pressed shirt that didn't belong in this neighborhood. His eyes were glacier-cold, unblinking. He didn't browse. He didn't buy. He just stood there, watching the reflection of Michael's back in the freezer door, pretending to compare brands of milk.

When Michael finally turned to leave, the man turned too, perfectly timed, as if their movements were rehearsed.

And then the subway. Always the subway. He felt the presence before he heard it, that subtle weight of another body matching his rhythm too precisely. The air down there was always damp, heavy with rust and brake dust, smelling of sweat, urine, and wet stone.

The lights flickered in the tunnels, casting everything in intervals of brightness and black. The footsteps came behind him, not rushed, not casual, but deliberate. One beat too many, the echo of a pulse not his own. He slowed. So did they. When he turned, the stairwell was empty.

Just the flicker of the fluorescent above, the faint drip of water tracing the concrete. But the sound hadn't been an echo. He knew echoes. This was weight. Flesh. Intent. He gripped the railing until the metal groaned beneath his palm, his reflection fractured in the grime of the wall tiles.

A train roared into the station, scattering wind and wrappers. The lights cut through the tunnel like blades, and for a moment, in the blur of motion and shadow, he saw it.

A figure at the far end of the platform, standing too still, head slightly tilted. Watching. Then gone. He boarded the next train without thinking. His heart pounded in time with the rattling steel beneath his feet. The windows turned black as the train shot into darkness, and for a heartbeat, he saw his own reflection in the glass.

Pale, hollow-eyed, and behind it, another shape that wasn't his. By the time he looked again, it was gone. The city pulsed on, indifferent. But Michael Harris knew. He wasn't walking through Manhattan anymore. He was walking through Lucian Alden's maze, and the walls had eyes. Lucian was no longer a man. He had become an atmosphere.

Something breathed in, something impossible to scrub from the air. He was the whisper that slipped through vents when the city slept, the ghost-static that hummed between radio frequencies, the subtle distortion in a security camera feed that made every still frame look like it was holding its breath.

He lived now in the in-betweens, between a flicker and a shadow, between a heartbeat and its echo. A presence without form, yet everywhere. Sometimes, when Michael passed beneath the streetlights on 2nd Avenue, one would sputter. Blink once, twice, then steady itself again, as if it had just remembered it was being watched.

The faint buzz that followed wasn't electrical; it was Lucian, breathing through the current. The whisper in the vents. The flicker in a streetlight's bulb. The soft creak of a door Michael knew he had locked. Lucian had woven himself into the very pulse of Manhattan, the veins of subway tunnels, the nerves of power lines, the digital ghosts that flickered behind every glowing screen.

He no longer needed proximity to control. Fear itself had become his instrument, and he played it with the precision of a surgeon. The zip tie on Claire's pillow had only been the beginning; a seed planted in both their minds, its roots twisting through their sleep, its vines wrapping around their waking hours.

It bloomed now into something far more potent: a terror that no longer needed proof to survive. Lucian's art was subtle. He didn't chase. He haunted. He didn't strike.

He waited. Every mirror became suspect. Every reflection felt delayed by half a second, as if reality itself were lagging behind his intent. The city's hum grew discordant, its rhythm off by a single, maddening beat.

Michael began to feel him in his chest. A weight that pressed just beneath the sternum, not quite pain, but close. The kind of pressure that comes before confession, or collapse.

And Claire, Claire dreamt of him. She dreamt of footsteps that echoed in reverse, of a voice that crawled up the back of her skull and whispered her name in tones she could feel but not hear.

She woke some nights with the faint impression of fingers at her throat, as if someone had traced her pulse just to remind her it could stop. Lucian existed in the pauses now. Between words. Between breaths. In every silence too long, every light too dim. He was not flesh anymore.

He was suggestion; an infection of thought, a presence carried in sound and shadow. Michael could sense him everywhere. In the static before a voicemail connected. In the pulse of his own veins when the city went still.

Even in the spaces between his thoughts, where fear ceased to be external and became him. Lucian Alden had ascended past vengeance. He had become the architecture of dread itself.

And Michael Harris, once a man who studied trauma, now lived inside it.

Michael knew panic was death. Lucian fed on it.

Not in the wild, cinematic sense of a monster tearing flesh, but in the quiet, deliberate way of a spider that waits.

Every fear sent through the web trembled its lines, calling him closer. He listened for it, the rhythm of dread, the small, quickened heartbeats that meant his prey was still moving, still alive enough to taste.

So, Michael did what he had always done best, he thought to himself. He forced stillness where instinct begged him to run. He slowed his breathing until even the room seemed to hesitate with him. Panic was Lucian's language. Logic, then, would be his rebellion. He turned inward. Cold, methodical, wielding his intellect like a scalpel.

He dissected the fear, laid it open on an invisible table, and examined its anatomy. Every pulse, every tremor, every whisper in the dark had a pattern. And patterns could be mapped.

Controlled. Countered. Lucian Alden wasn't chaos; he was choreography. His cruelty was mathematical, his malice deliberate. A series of gestures repeated until they stopped being human and became ritual. Michael studied him the way he once studied trauma itself. As both disease and design.

He cataloged every intrusion:

– *Anonymous emails, time-stamped* 3:03 a.m., always from addresses that didn't exist by sunrise.

– *Photographs,* slipped into mailboxes without stamps, edges damp with rain, the ink smudged just enough to feel touched.

– *Zip ties*, melted at one end, reshaped into circles. Not restraints, but symbols. Endless, recursive, choking.

– *The half-voice on the answering machine*, breathless, whispering a name. Claire, before the static swallowed it whole.

– *The timing.* Always just before dawn, always when the world was most defenseless.

Each act wasn't random; it was rhythm. Each reminder was part of a tightening ritual, a slow constriction that turned life itself into a living autopsy. He could feel Lucian's method beneath it all. Every move was meant to teach fear, to condition, not to crush. A psychologist's cruelty.

A god's patience. Outside, the wind picked up, slapping against the windows with sudden violence. A sign on the corner rattled its chains. Somewhere distant, a dog barked once, then went silent. Michael's pulse matched the storm's rise and fall, yet he refused to flinch. He scribbled in his notebook, not case notes, not therapy, but defense.

He wants panic, he wrote. He feeds on chaos. Starve him. But even as the words formed, the lights flickered once, twice, and held steady again. And for a heartbeat too long, the hum in the walls sounded like breathing. Lucian was near. Not in body. In presence. Watching from whatever dark machinery he'd built for himself, patient as the spider that knew the web was already trembling.

So Michael began to maneuver like prey pretending to be predator. He moved through Manhattan like a ghost studying its own haunting. He changed subway routes daily. Never boarding at the same platform twice, never trusting the rhythm of the trains that once felt like the city's heartbeat.

He memorized exits the way others memorized prayers, counting steps between staircases and side doors, marking which ones opened onto crowds and which spilled into dead alleys slick with rain.

He walked with mirrors in his mind. Knowing where each security camera blinked, when each lens turned its gaze away. He learned which station lights flickered in intervals long enough to let him vanish between frames, which corridors swallowed sound. Every corner became geometry.

Every reflection, reconnaissance. He carried the city in his head like a sacred manuscript of survival, its margins annotated in instinct. And at the clinic, the ruins of his old life, he built decoys. He left false files with fabricated client histories, notes in a hand too precise to be doubted. Addresses led nowhere.

To abandoned laundromats in Queens, to shuttered bakeries and condemned lots wrapped in rusted fencing. He wanted them to search. He wanted them to waste their certainty. A hunter spends most of his time waiting for prey to run the way he expects it to.

Michael made sure he never ran that way twice. With Claire, life became an exile inside the familiar. They lived as fugitives from their own names, drifting between borrowed spaces that offered no permanence and asked for none.

They met only where belonging was impossible. In libraries, where the air carried the dry, papery scent of forgotten stories, and their whispers hid beneath the turning of pages.

In public gardens, where fountains whispered louder than their fears and children's laughter became camouflage for confession. And sometimes, when the city's noise fell away and the wind carried church bells through narrow streets, they found themselves drawn to sanctuaries.

In old cathedrals, where saints stared down from stained glass and candles trembled in pools of wax, they sat together in pews polished by a century of knees. The scent of incense clung to their coats; their fingers brushed between prayers neither believed in. And sometimes, between the cold marble and the echo of whispered forgiveness, they kissed.

Not like lovers seeking passion, but like survivors passing warmth in a collapsing world.

Their lips carried no promise, only the trembling relief of not being alone in the dark. But the shadows followed anyway. They always did. One night, leaving the library on 42nd Street, he felt it; the air thinning behind him, charged, wrong

The kind of stillness that doesn't belong in a city that never sleeps. Even the traffic seemed to hesitate, the hum of engines swallowed by something colder. He adjusted his collar, stepped into the rain, and began walking down Fifth Avenue. Neon lights fractured across the puddles, bleeding red and blue into the wet asphalt like oil-slicked veins.

Reflections of storefronts slid past him in jagged streaks, mannequins frozen mid-laugh, windows like glass coffins. Then came the sound. Footsteps. Measured. Heavy. Too close to be chance, too steady to be coincidence. When he slowed, they slowed. When he turned at the corner, they paused, just long enough to let him know they were listening.

He could smell rain on the air, mixed with exhaust and the faint, sour tang of adrenaline. He slipped his hand into his coat pocket, fingers brushing against the small folded map he no longer needed, a relic now, a ritual of control. Then, without breaking stride, he veered right into the bright chaos of a hotel lobby.

The sudden shift hit him like oxygen after drowning. Color. Light. Movement. Crystal chandeliers shimmered overhead, scattering fractured rainbows across the marble floor. Bellhops in crimson jackets wheeled luggage carts that chimed softly against the tile. A woman's perfume, sharp, citrus and smoke, drifted past.

Tourists laughed at the bar, their voices sharp and careless, like they didn't know monsters could wear human faces. Michael kept moving.

He crossed the lobby, pulse quick but face calm, using reflections in the glass doors to search behind him. The footsteps had stopped. For now. He paused by the revolving doors, his hand hovering over the brass handle.

Outside, the city waited; black umbrellas, steaming gutters, a world pretending it wasn't falling apart. In the glass, he caught his own reflection, pale, drawn, eyes ringed in sleeplessness, and behind it, for a fraction of a second, another figure. Tall. Still. Watching.

Then the light blinked. And he was gone. The rain outside hissed against the street like static. Michael stepped into it, each drop a heartbeat, each shadow a test. He walked on. Not because he felt safe. But because stopping would mean admitting he never would be again.

Inside, the world exploded into sound and color. Crystal chandeliers scattered light across marble. Bellhops in scarlet jackets wheeled luggage carts that thudded and rattled across the floors. Tourists argued over drink orders at the bar, their laughter too loud, their gestures too wide. Phones rang. Keys jingled.

Doors sighed open and shut. The air smelled of cigar smoke and wet leather. He moved through it like a ghost trying to borrow humanity, his reflection flashing across gold mirrors as he went. He didn't look back until he was already outside again. The footsteps were still there.

At Madison and 39th, Michael stopped. The man following him did too. Tall. Broad-shouldered. Black coat. Gloves. Eyes that didn't blink. Michael recognized the stillness immediately, not hesitation, but patience. The kind of stillness predators learn before they strike. He didn't back away. "Tell him," Michael said, voice low, trembling but steady, "I'm not prey." The man smiled, thin, humorless.

He didn't reply. He simply stepped forward and slipped something into Michael's coat pocket with the ease of a thief. Then he stepped into the crosswalk. Horns blared. Headlights flared. Cars surged forward.

The man moved through it all without flinching, vanishing into the blur of motion, as if the city itself opened to let him pass. Michael stood under the traffic light's yellow wash. The rain made halos around the lamps. He reached into his pocket, fingers closing on folded paper. The ink had bled from the damp, but the words were still legible.

"Every maze has a Minotaur." Lucian's handwriting.

Precise. Elegant. Deadly. That night, Claire trembled in his arms. "He's circling," she whispered. "I can feel it. He won't let us go." Michael kissed her temple, holding her face in both hands, forcing her to look at him. "Then we don't play by his maze," he said. "We build our own."

She nodded, but her body shook as she spoke. "What if he's already inside it?" He didn't answer. He couldn't. Instead, he kissed her, fiercely, hungrily, as though her lips could keep the darkness at bay. Their lovemaking that night was not gentle. It was rage and fear turned to heat, bodies colliding in an act that was half-love, half-survival.

She clutched him like drowning demanded hands, nails cutting into his shoulders. He moved against her with the desperate rhythm of a man defying his own ending. Their gasps filled the small apartment, not pleasure, not entirely; something rawer, more feral.

When they finally collapsed, slick with sweat and exhaustion, Michael whispered into the hollow of her throat, "If he watches, let him choke on the sight." Claire's laugh broke, half sob, half fire. "Then we'll give him a tragedy worth watching."

But Lucian Alden was not merely watching anymore. He was rehearsing. Planning his grand unveiling, the final act of the play they didn't know they'd been written into. And somewhere, beneath the city, among his screens and wires, the red light blinked once.

Like a heartbeat. Like the signal that the end had already begun.

That night, in his sanctuary, he spread maps across his desk. Subway lines, neighborhood grids, Boston streets. The desk itself was scarred oak, its surface littered with pins and scraps of paper, the faint scorch marks of cigarettes long stubbed out. A brass lamp threw a cone of yellow light, its shade tilted so the rest of the room drowned in shadow.

The walls were crowded with cork boards layered in photographs. Michael at the courthouse steps, Claire slipping into her building, Eva laughing with friends outside her school. String connected them in red and black lines, a web that grew denser with each new obsession.

Beneath the boards, a radiator hissed, and the smell of iron and dust thickened the air. Lucian traced routes with gloved fingers, the leather whispering against paper. Circles marked Michael's patterns, train stops, coffee shops, office lobbies, and beside them, smaller loops: Eva's ballet rehearsals, the library where she studied, the playground where her innocence still bloomed.

"She is the thread," he murmured to the empty room. His reflection flickered faintly in the darkened window, city lights bleeding through like distant stars. "Pull her, and the whole tapestry unravels." He closed his eyes, savoring it.

The collapse not just of Michael's career, not just of Claire's sanity, but of their very souls. Michael sensed it before he knew it. A father knows when his child is in danger, the way animals know storms before the first drop of rain. Eva's laughter on the phone that evening carried an echo he couldn't name, a hollow behind her words.

Evelyn had brushed it off, "She's fine, Michael, don't project your paranoia", but paranoia had kept him alive this long. He remembered the clinic in Manhattan: the way conversations died when he entered a room, how nurses' eyes slid past him as if he weren't there. The barista's smirk with his coffee. The woman in the elevator who whispered "Shame" as though she'd been waiting just for him.

He had felt Lucian in all of it, a shadow leaking through the cracks of ordinary days, staining them. And so, he maneuvered again. He called in favors. He moved money into accounts Lucian couldn't trace. He began the relocation to Boston in secret, not as an exile now but as an escape route through a burning labyrinth. But Lucian was already waiting at the other end.

That night, Michael dreamt of Boston Harbor. The water rippled black beneath the moon, and dozens of zip ties floated on the surface, bobbing like broken rings. Each one clicked shut on its own, the sound echoing across the harbor like a hundred locks closing.

The ties sank one by one, dragging invisible weights into the deep until the water swallowed every reflection.

When he woke, Claire was gone from the bed, the window half-open, the curtain stirring like a breath.

On the sill, a zip tie. Black. Scorched. Waiting.

The Chessboard

Every move mattered now. Every breath was an equation. Every step a negotiation with fate. Every corner of every street held the quiet question, is this the one he's waiting around? Even the city's pulse had turned against him. Neon blinked in coded rhythms. Traffic lights felt deliberate, almost sentient, holding red just long enough to make him visible, to make him wait.

He noticed patterns everywhere now; the flicker of a light in a high-rise window, the rhythm of passing cabs, the cadence of footsteps on wet pavement. Once, these were nothing but the heartbeat of New York. Now, they were tells. Michael had begun to think in terms of strategy, his instincts reshaping themselves into something colder, sharper.

His life was no longer a narrative. It was a board, and he was a piece being moved across it. Every choice had weight. Every mistake left residue. Sleep became an indulgence he couldn't afford. He studied streets the way others studied scripture. Memorizing angles, counting windows, noting how sound carried differently between brick and glass.

Except this wasn't chess. This was survival played on the raw edge of fear. No tidy moves, no resets. Only the slow bleed of endurance. And the stakes weren't abstract. They had names. His. Claire's. Eva's. He could feel their lives threaded through his every motion; fragile, luminous, and breakable.

When he pictured Eva's face, her small hands folded around a crayon or her voice asking if he'd be home for breakfast, his resolve hardened.

He could lose the world, lose his license, his reputation, but not her.

Not the one thing he hadn't already corrupted. And yet the game was never his to win. Lucian Alden had carved the board itself. Every line etched in advance, every square a preordained trap. Lucian didn't play, he designed.

He'd built the rules, the boundaries, the illusions of choice. The city was his labyrinth, and Michael its reluctant Minotaur, hunted, cornered, condemned to his own intelligence. He knew Lucian's kind of power. It wasn't brute force. It was precision; the art of pulling one thread and watching a man unravel without ever laying a hand on him.

Every streetlight. Every photograph. Every whisper in a hallway was part of the architecture of Lucian's control. And so Michael moved carefully through the dark machinery of a world designed by someone else's cruelty, knowing that one misstep wouldn't just end him. It would erase everyone he still dared to love.

Michael struck first. Not loudly, not recklessly, but with the precision of a man who'd finally accepted that decency had no place in a war built on deception. His moves were small, invisible to most, yet deliberate enough to shift the ground beneath Lucian's reach. He started with Eva. Her safety was no longer a hope; it was a strategy.

Her dance rehearsals, once routine, predictable, marked neatly on a calendar Lucian's people could've memorized, were moved without warning. No announcement. No pattern. The old studio downtown, with its cracked mirrors and open street view, was abandoned overnight.

In its place, a new location: an uptown studio hidden above a florist's shop, its scent of lilies masking the stale air of vigilance. The building had two exits, one that led to the street, the other to a narrow alley spilling into a busy café. Cameras covered both, their red lights faint but steady.

He checked them himself, tracing the angles, memorizing the blind spots. Then came the phone. He destroyed the old SIM card, pressing it between his fingers until it splintered with a brittle snap.

The sound sharp and final, like breaking a promise to a past life. In its place: a burner. Cheap plastic, gray as hospital light. No contacts but three. Evelyn, Claire, and the director in Boston arranging what was supposed to be his new beginning.

He left the rest of the world behind. Clients. Colleagues. Friends who'd stopped calling once the rumors began. Gone. He built his life out of layers of silence. No pattern. No trace. No trust. He became methodical. Paranoid. Maps of the city replaced case notes on his desk.

He studied them until the lines became rivers of thought, until he could see their intersections even when he closed his eyes. He memorized transfer stations, counted how long it took to move from one to another, learned which staircases circled back and which ended in dead ends that reeked of old rain and loneliness.

He changed routes daily. Sometimes twice within the same hour. He'd step onto one train, feel a pair of eyes linger too long, then switch lines mid-ride. Sometimes he'd surface blocks away from where he meant to be, drenched in sweat, pulse stuttering in rhythm with the city's electric veins.

The New York he once loved, the city that had raised him, that had whispered opportunity in his youth, was gone. What remained was a labyrinth made of glass and asphalt, each pane reflecting his own hunted shape back at him.

The skyscrapers loomed not as symbols of ambition, but as silent sentinels.

Watching. Waiting.

And still, the feeling never left him, that hum just beneath the noise, the static thread between him and them. He could feel it in the weight of shadows, in the way the world slowed at intersections as if holding its breath.

A man in a baseball cap, loitering too long at the corner. A woman on the train, eyes locked not on her phone but on his reflection in the window. A faint click echoing down an empty hallway, camera shutter or lighter, he could never tell. The air itself seemed wired. Every silence carried a pulse. Every movement, a witness. It wasn't paranoia. It was certainty dressed in silence.

The terrible knowledge that Lucian Alden had already woven his presence through the city's circuitry, and that even when unseen, he was always there. Claire tried to laugh it away. She tried to fill their nights with wine and soft music, to remind herself what it felt like to exist without trembling.

But her eyes betrayed her. One evening, she froze in front of her mirror. At first, she thought it was a trick of reflection, until she saw it clearly. A single feather taped dead center to the glass. Not on her pillow this time. Her mirror. White and small.

A mark of ownership. A taunt. Lucian's hand, invisible but unmistakable. She tore it down, fingers trembling, voice cracking into sobs. "I can't breathe here," she said, collapsing into Michael's chest. "Every wall has ears. Every lock is a joke. I can feel him even in my dreams."

Michael stroked her hair, whispering into the crown of her head. "Then dreams are what we'll use," he murmured. "Let him haunt. Let him watch. We'll give him illusions until he can't tell truth from shadow." And so he began to fight not with fists, but with mirrors. He turned his apartment into a stage of false images. Lights left burning in empty rooms.

Curtains drawn half-open to reveal silhouettes, not theirs, but the outlines of mannequins he'd bought from a closing boutique downtown.

He staged phone calls in public, his voice loud, careless, naming false addresses. He let Lucian listen, let him chase ghosts. And for Eva, sweet, oblivious Eva, he arranged something darker.

A friend of Evelyn's, roughly Claire's height and build, walked her home from school twice that week. Her hood pulled low, her stride deliberate. From a distance, it looked like Claire and Eva together. Michael wanted Lucian's men to think they had already fled.

The city itself became his accomplice. Its shadows became allies. Its noise became cover. And still, he felt Lucian's gaze on the back of his neck like static. In his private room of screens, Lucian smiled. "Good," he said softly. "Run. Hide. Pretend. The clever mouse makes the chase worthwhile."

He adjusted the camera feed, zooming in on Michael's dim apartment. The mannequins fooled his men once, but not him. "You think in traps," he murmured to the flickering monitor. "But I build labyrinths." He didn't need to win every move. He only needed to win the last. Then came the threats. Sharper now. Personal.

A note slipped under Michael's office door: Your daughter has beautiful eyes. They deserve to stay that way. A voicemail, nothing but the sound of breathing; slow, steady, listening. And then the package. Claire opened it. Inside, a broken watch. The glass cracked, its hands frozen at 4:06. The hour of her first session with Michael. The hour everything began.

Her scream tore through the room.

Michael caught her before she hit the floor, her body shaking as she whispered, "He's in my head. He'll never stop." He held her tighter, trying to believe the words that left his mouth.

"Boston is coming. Just a little longer. Hold on." But his voice trembled. Because somewhere deep inside, he knew shadows don't respect borders. That night, they didn't speak. They just held each other, skin against skin, breath to breath, the fear pressed between them until it burned.

Their lovemaking wasn't tender. It was survival. Each movement was a plea; don't disappear, don't vanish, don't leave me to face this alone. When they finished, Claire lay trembling, her lips against his ear. "Do you think he watches us even now?"

Michael exhaled, eyes fixed on the dark ceiling. "Yes," he said. "But let him choke on it." Claire gave a broken laugh that twisted into a sob. "Then we'll give him a tragedy worth watching."

Across the city, Lucian didn't choke. He savored. He sat surrounded by screens, the glow painting his face in cold light, his glass of whiskey catching gold in the dark. Michael's voice echoed faintly from a speaker, distorted but clear enough. Lucian swirled the glass, his smile widening.

"Every chess game has an end," he whispered. "But the most exquisite part isn't the checkmate, It's the moment the king realizes he was doomed all along." He smiled to himself as he said it. He closed the laptop, the hum of machinery falling away into silence. The room seemed to inhale, vast, suffocating, triumphant.

And somewhere, across the city, Michael Harris lay awake beside Claire, his eyes wide open, his heart pounding. He stared at the shadows on the ceiling, listening for breathing that wasn't there.

He knew what Lucian knew. The game was far from over.

And every night they survived it, they were only being moved closer to the end.

The Trap

The nights stretched long, and the days turned brittle. Thin glass hours, fragile and transparent, ready to shatter beneath the smallest touch of unease. Time no longer passed for Michael; it stalked him. It circled quietly, patient, and deliberate, a predator pacing the perimeter of his thoughts. Sleep came in fragments, brittle and feverish.

He'd drift under, only to jolt awake at the faintest sound, the whisper of pipes expanding, the sigh of the old radiator exhaling steam like a wounded animal. The city outside had a voice of its own, and every tone felt sharpened against his nerves. A horn in the distance, a siren wailing up Lexington, a slamming door several floors below. Each became a signal. Each became a threat.

He began to move through his apartment like a soldier clearing hostile ground. Every night, he checked the locks twice, then three times. The bolt. The chain. The window latches. He'd run his fingers along the edges of the frames, feeling for the faintest shift of air.

He learned the cadence of his building. The steady rhythm of Mrs. Han's slippers in 3B, the squeak of the mail slot when the superintendent made his rounds, the echo of the elevator cables groaning with age. He could tell, by sound alone, which footsteps belonged to which neighbor and which ones didn't.

But even vigilance came at a cost. It crept into him, filling the hollows of his body like smoke. His hands developed a tremor so fine it was nearly imperceptible until he tried to write, his pen shaking against the paper.

The mirror in his bathroom became a stranger, eyes sunken, jaw tight, the ghost of stubble shadowing his cheeks.

He looked like a man perpetually bracing for impact. His heartbeat had learned to live in his throat, ready to sprint before he did. Coffee no longer helped; it only made the trembling worse. Food lost its taste. Everything metallic, everything dust. There were moments, brief and treacherous, when exhaustion dragged him to the edge of surrender.

When he'd lean against the wall, eyes closed and wonder what it would feel like to stop fighting. To open the door, step into the dark, and let the inevitable come. But then he'd think of Eva, her small voice calling him Daddy, the way her hand had once fit inside his like something sacred. That memory was the only thing that steadied him, the last unbroken piece of himself.

So he executed, hollow-eyed and sleepless, a man made of vigilance and fading hope, haunted not just by what hunted him. But by what he was becoming to survive it. Claire noticed before he did.

"You don't sleep anymore," she whispered one morning, brushing the hollow beneath his eye with a trembling fingertip. Michael gave a humorless laugh. "If I close my eyes, I'll miss the move."Her lips tightened. "You'll break before he does."It wasn't an accusation.

It was prophecy. Michael said nothing.
The truth of it was too close, too raw. The threats no longer whispered. They began to announce themselves.

One Tuesday afternoon, Eva came home pale, her backpack clutched to her chest. "Daddy?" She said softly. "Someone left me a present at school."

Her voice was too careful, too adult. Michael's stomach dropped. He opened the backpack and pulled out the stuffed rabbit. It had been white once. Its seams were split, its cotton guts spilling out, the edges of the fluff smeared a dark, rusty red. The smell, faint iron, confirmed what his mind refused to believe.

Eva's teacher had thought it was a cruel prank. Michael knew better. He recognized the precision. The message. He told Eva it was nothing. That someone had played a trick. Then he locked himself in the bathroom, turned on the faucet, and vomited until bile scorched his throat.

Three days later, he found Claire on the bathroom floor. At first, he thought the sound was the shower. A steady hiss behind the door, but as he got closer, he heard something else beneath it. A rhythm. The harsh, relentless scrape of bristles against porcelain.

When he pushed the door open, the smell hit him first. Bleach, sharp and chemical, biting at the back of his throat. The mirror was fogged, the air thick with steam, the lights humming faintly overhead like an insect trapped in glass. And there she was. Claire was on her knees, hair plastered to her temples, her breath coming in small, broken gasps.

The scrub brush in her hand moved with mechanical precision. Back and forth, back, and forth. Her knuckles raw, the water swirling pink around the drain. Feathers clung to her skin. Dozens of them. Maybe hundreds. White, gray, and a few stained a dull, terrible red. As though whatever bird they came from had fallen through something it shouldn't have. The tub was full of them.

A graveyard of softness. They floated on the water's surface, matted and torn, sticking to her arms, her wrists, her throat. She didn't even look up when he stepped inside.

Her voice was small, almost childlike, trembling in the mist. "I can't get them out," she whispered. "They're everywhere. He put them here. I can feel them." Her words shuddered, and for a moment, Michael didn't know whether she meant the feathers or the memories.

He crossed the room and shut off the water, but it didn't stop her movements. The brush kept scraping, hard enough to strip the porcelain. "Claire." He knelt beside her, took her wrist, gentle but firm. Her hand twitched, resisting, then went limp.

When she finally looked at him, her eyes were wide and wild. Pupils, huge and dark, rimmed with the faintest trace of bloodshot veins. There was madness there but not born of delusion. It was terror, rational and real, the kind that takes root in truth and grows until it strangles everything else.

"Why won't it stop?" She whispered. "I hear him when I close my eyes. He's in the vents, in the walls… he's in me." Her voice cracked. A feather slipped from her hair, landed in the puddle between them. Michael gathered her in his arms, her wet skin cold against his chest, her trembling body folding into his.

He could smell the bleach on her, the sharp ghost of panic that never really left their apartment anymore. "It's over," he said, though his voice betrayed him. "He's not here." But the lie barely lasted the breath it took to say it. Because even as he held her, the pipes groaned. Somewhere deep in the walls, a faint click echoed; soft, deliberate.

A lighter. Or a camera. And both of them froze. "He was here," she whispered. "He was here." Her fingers were raw, bleeding where the bristles had torn skin. Michael caught her wrist gently, pried the brush from her grip, and pulled her into his arms. "Boston," he whispered against her hair. "Just hold on. We're almost out." Her laugh cracked into a sob.

"Almost," she said bitterly. "Always almost." He couldn't argue. The word almost had become their religion, a faith in escape that never came. Across the city, Lucian's sanctuary of surveillance glowed like a cathedral built from sin. It sat high above the street. A penthouse stripped of warmth and reimagined as something between a confessional and a command post.

The curtains were always drawn, sealing out the skyline. The air was cool, recycled, carrying the faint smell of ozone from the machines. A dozen screens lined the walls. Flickering in uneven rhythm, their light washing his face in alternating shades of gold and blue.

Each hum from the processors sounded like prayer. Low, constant, reverent. If one stood outside the door, they might mistake the glow for something holy. But this was no place for redemption. It was a chapel for control. Lucian Alden sat at the center of it, elbows on his knees, hands clasped loosely beneath his chin.

His face was calm, composed, the faintest hint of a smile curling his lips. The look of a man admiring the precision of his own cruelty. On one screen, Michael paced the perimeter of his apartment checking locks, drawing curtains, muttering to himself in the half-light. On another, Claire knelt on the bathroom floor, her hair sticking to her cheeks.

Her fingers bleeding as she scrubbed at feathers that would not vanish. And on the smallest screen, almost an afterthought, Eva sat at her desk, tracing circles in her notebook, her small brow furrowed in concentration. Lucian watched them all. The therapist. The woman. The child. Each screen was a confession. Each movement, a hymn.

He studied them like case files, eyes unblinking.

Every flicker of emotion, every hesitation cataloged.

He saw when Michael's hand shook while locking the door. He saw when Claire's lips formed his name in the dark. He saw the child look up toward an unseen shadow on the wall. As if some part of her already knew she was being watched.

The hum of the monitors filled the room. Lucian leaned back, letting it wash over him, the chorus of their unraveling. He had built this world from wires and whispers, and now it sang for him. One screen crackled. Static rippling across Michael's image, and Lucian's eyes narrowed, almost fond.

He reached for his glass of whiskey, the ice clinking softly against the crystal, and raised it in a slow, deliberate toast to the ghosts on his walls. "To devotion," he murmured. "To the art of breaking." He took a sip. The liquor burned his throat in the most satisfying way. Outside, thunder rolled faintly over Manhattan; a slow, rolling growl that seemed to echo his mood.

Lucian didn't flinch. He simply turned up the volume, the static sharpening into breath, Claire's breath, and smiled. Because somewhere across the city, a man and a woman were losing their grip on sanity. A child was beginning to dream of shadows. And all of it, every trembling heartbeat, belonged to him.

"He's improvising now," Lucian murmured, voice low, amused. "Panic makes the mind inventive." Evelyn stood behind him, arms crossed, the only one whose reflection still seemed human in that metallic light. "And what happens," she asked quietly, "when he realizes you've already scripted the ending?"

Lucian turned slightly, the corner of his mouth curving. He swirled his whiskey, listening to the soft clink of melting ice. "That's the beauty," he said. "He will never realize. Not until the final breath." On the farthest screen, Eva appeared, her small form hunched over a notebook, doodling absentmindedly.

Circles, then smaller circles inside them, until the page looked like an eclipse of spirals. Evelyn's throat tightened. "And the child?" She asked. Lucian didn't even blink. "The child," he said, "is the queen. Remove her, and the board collapses faster."

Evelyn flinched. Her lips parted, to argue, to plead, but nothing came. She turned away instead, her reflection swallowed by the darkness at the edges of the room. Lucian watched her go, unbothered, almost tender. "Don't look so tragic," he said softly. "Even queens can be sacrificed. It's how the story stays interesting."

He raised his glass toward the screens. Toward the sleeping man, the trembling woman, the innocent child. "To endings," he whispered, and drank.

That night, somewhere above him, the rain began again, soft, relentless, and endless, like a city grieving for the ones who didn't yet know they were already ghosts.

Michael's paranoia became ritual, his new form of prayer to a god that never answered. It gave him structure, purpose, the illusion of control in a world that had stripped him bare. He checked every lock twice, then thrice, whispering the sequence under his breath like liturgy. Bolt. Chain. Deadlock. Again.

Bolt. Chain. Deadlock. The rhythm calmed him, if only for a moment. Each metallic click was a heartbeat, each seal a plea to whatever higher power might still be listening. He memorized the sound each lock made as it slid into place. The hollow clack of brass against wood, the faint vibration through the frame.

Learned to tell the difference between safety and deceit by ear alone. Some nights, he would pause, holding the key still in his hand, certain that the next click would sound wrong. A hair off-pitch, a whisper of tampering in the mechanism.

When that happened, he'd start again from the beginning. Bolt. Chain. Deadlock. Until dawn sometimes. He moved through the apartment like a man tending to a sacred space desecrated by ghosts. He unplugged the television first. The static hum had begun to feel sentient. Then the router, its blinking green light a pulse he didn't trust.

He tore the cables out, coiled them into neat circles, and sealed them in a drawer like relics too dangerous to touch. Every night, he drew new routes on paper. Subway transfers, alley shortcuts, exits. Hand-sketched maps that changed with the shifting patterns of his fear. When the ink dried, he burned them in the sink, watching as the flames devoured each line, each fragile plan.

The ashes curled upward, light as breath, drifting through the air like gray snow before settling in the basin. He'd stare at them until only black residue remained. Evidence of thought, erased by fire. He no longer trusted the city's hum. Metal, glass, signal, they were all accomplices.

Lucian lived in those things now. In reflections, in transmissions, in the soft electric pulse of modern life. Every screen was a doorway. Every reflection a mouth that whispered his name. So Michael turned primitive. He left notes for Claire in graphite on torn paper instead of text messages.

He bought candles to light their dinners, not for romance, but to avoid the flicker of the power grid. He stopped using mirrors. The one in the hallway he draped with a bedsheet, unable to stand the thought of being watched through his own face.

And each night, just before sleep, he took Claire's phone, her sleek, shining lifeline, and dropped it into a glass of water. He watched the bubbles rise, watched them pop one by one at the surface. It made a soft fizzing sound, almost delicate, like champagne.

He imagined it was the sound of drowning, the invisible eyes gasping, the signal suffocating. "Better," he'd whisper. "Better now." Claire would watch him from the doorway, her arms wrapped around herself, eyes tired and red.

She didn't argue anymore. There was no point.

The ritual wasn't madness to him. It was survival, a faith built on fear, a catechism written in static and shadow. Outside, the city pulsed on indifferent, alive, listening. Inside, the air grew thick with the smell of melted plastic, wet circuitry, and burnt paper.

And in that darkness, with the hiss of the radiator for company, Michael Harris prayed. Not for salvation, but for silence. "He listens through everything," Michael muttered. "Sound carries through metal. Even through air." Claire didn't argue. Not anymore. She had begun to fold inward, piece by piece.

Her laughter, once bright, startling, became a relic, something she remembered rather than felt. The circles beneath her eyes deepened to bruises. She flinched at small sounds now: a door creaking, a siren outside, the hum of the fridge turning on in the dark.

They lived in the same rooms but in different worlds, his built from logic and survival, hers from terror and exhaustion. Every night they lay in bed as if the air between them were wired. The only time she touched him now was in the dark, when her fear overpowered her shame.

That night, her hands were cold as she reached for him, pulling him close until her trembling stilled. Her voice came out a whisper, ragged and small. "Michael... what if Boston isn't real?" He stiffened. "What do you mean?"

"What if it's just another illusion he made? Another maze. We keep running toward escape, and it's just another one of his walls." She said with terror in her eyes. Michael's throat closed. The idea hit too deep. Too possible.

He wanted to tell her no, that Boston was real, that the promise of a new life wasn't another of Lucian's designs. But Lucian's reach had infected everything, even their dreams. Sometimes, when Michael blinked, he swore he saw the red light from Lucian's camera blinking in the dark behind his eyes.

So instead, he said nothing. He pressed his lips to her temple, tasting salt and despair. He held her tighter, breathing her in as if he could anchor them both. And as the room filled with the sound of rain against the window, he swallowed the truth he dared not say.

That even hope now felt like another of Lucian's traps.

That perhaps, in ways neither could admit, Lucian had already won.

Six Minutes Revisited

The night began with silence. Not the kind that soothes, but the kind that waits, heavy, sentient, aware. It filled the corners of the apartment like fog, thick and patient. As if the air itself knew the script and was holding its breath before the curtain rose.

Michael felt it before the sound ever came. That instinct, the one that had kept him alive this long, tightened in his chest like a warning. Something had shifted. Not outside, not yet. Inside. The atmosphere itself felt rewired, humming just below audibility, as if electricity were crawling along the walls, waiting for a place to strike.

The apartment had the hollow sound of a place already abandoned. Boxes sealed and stacked like gravestones. Books gone from their shelves, leaving rectangles of cleaner paint behind. Nails protruding where frames once hung. The ghosts of their life together.

Coffee rings, fingerprints, faint scuffs on the floor, were all that remained. The smell of cardboard and dust pressed in around them, dry and claustrophobic. The light above flickered, not with power failure but with exhaustion, as though even the bulb wanted to be done with this place. Claire knelt on the floor, pressing a final strip of tape along the top of a box marked LINENS.

Her fingers shook; the tape clung and fought her, squealing against the cardboard. The sound cut through the stillness like a scream.

She paused halfway through the motion, her breath catching mid-inhale. Michael watched her freeze, mid-kneel, head tilted slightly toward the door.

He didn't ask what was wrong. He already knew. It was that kind of silence, the one that doesn't end but breaks. He moved slowly, each step measured. His pulse pounded in his ears, synchronizing with the distant hum of the refrigerator and the faint ticking of the clock that hung above the door frame.

Then, beneath all of it, barely perceptible at first, came the sound. A low rumble.

Not mechanical, not thunder. Closer. The kind of sound a car makes when it idles too long outside your window. Claire's gaze flicked to the curtains. Her voice was barely a whisper. "Michael…" He crossed to the window, drew back the edge of the curtain with two fingers.

The city below was slick with rain, reflecting sodium light in liquid gold. But his eyes weren't on the street. They were on the vehicle parked opposite the building. A black sedan, engine purring, headlights dimmed but not off. Inside, through the windshield's reflection, a shape sat motionless.

A silhouette. Unmoving. Watching. Claire rose slowly, her hands curling into fists at her sides. "Michael," she said again, but her voice was thinner now, unraveling. "That's the same car. From last week. Outside the library." He didn't answer.

Didn't need to. He knew she was right. A tremor passed through her shoulders, subtle but visible. The apartment seemed to grow smaller by the second, the walls inching closer, the ceiling pressing down. The tape gun slipped from her hand and hit the floor with a hollow clack.

Neither of them moved to pick it up. Somewhere, a radiator hissed like a whisper too close to the ear. Michael turned from the window and met her eyes.

"It's time," he said. Claire nodded once, her throat tight, and moved toward the suitcase by the door.

Her fingers fumbled on the zipper, every sound amplified in that oppressive quiet, the rasp of metal teeth, the scrape of the handle against the floor. And then, faint, deliberate, a car door opened below.

A pause. Another. Footsteps. Slow. Unhurried. Claire's breath hitched audibly. The silence shattered like glass. "Michael," she whispered, the tape dangling from her fingers. He looked up.

Across the street, beneath a sickly yellow streetlight, a car idled. Black sedan. Windows tinted. Harmless, at a glance. But not to her. Claire's voice cracked like thin glass. "That's her."

"Who?" He asked wondering who she was referring to. Her pupils widened, her throat bobbing as she swallowed. "The woman I saw the day I came to your office. The day I was late." Her voice faltered, then steadied with dread. "She was standing outside watching. I thought she was just… no one. But it's her."

The silhouette in the driver's seat didn't move. A figure perfectly still. Waiting. The engine purred, exhaust coiling up into the misty air in slow, deliberate ribbons. Michael's stomach turned cold. He knew. "Evelyn?"

Claire's breath hitched like a gasp that didn't know if it should escape. "Your ex-wife." And then, as if conjured by the sound of her name, the driver's door opened. A figure emerged, the shape of a woman carved from the shadows, elegant, composed, almost Spectral. Evelyn Stone.

She walked slowly, heels clicking against wet pavement, her reflection shattering in puddles as she crossed the street. When she reached the curb, she stopped beneath the flickering streetlight and smiled faint, knowing, merciless.

"Hello, Michael," she said softly. Her gaze slid past him to Claire. "Hello again."

Claire recoiled, her back pressing to the wall. "You, you were there." Evelyn's smile deepened, almost kind. "I've always been here."

The silence that followed was a knife; sharp, gleaming, suspended in the air between them, waiting for a pulse to cut through. Evelyn stood just inside the doorway, framed by the weak amber glow of the hall light.

The rain behind her hissed against the threshold, dripping from her umbrella in slow, rhythmic taps that sounded almost deliberate. Each drop marked time like a countdown. She didn't speak. She didn't have to. Her presence alone was intrusion enough. Michael's apartment, stripped bare for departure, looked more like evidence than home.

The walls were ghosts, pale outlines of paintings and photographs where sunlight had once touched. Cardboard boxes stood like sentinels, sealed and labeled in his careful handwriting. A coffee mug sat abandoned on the counter, half-drunk and cold. The faint scent of dust, rain, and something burned; maybe from the last time he'd scorched one of his maps, lingered in the air.

Evelyn stepped further inside, the echo of her heels soft but deliberate on the wood floor. She didn't belong here, not in this version of his life. And yet, she moved as though she did. Slow, assured, the way someone moves through a place they've memorized long before it changed. Her eyes swept the room, clinical, dissecting.

She took in the taped boxes, the absence of color, the faint indentation of a sofa recently moved. Her gaze lingered on the window, where the curtain still trembled from being drawn back too fast. Then on the glass of water on the table, a drowned phone resting at the bottom like a dark fish. It was the sort of detail only Evelyn would notice.

Her lips curved, not quite into a smile. "So," she said finally, voice low, even, disturbingly calm. "This is what desperation looks like." Michael's jaw tensed. "Get out." But she didn't.

Instead, she turned her head slowly toward him, her expression unreadable. Not anger, not pity, something colder, more analytical. The gaze of someone cataloging the remains of what used to be a man.

Claire hovered near the wall, pale, trembling, her eyes darting between them. Evelyn's presence seemed to drain the air from the room. Even the hum of the city beyond the window sounded farther away. Evelyn tilted her head slightly, as though studying Claire under glass. "So this is her," she murmured. "The patient who made you forget who you were."

The words weren't loud, but they landed with the weight of a confession. Michael took a step forward, his fists tight, the movement instinctive. "Enough." Evelyn's gaze returned to him, steady and cold, and for the briefest flicker of a second. Beneath all that composure, he thought he saw it: not hatred, but grief. A grief so old it had calcified into cruelty. The silence stretched again, thinner this time, dangerous.

It wrapped around the three of them like wire, one breath, one wrong word away from breaking skin. Evelyn took a single step closer, her perfume faint and familiar, lavender and rainwater, the ghost of a life that had already died. Her hand brushed one of the boxes, tracing the ridged seam of tape with her fingertips.

"You always were good at packing things away," she said softly. "Just not the right ones."And then she looked at him. Not like an ex-wife, not even like an enemy, but like a witness to his final undoing. The knife of silence pressed closer. And no one moved."Packing already," she said. "Running never suited you, Michael."

He stared at her, voice low, dangerous. "What are you doing here?" "Closing a chapter," she replied simply. "Lucian wanted me to say goodbye." Claire's knees weakened. "Lucian?" Evelyn turned her gaze on her, steady, almost pitying. "You really thought he didn't know every move you'd make? You thought he hadn't planned the timing of every heartbreak, every compromise, every photograph?"

Her eyes glimmered with something almost human. Regret, maybe. But it was tangled with something darker. "You were never just a victim, Claire. You were the variable. The test. The wound that needed reopening." Michael stepped between them, his voice low but trembling. "What are you saying, Evelyn?"

She looked at him for a long moment, then closed her eyes, and the memories flooded back.

It had begun at a gallery. Months after their divorce. The walls hung with black-and-white photographs of cities in ruin, bridges collapsing, windows shattered, statues eroded by time. Evelyn remembered thinking how beautiful destruction could be when it wasn't your own.

And then Lucian Alden had spoken her name. His voice smooth as polished obsidian. When she turned, he was already smiling. "You wear grief well," he said. He bought her a drink. Then another. He spoke like a confession disguised as charm. And she, hollow from years of silence and resentment, let him fill her.

That night, she followed him home.

She remembered the first time he touched her; the heat, the violence wrapped in elegance, the way his hands claimed without question.

He had undressed her like a man peeling open a wound, slow, clinical, deliberate. And she had let him. Because he made her feel alive. Dangerous, needed, aflame. Every bruise he left became a reminder that she still had a body that could ache. "He undressed me like a thief," Evelyn said now, her voice trembling, "and I wanted to be stolen."

Tears welled but did not fall. "It wasn't love. It was hunger. I mistook his cruelty for passion. And when I finally understood the difference, it was too late. He had already hollowed me out." Her gaze met Michael's. "You were never meant to survive us both."

Claire's voice broke, shaking with both horror and rage. "And me? What am I to you?" Evelyn's expression faltered, for the first time, she looked fragile, even human. "Collateral," she whispered. "You're the wound that won't close. Lucian needs you gone because he can't stand to lose control. I…" She paused, her throat tightening. "I helped him because hating you was easier than hating myself." Michael's breath hitched. "You collaborated with him?"

"From the beginning," she confessed. "We knew you and Claire would fall. That was always the design."Claire's knees buckled. Her back hit the wall as if her body refused to carry the weight of the truth. "You planned this?" She whispered. "All of it?" Evelyn nodded. "From the moment you were six minutes late."

Michael's world collapsed inward. He saw the whole board now, the pieces rearranging themselves in hindsight. The photographs. The USB drives. The whispers. The surveillance. Lucian's cruelty had been surgical, but Evelyn's betrayal was the scalpel he hadn't seen coming.

"Why?" He rasped. "Why destroy me too?" Evelyn's lips parted, and something inside her cracked.

"Because you were never mine, Michael. Not really. You were always reaching for something softer, something purer." Her eyes flicked toward Claire. "And she was it. I couldn't stand to watch you find what I lost." The silence after was unbearable. The city outside groaned in wind and distant sirens, a dirge that fit too perfectly.

Claire began to cry, quiet, shaking sobs that made the walls feel closer. Michael caught her, held her, his own voice breaking against her hair. "Who? What? Why? When?" He whispered. "How far does this go?" Evelyn's eyes gleamed wet in the dim light.

"Farther than you think," she said. "Lucian doesn't just want her gone. He wants you hollow. He wants your daughter hollow. And I…" her voice cracked, "I let him. Because loving him was easier than living without meaning." The words lingered like smoke. Michael looked at her then, really looked, and saw the ruin behind her calm.

Two women. One broken by Lucian's love, one hunted by it. And him, the thread binding them both to the same damnation. He understood, finally, that this wasn't just vengeance or madness. It was architecture. Lucian hadn't built a trap for them, he'd built a cathedral.

A monument to control, and they were all the stained glass inside it. And Evelyn, trembling but defiant, had been the final piece of glass to fall. "He's coming for you," she said quietly, almost tender. "But not for death. Death is mercy. Lucian doesn't believe in mercy."

She stepped back toward the door, her shadow stretching long across the bare floor. "I'm sorry," she whispered. "Truly. But by now, the ending's already written." The door clicked behind her.

Outside, the car engine roared to life.

And Michael, standing in the ruins of everything he'd tried to save, realized what Evelyn had meant.

He wasn't just in Lucian's story.

He was the concluding chapter.

The Last Move

For days after Evelyn's confession, silence became their language. Not the kind that soothes or shelters, but the kind that lingers. Heavy, watchful, thick as smoke that refuses to clear. It crept into everything. Into the walls. Into their sleep. Into the tiny pauses between breaths that used to feel tender but now felt fatal.

The silence accused. It carried questions neither of them could bear to ask aloud. Questions that hung in the air like dust caught in weak morning light. What if she was telling the truth? What if we were only pieces in someone else's game? What if we were never real?

Michael and Claire moved around each other like ghosts bound to the same haunting, sharing space but not warmth. The apartment had become a mausoleum for the life they'd tried to build. Boxes sat half-packed, their contents stripped of meaning. Photographs turned face down.

Clothes folded without care, books stacked in uneven towers that reached toward the ceiling like unspoken confessions. Curtains half-drawn let in slashes of gray daylight that turned everything the color of old film. The air smelled faintly of rain and cardboard, of endings that refused to end. The city beyond their window blurred into a fever dream.

Sirens fading in and out like distant cries, headlights streaking through fog, rain tracing frantic patterns down the glass like veins of light on dying skin.

Claire moved through it all like she was underwater. He watched her when she thought he wasn't looking, the way she pressed her fingers to her temples as if she could quiet the noise inside her skull.

The way her shoulders flinched at sudden sounds, the way she avoided her own reflection in the mirror above the sink. Even her simplest gestures, making coffee, folding a sweater, turning on a lamp, had become acts of quiet collapse. Once, he caught her standing by the window long after midnight, her hand resting on the pane.

Her breath fogged the glass, and with one trembling finger she wrote a single word before wiping it away so fast he almost doubted he'd seen it. Why. Michael tried to speak once, to reach her, but the words turned to ash before leaving his mouth. He didn't know what to say anymore. "I'm sorry" had become meaningless, and "I love you" felt like a lie they'd both already lived through.

Instead, he lingered in doorways, staring at her silhouette bent over the table, the soft rise and fall of her back as she breathed, the curve of her neck haloed by the dim light. He wanted to touch her. To remind her they were still alive, still here.

But she had begun to look at him differently, not with suspicion, not exactly, but with study. Like he was a riddle she couldn't solve, a stranger who wore his face. The weight of it was unbearable. He could feel the silence pressing into his ribs, expanding, demanding. Every heartbeat louder than speech. Every glance between them another fracture forming.

Finally, one night, he couldn't take it anymore. The words clawed at his throat until they broke free. "Say something," he whispered, his voice raw, desperate. "Please." Claire looked up from where she sat, her eyes wide, rimmed red, not from tears, but from exhaustion that had gone bone-deep.

"What's left to say?" She asked quietly. Her tone wasn't cruel. It was worse, it was hollow. The kind of hollow that meant she'd already started to let go.

"You knew," he said one night, the words cutting through the quiet like a blade unsheathed. "That first day you saw her. You saw Evelyn. Why didn't you tell me?" Claire froze. The mug in her hands clattered to the counter, shattering.

Her tears came before her voice. "I didn't know," she whispered. "I thought she was no one. A stranger. And now…" She shook her head. "Now I don't know who anyone is anymore." Michael's anger folded in on itself, collapsing into guilt. He reached for her hand, but she hesitated before letting him take it.

Her palm was cold, her grip fragile, a truce written in sand. They made love that night because neither knew what else to do. It wasn't passion. It was penance. Their bodies collided out of need, for proof that they were still alive, still tethered, still them. Their passion was a tempest devouring itself, two storms drawn together by gravity and doomed to destroy everything between them. They reached for one another like fire reaching for air.

Michael's grip firm, reverent, desperate to memorize every inch of her grasping her breasts as he began to suck and lick each one of her nipples. He lingered, drawing out each moment until time lost its meaning, leaving only them and the rhythm of their breath.

But afterward, the silence returned, heavier, older, as though it had been waiting just outside the door for permission to come back in. The air between them thickened, humid with sweat and regret. The sheets tangled at their feet like evidence of something neither could name.

Claire turned away first. Her back curved like a question mark beneath the dim light, her breathing uneven, her body still trembling. Not from pleasure anymore, but from everything that pleasure had failed to erase.

Michael stared at the ceiling, the faint buzz of the light fixture filling the room like static, a ghost of sound that made the quiet unbearable. His hand twitched, wanting to reach for her, but he didn't. He couldn't. Touch, once a refuge, had become another trespass.

He tried to count the hums between flickers, as if numbers could anchor him; three, then five, then nothing. It didn't matter. The silence swallowed the count whole. Trust, he realized, wasn't something they had lost. It was something they had killed.

And now it lay between them, a corpse cooling beneath the sheets, impossible to bury, impossible to ignore.

Far away, in Lucian's cathedral of glass and glow, the watchers never slept. The room was colder than logic, sterile as a morgue dressed in mirrors.

Rows of monitors lined the walls, stacked like altars, their shifting blue light pulsing in steady rhythm, a heartbeat for the damned. Screens hummed and flickered with images of other people's lives: stairwells, streets, doorways, beds. The sound was a collage of distant echoes.

Whispers caught on hidden mics, rain hitting concrete, the faint hum of electricity crawling through cables like veins. Lucian stood before it all, the architect of the unholy. His reflection multiplied across a dozen panes of glass.

One man rendered into many, fractured and infinite. In some, he was motionless; in others, distorted, his features bending under the ghost light. He clasped his hands behind his back, the gesture calm but rigid, his knuckles white where the skin stretched too tight.

His face, caught in the flicker of alternating screens, was neither fully human nor fully monstrous, just something perfected by control. The glow of the monitors made his eyes seem hollow, twin wells reflecting the ruin he'd built.

A cigarette smoldered in an ashtray beside him, the smoke curling upward like incense at a desecrated altar. The scent of burnt tobacco and ozone hung thick in the air, ritual and rot entwined. Behind him, the watchers worked in silence, heads bent, fingers ghosting over keyboards.

None spoke unless spoken to; they moved like acolytes before their god. The hum of the machines drowned out any trace of humanity left among them. On the central screen, larger than the rest, framed in brushed steel, Michael's apartment glowed in ghostly color. He and Claire moved within it, slow and fragile, their lives rendered in pixels and shadow.

Lucian watched them with a kind of reverence. His lips parted slightly, as though he were listening to a private hymn. He didn't blink. Every motion was cataloged. Every glance, every hesitation, every moment of tenderness or fracture became another thread in his web. He leaned closer, murmuring to no one, or perhaps to himself. "They think the world outside this room still belongs to them," he said, voice quiet, nearly tender. "But it doesn't. It hasn't for a long time."

His hand brushed the surface of one monitor, fingers tracing Claire's face through the static. The image rippled, her expression distorting under his touch. Lucian smiled faintly.

In this light, it was easy to believe he wasn't merely watching, he was conducting.Every heartbreak. Every silence. Every collapse. His masterpiece wasn't chaos. It was order. His order. The watchers behind him shifted uneasily, though none dared speak.

The hum of the machines deepened, as if the room itself were breathing with him. Lucian straightened, shoulders rolling back with slow, deliberate grace. His reflection shimmered across the glass.

One man, a thousand faces, and in each, the same glint of satisfaction. "Let them think they've escaped," he said softly, almost to the dark. "Every story needs a moment of hope before it ends."

"She's unraveling," Evelyn murmured. Her voice carried both fascination and remorse, as if she couldn't decide whether she wanted to watch Claire fall apart or reach through the screen to save her. Lucian's smile was a blade's edge. "So is he," he said softly. "And when the king and queen fall apart, the board collapses."

He leaned closer to the monitors. Michael's image flickered, sitting at the edge of the bed, his face buried in his hands. Claire asleep behind him, her fingers twitching in some half-remembered nightmare. "They still cling," Lucian said. "Even after all this. Isn't that beautiful? They think love is resistance.

"Isn't it?" Evelyn asked quietly. Lucian turned toward her, eyes gleaming under the silver light. "You envy her." It wasn't a question. Evelyn's jaw tensed. She didn't deny it. Couldn't. Her silence was confession enough.

Lucian chuckled, low and cruel, swirling the amber in his glass. "Of course you do. She's still capable of hope. That's the difference between you and her. Between prey and participant." Evelyn's gaze stayed on the screen, on Claire's face, soft in the dark, pressed against Michael's shoulder.

Her voice came out almost as a prayer.
"Hope," she murmured. "That's what kills first." Lucian smiled wider. "No," he said. "That's what kills last."

Outside, the city kept breathing, indifferent and vast. But inside that small apartment, Michael and Claire had already stopped. Not their hearts, not yet, but something deeper.

Something that Lucian and Evelyn had learned to hollow long ago. And though dawn would come soon, with its thin gray light and promises of distance, it would bring no reprieve.

Because even as they packed to flee, neither of them understood that Lucian's reach didn't end at the city line.
He was already in the wires.
Already in the air. Already in them.

The end came quietly. Not with sirens or screams, no gunfire, no chase, but with the soft, almost cruel indifference of dawn. There was no reckoning, no thunderclap to mark their undoing. Only the sound of their footsteps and the distant sigh of a city that had already forgotten them. The air was pale with fog, a low mist that blurred the edges of the world.

Streetlights flickered out one by one, their orange glow dying as daylight crept reluctantly across the asphalt. It was that hour when even New York seemed exhausted. The heartbeat of the metropolis slowing to a fragile murmur, as if the city itself were pausing between dreams.

Michael and Claire moved through it like phantoms. Bags slung over their shoulders, eyes hollow from too many sleepless nights, they looked less like lovers escaping and more like survivors being quietly erased.

Their clothes still smelled faintly of cardboard and rain. The cuffs of Michael's coat were frayed, Claire's scarf snagged from catching on a nail in the stairwell as they left.

Insignificant details that shouldn't have mattered but somehow did. Reminders that they had once lived lives that contained color, texture, warmth. The world around them looked bleached, buildings reduced to silhouettes, windows veined with condensation, the skyline a watercolor smudge bleeding into the clouds. Even the sun seemed reluctant to rise.

Its light thin and brittle, spreading across the streets like a secret it didn't want to share. They didn't speak much. There was nothing left to say that hadn't already been bled dry in whispers, apologies, and trembling promises made in the dark. Words had become dangerous; too loud, too final.

Michael's fingers brushed Claire's as they walked, a small touch that carried the weight of everything unsaid. Her hand found his and held, their palms cold, trembling, but locked all the same. It wasn't love anymore, not really. It was something quieter. A pact. A prayer.

A plea for one more breath of peace before the world came calling again. The faint rattle of a delivery truck echoed down the block, metal on stone. A newspaper, thrown too hard, slapped against a nearby stoop. Somewhere above, a window creaked open.

A woman watering plants, unaware of the two people walking below her who were already ghosts. Claire's eyes lifted toward the horizon, the fog swallowing the edges of the street ahead. "It doesn't feel real," she whispered.

Her voice was so soft it almost dissolved into the air. "It's not supposed to," Michael said. His voice was flat, steady, but his eyes betrayed him, restless, darting to every corner as if expecting the fog itself to move against them. "Real is gone." A gust of wind rolled down the avenue, scattering leaves and old flyers.

Claire's hair whipped across her face, and Michael reached out to tuck it behind her ear. The gesture was automatic. Tender, familiar, and for a moment, the exhaustion in her eyes broke, revealing something fragile and luminous beneath. She smiled faintly, the kind of smile people give when they know they're being watched by fate.

Boston," she said. The word sounded like a wish she didn't quite believe in. He nodded. "Boston." But even as he said it, the word rang hollow, too clean, too distant, a promise made of air. They turned the corner onto Lexington, where the fog thickened, swallowing the streetlights until all that remained was a dim silver glow.

The city behind them faded, and for the first time in months, the noise fell away. Only their footsteps remained, soft against the wet pavement. For a brief, impossible moment, it felt like freedom, fragile, weightless, unpromised. Michael squeezed her hand once, as if to anchor it. And then, somewhere in the mist, an engine turned over.

A sound too measured to be coincidence. Claire's fingers tensed. Michael's breath caught. And the morning, pale, indifferent, merciless, kept unfolding around them. "Almost there," he murmured. Her smile was a ghost, there and gone in the same breath. "Almost," she echoed. But the word almost has always been the cruelest kind of hope.

They turned onto Lexington, where puddles mirrored the pale sky, and for a heartbeat, the city seemed to hold its breath with them. The cab they'd called never came. The hum of an engine approached instead, heavier, deeper.

Then the van. Black, unmarked, its windows tinted to liquid. It glided to the curb without rush or urgency. As though this moment had been written long before either of them was born. The door slid open.

The men who stepped out were ghosts made flesh, their faces obscured by balaclavas, their movements rehearsed. There was no shouting, no chaos. Just precision. A hand on Michael's shoulder.

A needle glinting in morning light. Claire's gasp, small, startled, the sound of someone realizing too late that hope had been the final illusion. "Michael!" She tried to scream, but it came out fractured. He turned to her, eyes wide, heart hammering. Just in time to see her knees buckle, her body folding like paper as one of them caught her mid-fall. "No…" The word never finished. A sting. A fading pulse.

Darkness blooming behind his eyes like ink spilling through water. His last sight was her face. Pale, peaceful, her lips shaping his name as everything slowed, dissolved, and went still.

By the time the city woke, there was nothing to find. No blood. No signs of struggle. Only two coffee cups cooling on a counter upstairs and the faint impression of a hand against the apartment window, a smudge, a goodbye.

No police report. No search. No questions worth asking.
Manhattan swallowed them whole, as it always does its dead.

In a quiet suburb miles away, Evelyn sat at Eva's bedside, brushing the girl's hair back with trembling fingers. The child's eyes, bright and trusting, lifted toward her.

"When's Daddy coming home?" Evelyn's throat constricted. She could still smell Lucian's cologne from earlier, the echo of his instructions humming behind her ribs. "He's… gone away for a while," she said softly.

"Why?" She questioned with innocence in her eyes. Evelyn hesitated, then bent to kiss her forehead. "Because he loved you more than anything." And for once, she didn't have to lie. Within a week, Claire's apartment was stripped bare. Furniture gone. Curtains torn down.

Her landlord shrugged when asked, she left no forwarding address. The neighbors forgot her name by month's end. The mail stopped coming. Her digital records vanished, erased line by line until even search engines could no longer conjure her existence. It was as if she'd been unmade.

Lucian watched from his high window, whiskey in hand, the skyline spread before him like a trophy. The city lights blinked below, each one a confession, each one a story. "Silence," he murmured. "The most elegant ending of all." Behind him, Evelyn stood in the doorway, pale and hollow. "You promised no harm." Lucian didn't turn. "They're not harmed. They're gone. There's a difference."

She flinched. "You think that's mercy?" Lucian's smile was faint, reflective. "No," he said. "It's permanence." But some things do not vanish, no matter how meticulously erased.

In the final moment, before the dark fully claimed them, Michael's hand had found Claire's. Their fingers had tightened, blood mixing with the cold of the needle.

They had looked at each other not with fear, but with recognition. If this is the end, let it be ours. His last breath had been her name. Her last breath had been his.

And somewhere, beyond the reach of Lucian's cameras, beyond the wires and the lies and the quiet cruelty of the world, something lingered.

Not a ghost, not a curse, but the echo of a love that refused to be silenced. Two souls broken by life. Bound by love.
Erased by design. Never heard from again.
But never, in truth, gone from one another.

Epilogue Echoes

I was seven years old when my father vanished. Old enough to remember the sound of his laugh. That full-bodied, unguarded kind of laugh that didn't just echo, it lived in a room. It filled corners, chased away the stillness, and made even silence seem friendly for a while.

It was the kind of laugh that could turn the dullest evening, grocery trips, burnt dinners, power outages, into something warm, something worth remembering. Old enough to remember the warmth of his hand as he walked me home from school. His smile carrying the quiet proof of a man who fixed things for a living, who believed that anything broken could be made whole again, if only you had the patience to try.

He always slowed his stride to match mine, his thumb tracing lazy circles on the back of my hand whenever I got nervous crossing the street. I used to think those circles were magic, tiny spells he drew just for me, to keep the world gentle. Old enough to remember how he called me moonbeam when I couldn't sleep.

He'd sit on the edge of my bed, voice low and steady, telling stories about the stars. About the ones that burned too bright and too long, and how even when they collapsed, their light traveled for years, reaching eyes that would never know the pain of their dying.

He'd say that's what love was: light that outlives the fire. But I was too young, far too young, to understand why no one ever said the word dead.

At first, I thought it was kindness. That maybe grown-ups avoided the word because they were trying to protect me. But kindness doesn't look like silence.

And silence doesn't feel like protection. It wants to stand in a house after the storm, surrounded by the hum of everything that didn't survive. They told me he went away.

They told me he loved me. They told me nothing else. I watched their mouths move and saw how careful their words were, how they avoided the truth like it was sharp enough to draw blood.

My mother's eyes, always so alive before, became mirrors that didn't reflect anything back. She moved through rooms like a ghost trying not to wake herself. Neighbors brought casseroles and pity. Teachers whispered when I passed. And I learned what people mean when they say grief changes shape but never disappears.

I didn't know it then, but that was the moment I stopped believing in closure. Because closure is just another word adults use when they can't find the courage to tell a child that some doors never open again. I used to wait by the window after that. Tracing raindrops on the glass, connecting them like constellations. Every headlight that turned onto our street made my chest tighten.

Every footstep in the hall made me hold my breath. But the door never opened. And his voice never came. I grew up in the echo of that absence. And sometimes, even now, when the world goes too quiet, I swear I can still hear his laugh distant, fading, but real enough to make me look up.

They told me he went away. They told me he loved me. They told me nothing else. For years, I believed them. I waited by windows like waiting was a prayer. The kind that had no words, just breath fogging the glass. The pane became my church, the rain my congregation.

I'd trace the trails of water with my fingertip, connecting each droplet into constellations the way he once showed me. *Orion. Lyra. Cassiopeia.* I whispered their names like passwords, believing if I got the pattern right, they'd open some secret door back to him. That maybe he was up there, rearranging the stars, trying to spell his way home.

Every car that slowed near our house made my chest tighten. Every set of headlights that swept across my bedroom wall made me sit up, pulse fluttering in my throat. I memorized the rhythm of the neighborhood. The late-night hum of the delivery trucks, the flicker of motion-sensor lights, just to know when something different came.

But nothing ever did. The door never opened. His voice never came. And the quiet that followed stopped being absence, it became a presence of its own.

By the time I was old enough to stop hoping, I had learned the language of silence. I learned how adults talk in circles when they mean he's gone. How they replace truth with phrases that sound gentle but cut just the same.

"He's somewhere better." "He's watching over you." "He loved you so much." I learned how pity sounds different from comfort, softer, but heavier. How people lower their voices when grief enters a room, as if loss were something contagious, a sickness that might spread if you spoke too loudly.

I learned how to smile and nod in the right places, how to make my sadness small enough that no one had to look at it. So I stopped asking. Stopped waiting at windows. Stopped listening for footsteps in the hall. But I never stopped remembering. Because memory is stubborn. It doesn't fade when you tell it to.

It just waits, patient, watchful, for the night to get quiet enough to return.

And sometimes, when the wind moves through the trees exactly right, I swear I can hear his laugh Again, faint, echoing down the years like a song that refuses to end. Because memories are stubborn things.

They don't obey the rules of time or reason. They live where they please; in smells, in sounds, in small, traitorous moments that refuse to fade. They linger in the scent of rain hitting warm pavement. In the click of a light switch in an empty hallway. In the way a voice on the radio bends around a certain word that sounds just like his.

I still remember the last night I spoke to him. The phone line crackled like static rain, that hollow, endless hum of distance that comes when someone you love is too far away for comfort but too close to let go. He sounded tired. Not sick. Not scared. Just... tired. The kind of tired adults never explain to children. The kind that seeps into the soul, the kind that sounds like surrender dressed up as peace.

He told me about the stars again. He always talked about the stars. How the light we see from them is ancient, already dead, in some cases, and yet it still finds us, crossing years and darkness to reach our eyes. "Remember that moonbeam," he said. "Just because something's gone doesn't mean its light stops shining."

He told me I was his sun, that even if I couldn't see him, he'd still be circling somewhere close, still pulling toward me. Then his voice softened, thinning through the static until it sounded like it was coming from another world entirely.

"Nothing," he said, "not distance, not time, not even silence, can make me stop loving you." I've carried those words like scripture. Some people keep faith in gods or promises, I kept mine in that sentence.

Sometimes, when the world feels too heavy, I close my eyes and hear it again, wrapped in that same warmth, that same steady certainty, like he was saying goodbye without using the word.

And her name, Claire, lingers too. I never met her, not really. But she existed in the margins of my father's voice. A soft echo behind him sometimes, laughter half-swallowed, like wind through a half-open door. A whisper when he thought I couldn't hear.

He never said her name during those calls, never explained who she was. He didn't have to. You can hear love, even when it hides. It hums beneath everything. The pauses, the breaths, the way someone's tone changes when they speak of light instead of loss.

I used to imagine her, not the way jealous children imagine rivals, but the way lonely hearts fill in the blanks of a story they were never allowed to finish. Maybe she had kind eyes. Maybe she made him laugh the way I remembered. Maybe she was the reason he still sounded human in those final calls.

Why his voice hadn't yet gone hollow from whatever darkness he was walking through. Then, one day, both their voices vanished. No warning. No goodbye. Just... gone. The world didn't stop. But mine did. Days blurred. Weeks passed.

And every time the phone rang, I ran, half hoping, half dreading. Until even hope began to taste like humiliation. They disappeared quietly, without a trace, leaving behind a silence too vast for words to fill.

The kind that moves into your chest and stays there, breathing for you when you forget how.

Years passed. I grew up. Life reshaped itself around the absence, as it always does.

But memory, memory is a parasite disguised as love. It never leaves the body it feeds on. Even now, when the night tilts toward stillness, I dream of them.

In those dreams, they walk down a long corridor where the light fades from gold to gray to nothing at all. But they don't rush. They don't stumble. They walk hand in hand, steady, certain, calm in the way only people who have accepted their ending can be.

They don't look back. They don't falter. And though the light dies around them, it never quite touches their faces. When I wake, my pillow is wet with tears, not from grief, not anymore.

Something else. Something quieter. Something like peace Because in those dreams, they are whole. They are not hunted. They are not haunted. They are not broken. They are together. And somehow, that's enough. They are whole. Finally.

And that knowing, that fragile, impossible peace, is what carries me forward. I live differently because of him. Because silence was the language of our home, and it starved us. I will not let my daughter inherit that hunger. I don't waste time on silence the way my family once did.

Silence that curdled into distance, that turned love into something polite and wordless. I speak love out loud, even when it shakes in my throat, even when the day has been cruel and exhaustion tries to make me forget how. I let her see me laugh. I let her see me cry.

I let her know that love doesn't vanish when things break, it lingers, patient, waiting to be spoken again.

Every morning before she leaves for school, I say, "You are loved." And every night before she sleeps, I say it again.

Because I know what it means to grow up wondering if silence meant you weren't enough. Our home is filled with photographs, not perfect ones, not staged.

Candid moments, crooked smiles, messy hair, half-light mornings Pictures that prove we existed together in all our imperfection. They live on every wall, every shelf, where eyes can meet them and remember.

No locked drawers. No dusty frames turned backward in shame. Sometimes, when the night settles and the house quiets to that soft, living hum, I step outside.

The world feels different after midnight, thinner somehow, as if the veil between then and now frays a little. I tilt my head toward the sky, find the familiar constellations, and whisper,

"I remember."

The streetlights buzz. A car passes somewhere far off. The trees rustle just enough to sound like an answer. And in that space, between sound and stillness, between breath and memory, I swear I hear it. Soft. Certain. Familiar.

"Be brave, sweetheart," my father whispers, his voice folding into the dark. "And remember, love isn't what saves us. It's what makes us worth saving."

Then the wind moves through the leaves like the turning of a page, and the night exhales. The stars blink, old light traveling through years just to remind me it's still there.

I stand there a little longer, hand pressed to my heart, smiling into the quiet. Because I know now what I didn't then.

He never really left.

He just became the light that finds me when the dark tries to take me back.

If this book resonated with you, the most effective way you can support my future is by leaving an honest review.

Scan the QR code below to go directly to the Amazon review page for this book.

If you're unable to leave a review on Amazon yet, your review on Goodreads is just as appreciated.

Scan the QR code below to rate and review the book on Goodreads.

Thank you for reading and for supporting me as an independent author.

Henry Daniel Archunde Jr.
True North Writings

Made in the USA
Coppell, TX
13 February 2026

71107757R00146